DARK GOD'S AVATAR

THE CHILDREN OF THE GODS BOOK 59

I. T. LUCAS

Also by I. T. Lucas

THE CHILDREN OF THE GODS ORIGINS

1: GODDESS'S CHOICE
2: GODDESS'S HOPE

THE CHILDREN OF THE GODS

DARK STRANGER

1: DARK STRANGER THE DREAM
2: DARK STRANGER REVEALED
3: DARK STRANGER IMMORTAL

DARK ENEMY

4: DARK ENEMY TAKEN
5: DARK ENEMY CAPTIVE
6: DARK ENEMY REDEEMED

KRI & MICHAEL'S STORY

6.5: MY DARK AMAZON

DARK WARRIOR

7: DARK WARRIOR MINE
8: DARK WARRIOR'S PROMISE
9: DARK WARRIOR'S DESTINY
10: DARK WARRIOR'S LEGACY

DARK GUARDIAN

11: DARK GUARDIAN FOUND
12: DARK GUARDIAN CRAVED
13: DARK GUARDIAN'S MATE

DARK ANGEL

14: DARK ANGEL'S OBSESSION
15: DARK ANGEL'S SEDUCTION
16: DARK ANGEL'S SURRENDER

DARK OPERATIVE

17: DARK OPERATIVE: A SHADOW OF DEATH
18: DARK OPERATIVE: A GLIMMER OF HOPE
19: DARK OPERATIVE: THE DAWN OF LOVE

DARK SURVIVOR

Books 7-10: Dark Warrior Tetralogy
Books 11-13: Dark Guardian Trilogy
Books 14-16: Dark Angel Trilogy
Books 17-19: Dark Operative Trilogy
Books 20-22: Dark Survivor Trilogy
Books 23-25: Dark Widow Trilogy
Books 26-28: Dark Dream Trilogy
Books 29-31: Dark Prince Trilogy
Books 32-34: Dark Queen Trilogy
Books 35-37: Dark Spy Trilogy
Books 38-40: Dark Overlord Trilogy
Books 41-43: Dark Choices Trilogy
Books 44-46: Dark Secrets Trilogy
Books 47-49: Dark Haven Trilogy
Books 51-52: Dark Power Trilogy
Books 53-55: Dark Memories Trilogy
Books 56-58: Dark Hunter Trilogy

MEGA SETS
INCLUDE CHARACTER LISTS

The Children of the Gods: Books 1-6
The Children of the Gods: Books 6.5-10

TRY THE CHILDREN OF THE GODS SERIES ON AUDIBLE
2 FREE audiobooks with your new Audible subscription!

Copyright © 2022 by I. T. Lucas

Published by Evening Star Press LLC

EveningStarPress.com

ISBN: 978-1-957139-15-9

TOVEN

*T*oven put his wine glass on the side table, propped his slippered feet up on the worn brown leather ottoman, and clicked the television on.

"Are you depressed?" asked the actor playing a sympathetic doctor. "Does your life feel like a long road to nowhere?" He looked directly at Toven. "Neurotap offers hope to those who no longer believe it exists. In clinical trials, seven out of ten—"

Annoyed, Toven clicked over to another channel.

That damn commercial had been popping up on different cable and broadcast stations for days. If he were human, he might have been tempted to give Neurotap a try, but no medication could alleviate a god's ennui, and neither could therapy sessions with the best psychoanalysts.

Philosophizing about the meaning of life with the greatest human thinkers was pointless as well.

He should know.

Toven had conversed with the most renowned philosophers humanity had produced.

Socrates, who had believed that the secret to happiness

was found in enjoying less, Confucius, who had advocated meditating upon good thoughts as a way to make the world a better place, and Seneca, who had preached that people should be happy with their lot and not strive for more. Lao Tzu advocated living in the moment, Nietzsche valued power above all, and Kierkegaard explained that life was not a problem to be solved but a reality to be experienced.

Ironically, most of those thinkers had been influenced in one way or another by Toven's own writings, and yet they had arrived at very different conclusions about the human condition and how to best endure it.

Toven agreed with some and disagreed with others, but he'd given up on solving that age-old problem centuries ago. Humans were doomed to their misery, and even a powerful god like him could not help them.

He'd tried, failed, tried again and again, but at some point, he had to resign himself to the fact that humans were bloodthirsty, power-hungry savages. Not all of them, but enough to make everyone else's life miserable.

Out of all the philosophers, Kierkegaard had been the wisest. Trying to solve humanity's problems was futile, and living in the moment and just experiencing life was all that was to be had, even for a god.

A god.

What a joke that was. He should've abandoned thinking of himself as a god eons ago. He was no deity, he was not deathless, he was just the scion of a superior race of people, who had long ago been worshipped by primitive humans.

But the gods were no more, destroyed by his own brother in what had turned out to be a suicide mission, and Toven was all that was left of that superior race of beings.

A rare burst of anger rising in his chest, Toven wished that Mortdh had survived the bombing so he could've killed the murderous bastard himself. His insane, power-hungry brother had dropped a bomb on the gods' assembly to escape his punishment for murdering a god, but the idiot had miscalculated the weapon's destructive range and had been swept away in its deadly wind.

His anger subsiding just as quickly as it had risen, Toven let out a sigh. Killing Mortdh would have been intensely satisfying, but he knew that he would not have prevailed against his older brother. Mortdh had always been more powerful, but since the bastard was dead, Toven could allow himself the fantasy.

Except, Toven was well aware of how absurd even fantasizing about it was.

He was a scholar, not a killer, which was probably the reason for his lack of effectiveness. The pen might be mightier than the sword, but the sword was still necessary to implement and enforce the pen's creations.

Toven had never wielded a tool of death.

Hell, he couldn't even bring himself to end his own miserable life.

Humans didn't realize it, but they had the better deal.

Their short lifespans were like rollercoaster rides, the slate wiped clean with each new rotation. Once they grew bored and disillusioned with life, which was inevitable, they didn't have to suffer long. Their lives ended shortly thereafter, and they were given a fresh start in a brand-new body and no memory of their previous incarnation.

Not all humans believed in the cycle, and even he couldn't be absolutely certain that reincarnation existed. But after witnessing too many cases of humans who'd remembered past lives and could prove that those memories were real, Toven had become a believer, and he envied humans for it.

A god who had lived for over seven thousand years and was tired and bored had limited options to end it all, and

Toven was too much of a coward to jump out off a plane or pay someone to behead him.

Instead, he tried to amuse himself the best he could, passing the never-ending time by traveling from one metropolis to another and penning romance novels about love he couldn't feel.

He used to enjoy his human lovers, but even that had become boring. Nowadays, he rarely sought out female company, preferring his solitude and the realities he created in his head to pleasures of the flesh that no longer excited him.

It took someone very special to stir even the slightest emotion in him.

As a loud car commercial began playing, pulling him out of his head, Toven groaned.

Why did he even bother watching television? It wasn't as if he was really interested in what was happening in the human world. The players and costumes kept changing, as did technology, but history kept its cyclical ebb and flow, and humans seemed to learn nothing from their ancestors' mistakes.

Was it morbid fascination that prompted him to follow global affairs? Or was it hope that humanity would one day break out of the cycle and reach the enlightenment he'd tried to steer them toward and failed?

Hope springs eternal.

Apparently not only humans fell victim to hope's allure. Toven had thought that his had died a long time ago, but perhaps a kernel of it still lived in a corner of his dark heart. Perhaps that little spark was what kept him from hiring a killer to behead him and end his misery.

As the car commercial finally ended and the news program tune started playing, Toven put the remote down and lifted his wine glass.

"In today's news, a Bayview resident is accused of..."

Toven switched to another channel. He wasn't interested in local drama.

It was time to move to his next destination.

The San Francisco home he was renting was lovely, but he didn't like staying in one place for too long, and he was looking forward to the change in environment his next stop would bring. The old-world charm of the Victorian house on Webster Street had inspired a historical romance, while the ultra-modern seventy-second-floor Park Avenue apartment in Manhattan would hopefully inspire a contemporary novel.

As a loud commercial for a cleaning product started, he clicked over to the next channel and yet another commercial, but the stunning visuals snagged his attention and he lingered to watch more.

Toven assumed that what was being promoted was a computer game, but as a pretty young lady walked in front of the screen and presented a service that was not about playing a game on the computer but rather playing inside of it, Toven's interest was piqued.

It was a fascinating idea.

"Are you a busy professional with no time to search for your soulmate?" she asked in a sexy, slightly raspy voice. "Are you tired of surfing endless profiles on dating apps and going out on disappointing dates?" Several snapshots of humorously overdone disastrous first dates flashed across the screen. "If so, then Perfect Match Virtual Studios has the answer for you. For more details, go to www.PerfectMatchVirtualFantasy.com. Your dream partner is only a few keyboard clicks away."

Intrigued, Toven pushed to his feet and walked over to the desk to retrieve his laptop.

Back in the armchair, he typed the URL into the search box and started reading the online brochure explaining the service. Could it be for real? Surely it was impossible to turn into someone else for the duration of the virtual adventure. A computer couldn't take over a person's mind and let them live out a fantasy. The brochure claimed that in the span of three hours, weeks of virtual adventure could be enjoyed. They promoted their service not only as the safest and most scientific way to find a soulmate, but also as the best vacation solution for busy people.

If genuine and not paid for, the numerous testimonials confirmed the service's claims, singing its praises. People were finding their perfect matches, and if the wedding photos of happy customers weren't fake, the number of featured couples was impressive.

Others were going on adventures with their spouses, rekindling their passion by either choosing beautiful avatars to represent them or going in as themselves.

It wasn't cheap, but the one thing Toven had no lack of was money. The savages he'd tried to civilize had paid him tribute in gold, and while it was the only tangible good he'd gotten from wasting centuries trying to improve their lives, there was lots of it.

There were many adventures in a variety of environments to choose from, and the service promised a perfect match with a real person who was interested in the same sort of adventure.

Toven wasn't hoping for a soulmate, and he'd been on enough real-life adventures not to crave fake ones, but what appealed to him the most was the promise of stepping out of his own mind and becoming someone else for a spell.

2

MIA

*M*ia turned the cream-colored envelope around, looking for a hint of what was inside, but other than the hand-scribbled *Happy 27th Birthday* there was nothing, not even a Hallmark logo or that of one of the other greetings card brands.

Patting the envelope didn't help either. It didn't feel like a gift card, which was what her friends had gotten her for her 26th birthday, or cash, which was what her grandmother always put inside the cards she'd gotten for her at Walgreens.

Margo and Frankie were smiling like a couple of fiends, so it was probably a gag gift.

"What is it?" She narrowed her eyes at her besties.

"Open it," Margo said.

Frankie waved the waiter over. "Another round of margaritas, please." She winked at Mia. "You're going to need it."

Mia rolled her eyes. "Did you get me a subscription to Boys Down Under?"

The three of them were obsessed with the Instagram sensation. They'd been tempted to subscribe to the private channel nearly every time the guys posted new pictures of themselves in provocative poses. Those who paid for premium access got to see more than just a sliver of muscular chests peeking from unbuttoned shirts, but Mia wasn't sure that she was ready to see more, especially if the guys exposed anything other than their abs and pectorals. She wasn't into pornography.

Frankie looked at Margo. "Damn, why didn't we think of that? That could have been so much cheaper."

"Indeed," Margo pretended to agree. "Next year, that's what we are getting you."

Laughing, Mia opened the envelope, and as she pulled out the card and saw the logo embossed in its center, her eyes widened. "You got me a Perfect Match adventure? Are you nuts? These cost a fortune!"

"It was on sale," Frankie said. "They opened a new studio a few blocks down from my office building. There was a big sign on the front window that they were offering fifty percent off to the first one hundred customers. I was sure that it was no longer available and that all one hundred were sold out." She waved a hand. "You know how everyone and their grandma is talking about it."

Mia laughed. "You're right. My grandma talks about it nonstop. She says that she's not interested in the hookups, and she just wants to try the Russian spy virtual adventure, but I think that she's full of it. She wants a hookup with 007. I know that she's been fantasizing about it ever since the Perfect Match commercials started."

"What does your grandpa have to say about it?" Frankie asked.

"You know him, he just smiles half-indulgently, half-sufferingly and goes back to his newspaper or his television show." Mia looked at the card. "But even at half off it is still a very expensive gift."

Frankie waved a dismissive hand. "Margo and I split

the cost. You can pay us back by telling us all about it after you're done. And if you find your perfect match, I'm going in there and buying a token at full price for myself even if I have to sell my vintage record collection to pay for it."

"It's just an advertising gimmick." Margo lifted her margarita and licked the salt from the rim before taking a sip. "To be able to find people their perfect matches, the Perfect Match Virtual Studios people would need to have hundreds of thousands of profiles in their database, which they can't have because their service is so costly that only the wealthy can afford it. But if I had the money, I would love to experience a virtual hookup, or two or three, in some exotic location just for the fun of it."

"You know what the best part is?" Frankie leaned forward. "Time moves differently in the virtual world. In the span of three hours, you can have a two-week romantic vacation with enough sex to last you for a year."

Mia forced a smile. "Awesome."

What Frankie had really meant to say was that in Mia's case it would have to compensate for the four preceding years, and unless she could afford another trip to cyber world, probably even more going forward.

Besides, there was no guarantee that she would enjoy it. The service was hyped up by a big advertising campaign and celebrity endorsements, but that didn't mean it was all that. It only meant that there was a lot of money behind the national chain of virtual adventure studios. Or was it international by now?

"Hey, maybe we should follow their website so we'll know where and when they open their next branch." Margo pushed her half empty margarita aside. "Maybe we can get more tokens at half off."

Mia lifted her purse from the back of the chair and put the envelope inside. "If my children's books gain some traction, I will buy you each a token for your next birthday."

Margo's lips twisted in a grimace. "Your illustrations are brilliant, but the stories suck. You need to find a different writer or write them yourself."

"I can't. That's the deal I have with my publisher. I'm just the illustrator."

Her agent had told her that they'd loved her illustrations but hadn't liked her stories, and the condition for a publishing deal had been that they provide the writer. The guy was okay, better than she was at coming up with compelling stories, but the books lacked something. They just weren't exciting, not to the kids, and not to the parents reading them to their children.

The publisher had said that her stories weren't happy enough, but they weren't supposed to be. Not everything in life was happy. In fact, most of it was not, and pretending otherwise was dishonest. Children should not grow up in a bubble, unprepared for life's challenges. Thinking that life was fair and that everyone got their happy ending was just setting them up for disappointment.

Margo lifted her margarita, took a sip, and as she put it down her expression was somber. "Just be careful with the type of adventure you choose, Mia. Don't go for the Russian spy one. Go for something sweet and romantic."

"You don't have to remind me. I know."

Too much excitement might kill her.

Literally.

Four years ago, it almost had.

KIAN

*K*ian closed the last of the files Shai had put on his desk and handed the stack back to him.

His assistant rose to his feet. "I'm going down to the café. Do you want me to get you something?"

"Only coffee, please. I'm having lunch with Syssi at home later." Kian swiveled his chair around and looked out the window at the village square below.

At this time of day, the café was teaming with people.

My people.

"I built this village for our clan, a safe place for the immortal descendants of Annani to live in and thrive as a community. I didn't expect to welcome the descendants of other gods, and I sure as hell didn't expect to invite three members of a different breed of long-lived people, who we had no idea coexisted with us and humans on this planet."

"The Fates have been busy lately," Shai said.

"Indeed, they have been, and they are not done yet."

Not too long ago, they'd discovered that Annani's half-sister had survived as well. In a bizarre turn of events, Areana had ended up being mated to Navuh, the clan's archenemy who was bent on the clan's annihilation. Areana had lived in seclusion for thousands of years, locked away in Navuh's harem and unaware that Annani was alive and that her mate sought her sister's demise.

But even more bizarre than Areana being mated to Navuh was that both their sons had joined forces with the clan.

And now they were searching for Toven, another god who'd been presumed dead.

The Fates had worked behind the scenes, weaving their plans and orchestrating the seemingly random encounters that had first led Toven's granddaughter and then his daughter and son to the clan.

Their invisible fingertips were all over it.

If not for the two immortal children Toven had fathered with human mothers finding their way to the clan, they would have never learned about Toven's survival.

Shai walked over to the window and peered at the busy café below. "When we built the village, we believed that the only other immortals on the planet in addition to us were the Doomers."

Kian chuckled. "I wonder if Navuh knows that we call his order DOOM and his followers Doomers. We couldn't have come up with a more fitting name for our enemies if we tried."

Shai shrugged. "That's their acronym in English. The Brotherhood of the Devout Order of Mortdh. It doesn't work out as well in the old language."

Kian turned to look at his assistant. "Do you speak the old language?"

Shai shook his head. "I never had the chance to learn it. Maybe I could ask Edna to teach me the basics, and then I could continue on my own."

With the guy's eidetic memory, he would have an easier

time than most learning the complicated language, but Shai had enough on his plate.

"When you hire an assistant, maybe you'll have time for a side project like that. Right now, you don't."

"No one wants to be the assistant's assistant. I can't find anyone for the job." Shai pushed his hands into his pockets and leaned back on his heels. "Maybe when we find more of Toven's children, one of them will turn out to be a capable administrator."

Kian chuckled. "If they are all like Orion and Geraldine, which given Toven's preference for artistic females they probably are, none will make good administrators."

It was ironic, or maybe fated, that Geraldine and Shai were truelove mates. The woman with memory issues had mated a man with an eidetic memory.

"You never know." Shai smiled. "Cassandra is artistic, but she's also good with numbers."

"True, but since she's Toven's granddaughter, she's further down the line and might have inherited a good head for numbers from her father. First, though, we need to find Toven himself. He's too smart to leave tracks for us to follow, and even if we somehow get lucky and find him, he might not want anything to do with us. If the god is so cold and indifferent that he turned away his own son, there is no reason to believe that he'll want to join forces with us."

"We will do what we can, and the rest is up to the Fates." Shai pulled his hands out of his pockets, turned toward the desk, and tucked the files under his arm. "I'll put these away and go get you your coffee. Your mood will improve after an infusion of caffeine."

"Thanks. Get me a pastry as well, please. It will tide me over until lunch."

"You've got it, boss."

13

When Shai left, Kian sighed, turned his chair around, and rolled it closer to the desk.

Perhaps when they found Toven and he met Annani, she would have a positive impact on him. She was the only one who had any hope of influencing the god to at least cooperate with the clan, and maybe to stay in touch with his children.

While Annani had despised Mortdh, she'd been very fond of his younger brother.

If Ahn had promised his daughter to Toven instead of Mortdh, the world would have been a different place today. Annani wouldn't have pursued Khiann in a desperate move to avoid marriage to the hateful god, and Mortdh wouldn't have murdered Khiann in retaliation for the humiliation. The gods' assembly wouldn't have sentenced Mortdh to entombment for the murder, and he wouldn't have bombed the assembly to avoid punishment, destroying the gods and altering the course of history. But engaging in a game of what-ifs was futile.

The past couldn't be changed.

Kian could only look to the future, and he hoped that Annani's upbeat personality and positive attitude would rub off on Toven. Perhaps her light could banish the darkness the god had allowed to smother his spirit. And if the Fates really wanted to do some good, Annani and Toven would be each other's second chance.

They could never be truelove mates, but they could at least have friendly companionship with benefits, which would solve the problem of replacing Alena as their mother's companion.

Kian shook his head. Once again, he was letting himself travel down the road of what-ifs, but unless those what-ifs had to do with clan security, he had no business engaging in them.

That brought to mind the next subject keeping him awake at night—the damn Kra-ell.

Discovering that two more gods had survived the bombing was a mere curiosity compared to discovering a different breed of long-lived people who, like immortals, had been living undetected among humans.

The Kra-ell were a potential threat to his clan.

The three hybrid Kra-ell they'd found so far were not much of a threat, but those who'd massacred the rest of their tribe were. If those other Kra-ell had no qualms about killing their own males so they could steal their females, they would not hesitate to do the same to his people, if and when they discovered the clan's existence. In fact, immortal females would be even more valuable to them than their own.

The Kra-ell were long-lived but not immortal, and mating with immortal females would be a new lease on life for their species. A daughter born to a hybrid Kra-ell male and an immortal female would transfer the immortality gene to her children. The Kra-ell did not have enough females, and breeding with humans was pointless for them because their longevity genes seemed to be recessive. The product of a union between a Kra-ell and a human produced a hybrid with longer life span than that of the human partner, but the children of the hybrids with humans did not inherit the Kra-ell longevity, which meant that the Kra-ell were doomed to eventually die out.

If he could avoid them detecting the clan for the next thousand years or so, the danger would be over, but Kian hadn't been as careful as he should have been.

He'd already taken a big risk by allowing two survivors of Jade's tribe into the village, and now he was admitting a third.

The rare hybrid Kra-ell female had lived in hiding, terrified of being found by the Kra-ell who'd massacred the males of her tribe. She had no one and nowhere to go, and he couldn't in good conscience turn her away, especially since Arwel had vouched for her.

The Guardian might be an empath, but that didn't make him soft-hearted. Arwel didn't vouch for Aliya out of pity but out of respect.

Perhaps the three hybrid Kra-ell arrivals were part of the Fates' grand design?

If that was the case, it was too early in the game for him to see what that design might be.

Kian just hoped that he wasn't letting a Trojan horse into the sanctuary he'd worked so hard to create for his people.

ANNANI

"I can't walk," Amanda complained. "I can't see my feet under my belly, and I'm afraid I'll stumble on uneven pavement or step in a doo-doo."

Annani laughed. "There are only three dogs in the village, and their owners are conscientious about cleaning up after them."

"Three? I only know about Scarlett. Who else has gotten dogs?"

"Ella and Julian. They got two little pups from a rescue shelter. One is a mix of Maltese and a West Highland White terrier whose name is Jo-Jo, and the other one is a mix of terrier and poodle. He's tiny and his name is Jack-Jack. They are adorable."

"When did they get them?"

"This Wednesday, I believe."

Amanda pouted. "I used to be the first to know things like that. Now that I'm stuck at home, I get second-hand news."

"You should not spend your time on the couch watching soap operas, my dear. I know that it is difficult for you to walk, but it is good for you. How about the two of us go to the café? It is not too far away, and we can rest along the way as many times as you feel you need to. If you want, I can call Ella and ask her to bring her new fur-babies to the café."

Annani had a feeling that Amanda's reluctance to move more than was absolutely necessary was caused by fear of inducing labor prematurely, which was not likely to happen three weeks before the due date.

"That's tempting." Amanda tried to heave herself off the couch. "Damn. I need a crane on standby." She smiled. "Fortunately, I have one."

As Onidu rushed over, Annani lifted a hand to stop him. "Let me help you." She rose to her feet and offered her daughter a hand up.

"Thanks, Mom." When she was on her feet, Amanda put her hands on the small of her back. "Let's go. I'm in a mood for a muffin."

"Whatever the motivation is, I am glad that you are willing to go on a walk. The fresh air will be good for you."

"It is nice outside," Amanda admitted as they made their way down the walkway.

Annani's two remaining Odus trailing behind them, they had covered no more than two hundred feet when Amanda spotted a bench and beelined for it.

"I look like I'm carrying twins." Amanda adjusted her T-shirt over her belly.

It was pink, the size of a tent, and had A BABY-GIRL'S BEST MAMA printed on it in bold black lettering.

"You are not. I can hear only one heartbeat."

"I do too, but then I had the thought that maybe their heartbeats are synchronized, and I even had Bridget do another sonogram on me to make sure that I didn't have two in there." She looked down at her cleavage. "I also went up two cup sizes, but I'm not complaining about that." She eyed Annani from under lowered lashes. "Sorry about being such a downer, Mom. I bet you can't wait to go home."

"I am not in a rush to go anywhere, and you are not a downer." Annani leaned over and kissed her daughter's cheek. "I am glad to be here for you, and if you need a sympathetic ear, you can have mine whenever you feel like complaining."

"Thanks." Amanda let out a breath. "Was Alena as whiny as I am during her pregnancies?"

Alena was meant to be a mother, and she had carried her pregnancies with a beatific smile on her face and no complaints, but that was not what Amanda needed to hear.

"It was so long ago that I do not remember."

"Liar." Amanda laughed. "But thank you for sparing my fragile feelings."

As Annani's phone rang, she was glad of the distraction. Searching for the hidden pocket in her gown, she patted the folds until her hand felt the device under the yards of silk. Pulling it out, she smiled. "Alena must have felt us talking about her."

Amanda frowned. "What time is it over there?"

"We shall soon find out." Annani accepted the call. "Hello, daughter mine. Were your ears burning? Amanda and I were just speaking of you."

Alena laughed. "My ears did no such thing. What were you talking about?"

"Amanda asked if you were also whiny during the last weeks of your pregnancies. I told her that I do not remember because it was so long ago."

"Then it is a good thing that I am pregnant again, so you'll be reminded of how elated I feel when I'm carrying a child."

Annani's heart leaped in her chest. "You are not jesting, I hope. Because that would just be cruel."

Alena and Orion had not been together long enough to

produce a pregnancy that could already be detected, and Alena had not been with anyone else for months before that. Unless medicine had made big strides in early detection of conception, and Alena had been checking every day whether she was pregnant, she should not have been able to find out so quickly.

Alena laughed. "You are probably making calculations in your head, and the dates don't add up. I still can't believe it either. According to Vrog, I got pregnant last night, and he detected the life growing inside of me this morning. Apparently, Kra-ell males can detect pregnancy right at the moment of conception. That's how Vrog knew right away that Stella had conceived."

Annani felt tears prickle at her eyes. "I am so incredibly happy."

"So am I!" Amanda screeched. "We will have little ones together. How wonderful is that?" Then her face fell. "Poor Sari. I hope she gets pregnant soon. She's the last one to become a mother. Did you call her?"

"Not yet. Orion and I wanted Mother to be the first to know."

"Congratulations, Daddy." Amanda's eyes were leaking happy tears, and her voice wobbled. "You must be over the moon."

"I am," Orion said. "I'm so grateful to Vrog. I want to get him a meaningful gift. Any ideas?"

"Get him a goat," Amanda suggested with a straight face.

"Why a goat?" Annani asked.

"My first thought was a puppy, but then I remembered that the Kra-ell love fresh blood, and a dog is too small to be a good blood donor. Besides, *ew*. A cow would be even better than a goat, but our backyards are not big enough for a cow."

"That's actually not a bad idea," Alena said. "Vrog

doesn't need much blood, but Aliya might need it from time to time. A couple of goats could be a great engagement present."

"Are they engaged?" Annani asked.

"They are in the initial get-to-know-each-other stage. The Kra-ell don't bond like we do, so their courtship will probably not be as intense as ours."

"When are you coming back?" Annani asked. "I cannot wait to hold you in my arms and congratulate you properly."

"The plan was to leave on Monday, but we are heading home sooner. We will be back Sunday afternoon. Carol and Lokan are a little disappointed because they were hoping for a full two-week vacation, and they got us only for ten days. Their plan is to stay in Lugu Lake until Thursday and return to Beijing Friday morning."

"I wish they could come to the village," Amanda said. "I'm sure that Carol misses home."

"She does." Alena sighed. "But it's too dangerous for them right now. Even coming to Lugu Lake was risky. But since it was also in China, and Lokan knows for a fact that he and his men are the only Doomers there, it wasn't as risky as coming to the village."

"All in good time," Annani said. "Lokan is playing a dangerous game, but he is a smart man, and he knows what he is doing. I hope that eventually, he will leave the Brotherhood and join us in the village."

DARLENE

*P*er Onegus's instructions, Darlene parked her car in the self-parking section of the office building. It was the same place as last Wednesday, but this time, Cassandra and not Onegus was supposed to pick her up.

The cloak and dagger evasive maneuvers made her nervous.

Immediately after Roni's escape, agents had watched her and Leo twenty-four-seven, and they hadn't been overly discreet about it. Darlene had been aware of their presence and unnerved by it, but it had lasted only a few months.

Naively, she'd thought that they'd given up on catching Roni and had left her and Leo alone. But Onegus had shattered that illusion. He'd told her that their phones were still being monitored, including location tracking, and if she or Leo veered away from their regular routines, an agent would be dispatched to check what they were up to.

Slumping low in the driver's seat, Darlene glanced in the rearview mirror. If anyone had followed her here from her home, they'd done a fantastic job of evading her detection. Driving over, she'd glanced at the rearview mirror every few seconds, but as far as she could tell, no one had been on her tail.

Nevertheless, she felt like a sitting duck while the seconds ticked away, and she was so stressed that her hands felt clammy, and her blouse was sticking to her sweaty back.

She was no movie heroine, and as much as Leo got on her nerves from time to time, Darlene liked her mundane, unexciting life.

Liar.

She was a lonely middle-aged woman who'd been offered the best gift anyone could hope for, but instead of feeling elated by the prospect of eternal life, she was terrified of changing her stupid routine.

The fight she'd had with Leo over the phone just before leaving the house had only added to the unease churning in her stomach.

After she'd told him that she was going to spend a weekend with her cousins, and that there was no phone reception in their mountain cabin, Leo had accused her of lying to him and asked who she'd been fucking on the side. She'd hurled similar accusations at him, and then disconnected without giving him a chance to retaliate.

The nerve of the guy.

Later today, she was going to find out whether she'd been right about him taking a lover on his business trip. Roni had promised to do some hacking and check whether her suspicions were justified, and unlike previously, this time Darlene wanted to know the truth.

About everything.

Cassandra and Onegus claimed that Leo had sold out Roni to the Feds, but she wasn't just going to take their word for it.

Darlene wanted proof.

For some reason, Cassandra really wanted her to leave Leo and attempt transition, and Darlene had a feeling that her sister believed in achieving her goals by any means, including fabricating Leo's guilt.

Why would he have done such a thing?

They weren't strapped for money, and Leo made enough to support them comfortably.

But perhaps he wanted more for himself?

Or maybe he wanted more for his mistress?

When a car pulled up into the parking spot next to her, Darlene's heart went into overdrive, but when she whipped her head to look at the driver, she was relieved to see Onegus's handsome face.

Never mind that she'd expected Cassandra. As long as it wasn't an agent coming to arrest her, she was good.

Darlene opened the driver's side door and stepped out. "Hi—"

Onegus put a finger to his lips. Miming, he indicated that he wanted her to hand over her phone, and when she did, he turned it off, put it inside a small box that looked like it was made from lead, and then slipped it into his pocket.

Retrieving from the other pocket the handheld device he'd used on her before, he swiped it over her front and then her back. When nothing beeped and no red light came on, Onegus indicated that he wanted her to give him her purse and open the trunk.

As she'd been instructed, Darlene had packed her most precious possessions into one suitcase, and Onegus used his device to check her belongings as well.

With that done, he smiled and motioned for her to get into his car. "Do you want me to forward your calls to the new clan phone I brought for you?"

She shook her head. "I told Leo that there is no reception in the mountains. I don't want to talk to him during this weekend." She grimaced. "Or ever."

"Did he give you grief about spending time with your so-called cousins?"

"He didn't believe me. You know how they say that everyone sees the world through the prism of their personality and belief system? He accused me of cheating on him because that's probably what he's doing. Right?"

Onegus lifted his hands in the universal sign for peace. "I didn't hear anything to that effect, so I can't comment on it." He patted the pocket where her phone went. "I'll put it in the locker and be right back."

"Okay." Darlene pulled her other leg inside and closed the passenger door.

When Onegus returned and sat behind the wheel, he reached into his pocket, pulled out a brand-new phone, and handed it to her. "It's already programmed with all of our numbers."

"Thank you." She cradled the device in her hands. "I didn't expect to see you here today. I thought that Cassandra would pick me up."

He gave her a smile. "I wanted to make sure that you weren't followed. I've been trailing you the entire way from your home."

"You have? I was constantly looking in the rearview mirror, and I didn't see you."

"That's because I'm good at what I do." He turned the engine on. "You weren't followed, but just in case, I stopped at the entry to the parking garage and watched the cars going in to make sure that you didn't have a tail that I'd somehow missed."

She'd been sitting in her car for at least twenty minutes. "You're very diligent."

"I always am, and especially when it has to do with my

sister-in-law and my mate's nephew. Cassandra is waiting for us in the Starbucks on West 9th Street. Once I'm a hundred percent sure that we don't have a tail, I'll drive you there." He cast her a sidelong glance. "I told Cassandra that I could take you straight to the village, but she wanted to be the one to do that. She wants to share the experience with you."

"That's sweet." Darlene forced a smile. "I can't wait to see it."

6

TOVEN

"*P*erfect Match Virtual Studios. Adele speaking. How may I help you?"

Toven cleared his throat. "Good afternoon. I have a question that I'm not sure you will be able to answer. Is it possible to design a custom-made environment for a fee? I've looked over the options, and none of what is offered appeals to me."

Over the past week, he'd read the entire online brochure, including all the reviews on the company's site and outside of it, and had watched all the sample presentation videos. But even though he was now convinced that Perfect Match Virtual Fantasy Studios really delivered what they promised, none of the adventures had all the elements he was interested in.

"You are right." She chuckled. "This is the kind of inquiry I can't answer. But I can have someone from our main office contact you. Can I have your name and phone number?"

Toven swiveled his chair and looked out his study's window. "If I give you my name, wouldn't it nullify my anonymity?"

When he'd prepaid for the service in their Manhattan branch, he'd received a digital token that allowed him to log in anonymously. Supposedly, the payment data was erased as soon as the funds were received, and his only proof of purchase was the token.

"Sir, I assure you that your inquiry will remain anonymous, and no one will have access to it. But if you wish, you can give me your chosen avatar's name and digital token number instead."

"That would be preferable. My avatar's name is Tobias Navón."

Toven smiled. His avatar's last name was borrowed from Navohn, Annani's father-in-law. Navón also meant wise, and since he was supposedly the god of knowledge and wisdom, that was appropriate. The first name he'd chosen for his avatar was a play on his real one and the closest he'd ever dared to use so far. Tobias was the Greek translation of the Hebrew name Tov-Yah, which meant 'God is good.' Perhaps that was why his father had given him the name Toven. Ekin had often referred to him as the good son, and he had considered Mortdh a dangerous bully.

Toven wondered whether their father's opinions had shaped their characters or had been shaped by them. In mythology, he was the good god while Mortdh was the bad one.

"Can I have your digital token number, Mr. Navón?"

"Of course." He recited the combination of letters and numbers and then added his phone number. "When should I expect a callback?"

"It will be later today. I can't promise that what you envision for your fantasy can be done, but we will let you know one way or another. Customer satisfaction is very important to us, and we strive to provide each client with the best experience possible."

"Thank you, Adele. I appreciate your help."

"You are most welcome, Mr. Navón."

Toven ended the call and put the simple burner phone he used for such purposes on his desk.

Propping up his feet on the windowsill, he gazed at Central Park sprawling below. The seventy-second floor Park Avenue apartment rented for thirty-five thousand dollars a month, which was an outrageous amount, but it was worth it. The place was beautifully furnished, had a great view, and was located in the center of one of the most vibrant cities in the world.

These days, Toven traveled lighter than ever. Now that books were available digitally, he no longer needed to haul chests full of heavy tomes with him. He'd even scanned the many journals he'd penned over the centuries into one tablet and left the originals together with his gold in a safe depository in Switzerland. He only took two with him. One was for gathering ideas, and the other for descriptions of his lovers. It was the newest one, the one he'd started after Orlando had stolen its incomplete predecessor.

Not a day had passed in the thirty-eight years since that encounter that Toven hadn't thought about the son he had turned away. But no matter how many times he'd turned it over in his head, he still didn't regret his decision. Orlando was a young immortal—he had feelings, desires, and goals. Being around a black hole like Toven would have sucked the light out of him.

Besides, it wasn't safe.

They would have become each other's Achilles' heel.

With a sigh, Toven turned around and flipped his laptop open. A long time ago, he'd let go of his regrets and failures along with any goals and aspirations he'd had and had decided to just live one day at a time.

Perfect Match offered him an exceptional opportunity to step out of his own mind and perhaps find those facets of himself that had atrophied but had not died out completely.

The problem was that none of the available environments and experiences appealed to him. He could see how they would seem exciting to humans who hadn't experienced much, but he needed something more. Thankfully, his imagination and creativity hadn't deteriorated along with his spirit.

His ability to imagine and create works of art was a part of what gave some meaning to his otherwise empty life and kept him from seeking ways to end it. Another part was the charities he contributed to, but to a much lesser extent.

Toven had given up on changing humanity for the better a long time ago, and his donations were just a tiny, inconsequential Band-Aid. He only donated earnings from the sales of his novels and gains from his investments. Those charities would have benefited much more if he was gone, and his large reserves of gold would have found their way into their coffers. But as in all things human, corruption was rampant, and only a small portion of the contributions would have found their way to the needy.

Pulling up the Perfect Match website, he logged in with his digital token and scrolled through the selection of environments.

The Krall one had vampire-like creatures that answered his need for a scenario that included fangs and biting, but he didn't like cold climates and had no wish to experience Greenland.

But even if the same scenario could be transported to a more hospitable climate, Toven didn't like the female-dominated society. He was by no means a proponent of patriarchy, but he was a dominant male, and he liked his partners soft and sexually receptive of his dominance. At the same time, though, he liked them to be intelligent, assertive, and successful in their endeavors. To enjoy a female's yielding, he needed it to be her choice, not something she considered a necessity given her gender or social standing, but rather something that she enjoyed.

A pleasure, not a capitulation.

7

DARLENE

*A*s Onegus pulled into the Starbucks parking lot, Cassandra got out of her car with a huge grin on her face.

"I assume operation evade and confuse worked as expected." She pulled Darlene into a bear hug. "Congratulations on swallowing the red pill. Welcome to the next chapter of your life, sister."

Darlene chuckled. "I thought that I already swallowed it on Wednesday. Is there more?"

"There is plenty more." Cassandra let go of Darlene.

Looping her arms around Onegus's neck, she kissed him long and hard.

Embarrassed to watch, Darlene took the suitcase Onegus had pulled out of the trunk and rolled it over to Cassandra's car.

The damn kiss lasted for more than a minute, and when Cassandra let go of Onegus, he pulled her back to him and kissed her again for another full minute.

"Don't you two have a room?" Darlene murmured under her breath.

"Wait until you meet your one and only." Cassandra opened the trunk, lifted Darlene's suitcase as if it were a paper shopping bag, and put it down gently before closing the trunk. "Did you pack all the things you absolutely couldn't live without?"

"I did, but I don't intend to stay forever. I'm just staying for the weekend."

"We will see about that." Cassandra smiled knowingly and opened the passenger door.

Darlene hesitated before getting in. "I want you to swear on Onegus's life that at the end of the weekend, you will let me go and that no one will try to stop me."

Cassandra gave her a pitying look. "If at the end of the weekend you wish to return to your home, I swear on the life of everyone I love that you will be delivered there."

"Alive," Darlene added, just in case.

"Alive and well." Cassandra motioned for her to get in. "People are looking at us."

Darlene glanced at the Starbucks patio where a group of four men were indeed staring at Cassandra, but probably not for the reason she suspected.

Her half-sister was enviably gorgeous, impeccably dressed, and radiated confidence from every pore of her long lean body.

"Your father must be someone special." Darlene sat down in the passenger seat. "Are you in touch with him?"

"My father is a lying, cheating scumbag who had an affair with our mother while he was married. I've never seen him, and I didn't even know who he was until Orion told me about him." She turned the ignition on. "Orion is our uncle."

"I know." Darlene fastened her seatbelt. "Once Onegus released my memories from the first red pill you fed me, I remembered everything. Our dear uncle is the one who took my mother away from me and didn't tell her that she had left a husband and a child to grieve her death while she was very much alive."

Cassandra shook her head. "Orion didn't take your mother away from you. The accident that nearly killed her did. But you are right that he could've told her about you. He thought he was doing the right thing."

"The road to hell is paved with good intentions."

"And so is the road to heaven. It all depends on whether you are a glass-half-empty kind of girl or a glass-half-full."

That shut Darlene up. Was she a glass-half-empty kind of person?

Not really, but she was angry and bitter, and she had a good reason to be. When she met their uncle, she intended to give him a piece of her mind.

"Don't be too harsh on Orion," Cassandra said. "He hasn't had it easy either, and right now, he's floating on a cloud of happiness. I don't want you to drag him down."

It was no big surprise that her sister was siding with their uncle. No one ever sided with Darlene.

"What is he so happy about?"

"He and Alena are expecting a child, which is a miracle of biblical proportions. Orion thought that he was infertile, and he had given up on ever becoming a father. Alena is the mother of thirteen children, but she had them all many centuries ago. She didn't expect to get pregnant again. But the Fates were kind to them and blessed them with a child."

The lifespans Cassandra was talking about were too fantastical to comprehend. "If I become immortal, would I be able to have another child even though I no longer get periods?"

Cassandra scrunched her nose. "Frankly, I'm not sure. Transitioning into immortality is supposed to restore your body to its optimal condition, but since females are born with all the eggs they will ever have, you might have used up all of yours. Immortal females ovulate on demand when their body recognizes a compatible mate and the conditions for conception are optimal. That way, they preserve their eggs."

"And those eggs don't age because the females don't."

"Correct. Do you want to have another child?"

Darlene shrugged. "Not anytime soon, but if I'm going to live indefinitely, I might want to have another baby at some point."

Reaching over the center console, Cassandra clasped her hand. "I hope you will have another one. I adore Roni."

Darlene chuckled. "Then I have to find another smart programmer to father my next child. Roni certainly didn't get his smarts from me."

Ignoring her comment, Cassandra smiled and pointed at the car's front window. "Watch this."

Suddenly, all the windows turned opaque, and Cassandra lifted her hands off the steering wheel.

"What are you doing?"

"Relinquishing control to the onboard computer. From this point on, the car is going to drive itself into the village parking structure. It's a safety precaution, so not even the residents of the village know where the entrance to the tunnel is, and no one can torture the information out of them."

"That's sounds terrible. Who would want to do that?"

"Who wouldn't? Humans would want the secret to immortality, and the clan's enemies would want to kill everyone. But let's not talk about depressing stuff. The village is beautiful, and I can't wait to show it to you."

"Does Onegus know where it is?"

"He's the chief of security, so of course he does. And the

head Guardians know as well. I'm very happy to remain ignorant."

The car drove itself for about fifteen minutes before entering a tunnel. Even though the windows were opaque, the sudden darkness, the drop in temperature, and the echoing of the car's engine gave it away.

"What if a police car drives past and sees a car with opaque windows going by?"

"It doesn't look opaque from the outside."

Darlene tried to imagine what the car windows looked like. Maybe they were like those special two-way mirrors in interrogation rooms—clear on one side and not on the other?

As the car slowed down and then stopped, it shook for a moment before lurching up. "Are we in an elevator?"

"Yes. It goes about a hundred feet up to the parking level, and then we need to take another elevator to the entry pavilion. It's made from glass and has a permanent exhibit of Sumerian and Egyptian artifacts, courtesy of Kalugal, who is the son of the clan's archenemy and the goddess's sister. But that's a story for another time."

Darlene chuckled. "Do you have a full bottle of those red pills that you intend to feed to me over this weekend?"

Cassandra smiled. "Only a few."

As the elevator came to a stop, the windows became clear again, and when Cassandra pulled out into the parking structure, a familiar figure waved at them.

When the car came to a full stop, Geraldine rushed over and opened the passenger side door. "I can't believe you are finally here. Someone pinch me, please, so I know I'm not dreaming." She pulled Darlene out and wrapped her arms around her. "I'm so happy." Her voice trembled.

When Darlene felt wetness on her neck, she pulled back and looked at Geraldine's teary eyes. "I hope those are happy tears."

"The happiest." Geraldine kissed her cheek and took her hand in hers. "You are staying with Shai and me. Tonight, we are having a family dinner at our place. I cooked five different main courses, so everyone would have something they like."

Behind them, Cassandra opened the trunk and pulled out Darlene's suitcase. "Did you invite Sylvia's mother and her mate?"

"Of course. We are one big family now. I just wish Orion and Alena were back already so they could join us, but you are going to meet them Sunday at Roni's. He's hosting a barbecue lunch. Syssi said that she and Kian would come to say hello, and I hope they bring their adorable baby girl with them. Maybe Amanda and Dalhu will stop by as well. Roni is known as the best barbecuer in the village."

"Is he now?"

Geraldine's excited babbling was infectious, and Darlene felt her anxiety slowly melting away.

"He is." Geraldine led her into the elevator. "I'm told that the competition is stiff, and that Roni needs to keep improving his technique to keep up with his main adversary, a guy named Turner, who I haven't met yet."

It was disappointing that Roni hadn't come to greet her, but since it was a weekday, Darlene assumed he was working and couldn't get away.

"Is Roni at work?" she asked Cassandra.

"He is. Roni is the clan's number one hacker, and he always has too much to do."

"Do you know if he checked up on Leo?"

"I don't. You can ask him at dinner."

As the elevator doors opened and the three of them stepped out into the glass pavilion, Darlene put a hand on her chest. "This is absolutely gorgeous. Look at that greenery. Is it real?"

"Everything is real." Geraldine took her hand. "Would you like to tour the exhibit first?"

Darlene was more interested in the village than in artifacts from Egypt and Sumer.

"Perhaps some other time."

8

TOVEN

*T*oven was surprised when his phone rang less than two hours after the receptionist at the Perfect Match Studios had promised him that someone would call him back. In fact, he hadn't expected to get a callback at all.

"Hello," he answered.

"Mr. Navón?"

"That's me."

"This is Brian from the Perfect Match Virtual Fantasy Studios. I understand that you wish to build a custom-made adventure."

"I do. Is that possible?"

The guy chuckled. "Of course it is possible, but it will cost a bundle and take time. Also, since it will require a large monetary investment, anonymity will be a problem." He chuckled. "Unless you want to walk into the main office and hand over a suitcase full of cash."

Brian was refreshingly blunt, which Toven appreciated. "I understand, and I don't mind bringing a suitcase full of cash to your offices, but I also don't mind issuing a wire transfer from my bank account. As long as I remain anonymous to the lady, I'm okay with your company knowing who I am."

One of his fake identities would wire the money, so that wasn't something he was worried about. He had plenty to choose from.

"Thank you for your trust, and I would be more than happy to take your money, but it might not be necessary. The environments and experiences are highly customizable. You can combine features from several to create almost any fantasy you can imagine. Did you fill out the questionnaire?"

"I did." Mostly. He still had several sections to complete.

The thing was extremely thorough, which could potentially be a problem. A personal profile could be compiled from the information provided, and even though Toven had used his creative imagination to describe his character, a powerful AI or a skilled psychologist could learn a lot about him just from going over that data.

After a moment of silence, Brian came back on. "I see that you haven't submitted it yet. At the bottom of the questionnaire there is a comment section where you can put in special requests and also upload pictures or stories that pertain to your fantasy. Did you make use of it, Mr. Navón?"

"I started writing down what I had in mind but then decided it would be better to speak to someone in your company first to see what's possible."

"The first step should be filling in that section. If you have trouble describing what you wish for, you can include names of movies or books that resemble the kind of adventure you wish to experience, and it's not limited to specific ratings. We are all adults here, and we deal with adult themes."

Toven got to his feet and started pacing. "I have no problem describing what I want. What I'm worried about is the ability of those reading my description to breathe life into it."

"That's what we do here, Mr. Navón. We bring fantasies to life. I will personally oversee your file, and after I read through your submitted questionnaire, I'll let you know if more customization is needed and how much it will cost."

"Fair enough."

"If you submit it within the next hour, I will probably be able to get back to you before the end of the day."

Toven doubted that he would be done so quickly. He was a fast thinker, but creativity required time. The brain needed to soak up ideas, turn them around, and then spit out possible scenarios. But even if he somehow managed to accomplish that in less than sixty minutes, Brian would probably not be there.

He glanced at his watch. "It's five in the afternoon where I am. What time is it where you are?"

"The Perfect Match headquarters are on the West Coast. It's only two o'clock here, but I'm not your typical nine-to-five kind of guy. If I leave here before ten at night, I call it a short day."

"Working so late on a Friday night means that you love what you do." Or had no prospects of securing a date.

"I do. Not only do I get to work with the best minds in the virtual industry, but my work makes people happy. Sometimes I feel like a god, granting wishes and making dreams come true."

Toven smiled. "Being a god is not all it's cracked up to be."

"Too much responsibility?"

"No, that's not it. A god can take as much or as little responsibility as he or she wants. It's just that some wishes even a god cannot grant."

"That's true. But I'm happy with those I can. I'll be

watching out for your submittal, Mr. Navón. I'm curious to see what kind of adventure you have in mind."

"I'll get right on it, but I doubt that I'll be done within an hour or even by tomorrow. May I call you if I have questions pertaining to the questionnaire?"

"Of course. The number I called you from is my personal cell phone. Feel free to call me back at this number. I'm available at all hours."

The poor guy had no life. "Thank you for giving it your personal attention, Brian. I appreciate it. Your dedication to your customers is commendable."

"It's my pleasure, Mr. Navón."

When Toven ended the call, he didn't pull up the digital questionnaire. Instead, he opened his desk drawer and took out a fresh journal. There was no substitute for hand-writing his ideas. It helped him focus his attention, sharpen his mind, and crystallize his vision.

Also, drawing what he had in mind might be easier than expressing his thoughts in words. He could scan his sketches and upload them into the comment section of the questionnaire. Perhaps he could even add a few pictures of exotic locales and beauty ideals.

Hand drawing had not been mentioned as an option, but then most people couldn't express themselves well in that medium.

Sitting back down, Toven closed his eyes and envisioned the world to which he wished to escape. Perhaps it wouldn't be on Earth at all. Some of the environments offered by Perfect Match were on alien planets, and Brian might be right that with some tweaking, they could serve as the backdrop for his adventure.

In fact, what Toven had envisioned before had been too limited. If he wanted to be someone completely different from who he was in reality, then he should let his imagination soar.

For example, he could be a dragon shifter or a dragon slayer.

Toven snorted. "Been there, done that, just not in the flesh."

The primitives had thought that his flying machine was part of him, and he'd been called a dragon, a winged serpent, and other similarly colorful names. But to actually have wings and fly through the sky without the help of a motorized contraption should be an extraordinary experience.

Almost as if in a trance, Toven sketched an image of a winged male who had his face. Neither an angel nor a demon, the male looked as sad and broken as Toven felt. Flipping the pencil around, he erased that sorry expression and drew a fierce one. Tobias would be a winged warrior, the last descendant of a proud race...

No, that was also too close to the truth.

Tobias would be part of an order of fierce warriors, the defenders of...what?

Toven was reminded of a line from a movie. "I give to you, the seeker of serenity, the protector of Italian virginity...the one, the only, Sir Ulrich..."

Toven chuckled. *A Knight's Tale* was one of his favorite movies. It was such a shame that the young star's life had been cut short prematurely.

With a sigh, he looked at his sketch and added a sword and a shield. Tobias Navón and his order were the protectors of a rare race of sprites, a sort of nymphs who were hunted by...demon-like creatures who coveted their shimmering wings.

Toven chuckled. That was too clichéd. He needed to come up with something more original. Then again, if he wanted a woman to match with him, he needed to keep the fantasy within the confines of known tropes. He could push the limits a little, though, make it more interesting for himself and for the lady who desired a similar fantasy.

After all, the type of woman he was interested in had a vivid imagination and a creative personality. She would appreciate a fantasy that was a little off the beaten track.

9

DARLENE

*T*he village was more or less how Darlene had imagined it, with lots of greenery, nice houses, and meandering pathways. The exception was the village square, with its office building, café, and clinic that made it different from other gated communities, and so was the lack of roads and cars. Everyone parked in the underground and continued on foot, which wasn't very convenient for bringing groceries home.

Supposedly, several golf carts were available for the village occupants' use, but Darlene hadn't seen any on her way to Geraldine and Shai's home.

It was clear that the village was designed for able-bodied people, which the immortals were.

Everyone looked so damn young, making Darlene feel even older than she actually was. She knew that some of them were probably ancient, but that didn't help her feel any better. So far, she was the only one around who showed any signs of aging.

Roni, Sylvia, and Nick were young for real, chronologically. But Ruth looked the same age as her daughter, and Geraldine looked much younger than even Cassandra, who was chronologically young and biologically even younger.

Shai was considered young for an immortal, and Onegus was really old.

"I invited William to the barbecue on Sunday," Roni said as he cast a meaningful glance at Cassandra. "Only the promise of good food can get him away from the lab. The guy spends every waking moment in there, and sometimes he even sleeps on a cot in his office."

"Who's William?" Darlene asked.

Given the look Roni had given Cassandra, William was someone her son wanted Darlene to meet. Hopefully, he wasn't setting her up on a blind date because she would be very upset if that was why he'd invited the guy.

"He's the clan's tech guy," Shai said. "William is a real genius who is in charge of developing all the cool gadgets we have. He was also involved in developing the Perfect Match virtual machine. I'm sure you've seen their commercials. They are all over the streaming channels and even some of the broadcast networks."

"I did, but I thought it was just a lot of hype over a new virtual reality game."

"It's much more than that," Nick said. "When you are hooked up to the machine, you get to experience living in a different world through an avatar of your choice. Kian and Syssi invested in the company when it was just in the development stages, and when the original inventors got stuck and couldn't solve a major problem with the software, William was brought on board to assist. Without him, there would be no Perfect Match."

"You might want to give it a try, Mom." Roni pulled the platter with baked fish toward him. "We have two machines in the village for our exclusive use. Maybe you'll find your perfect match that way."

So she'd been right, and her son was trying to get her to

meet a new guy before she even filed for a divorce from the man who was signed on his birth certificate.

"I'm still married to Leo."

Roni arched one brow. "That didn't stop you before."

Her cheeks heating up, Darlene cast her son a baleful glare. "We were separated at the time, and I was much younger then."

"You can think of yourself as separated from him now as well. Besides, a virtual hookup doesn't count. It's like watching porn, and I'm sure dear old Leo is doing a lot of that."

Swallowing the lump in her throat, Darlene asked, "Is that all he's doing?"

The silence around the dining table was so thick she could slice it with a knife.

"As far as I know," Roni admitted. "I hacked into the surveillance feed from the last two hotels he stayed in, and it seems that he spent his nights alone."

The relief made Darlene feel buoyant. "Thank heavens." She let out a breath. "We had a huge fight earlier today when I told him that I was going to spend the weekend with my cousins, and I said some things that I shouldn't have. I will apologize once I get my phone back on Monday."

The disappointment on Roni's face was like a punch to her gut.

"What's your hurry?" He glared at her. "He's not going to be home on Monday. You can stay longer."

"I need to call him and apologize. I don't want that stupid fight to be the last conversation between us."

Again, no one said a word, and other than Roni and Geraldine, everyone pretended to be very busy looking at their plates.

"You can't ignore what he did, Mother. He sold me out."

"What proof do we have of that? Maybe it was just hearsay?"

"It wasn't," Onegus said. "Syssi's brother works in the same government building where Roni was imprisoned. He asked around and was told that Leo sold out his son. Andrew has no stake in any of it, and he's a very trust-worthy guy."

"Andrew got me out of there," Roni said. "I owe my freedom to him." He turned to Sylvia. "And to you. If not for your ability to mess with electronics, I would still be rotting away in that tiny apartment on the fifth floor."

The lump in Darlene's throat had grown so large that she could barely breathe. She tried to take a sip of water but had difficulty swallowing through the constriction.

She wanted to cry, she wanted to holler, she wanted to strangle Leo and kiss Roni to make it better, but all she could do was sit like a dummy at Geraldine's dining table and choke on her own cowardice.

10

ALIYA

*a*s the jet started its descent, Aliya looked out the window at the mountains below. They weren't as green or as dense as the ones around Lugu Lake.

"Are you excited?" Vrog asked.

He'd been seated next to her during the long flight, which she'd feared would be uncomfortable, but he'd been pleasant company and had even held her hand during takeoff when she'd had a few moments of panic.

It wasn't natural for wingless creatures to be soaring through the sky inside a hunk of metal.

Aliya had to remind herself that her ancestors had traversed the empty space between the stars on a spacecraft, so flying a few miles above the Earth in a manmade machine was not such a big deal in comparison.

"I don't know how I should feel," Aliya said. "I'm looking forward to meeting new people, but I'm also wary of their reaction to me despite what Alena told me. They might be welcoming to others like them, I mean immortals who look human, but I'm not related to them, and some might see me as a threat or just an intruder who doesn't belong."

Vrog nodded. "People in the village are friendly, but I've gotten a few not-so-friendly looks. Although in my case, they were duly earned. I was the hothead who'd attacked Stella, and her mate didn't let me or anyone else forget it."

"Is he still mad at you?"

Vrog shrugged. "Richard doesn't like me, but that's understandable. He's mated to Stella and has a good relationship with Vlad. He perceives me as a threat to their family unit."

"Are you?"

"Maybe. Vlad appreciates Richard, but he will never think of him as a father, no matter how hard Richard tries to earn that title. Vlad considers him a good friend, but that's all. I hope to one day earn the title of father even though I wasn't there for Vlad when he was growing up."

"It's not the Kra-ell way." Aliya straightened in her seat and tightened the safety belt around her. "The children belong to the females, and the males protect and support all the children, not just their own."

"Vlad is only one-quarter Kra-ell, and our customs don't apply to him. That being said, the clan adopted similar attitudes toward its young. Although in their case, it was done out of necessity. The human fathers had no place among the immortals, and since up until recently the clan males couldn't have long-lived young of their own, they served as providers and protectors for all the clan children, the same way as the Kra-ell males did in our tribe."

"Not the same. The purebloaded males of our tribe were the fathers of most of the children born in the compound. The clan males were just the uncles and cousins. I think that makes a big difference."

"Does it?" Vrog lifted a brow. "They didn't act like fathers or even uncles or cousins. Most of the purebloods ignored their children, even the purebloaded ones.

Although in my case, it wasn't so bad. My father treated me kindly. He wasn't as indifferent or cruel as the others."

"Mine wasn't bad either," Aliya murmured. "I still miss him. We didn't have much of a relationship, but I knew who he was, and he knew that I was his, and I felt a little safer knowing that my father would protect me if needed. Although I never imagined that we would be attacked by others of our kind. The only protection I thought I needed was from bullying by the pureblooded children or their mothers."

Vrog tilted his head. "I thought that as a female you were spared their petty bullying."

"It wasn't as bad as it was for the boys, but I also got beaten up. Jade said that it was part of growing up, and that if I couldn't defend myself, I had no business belonging to her tribe."

"She was a sweetheart." Vrog's sarcastic tone didn't leave room for misinterpretation. "A true Spartan."

"What's a Spartan?"

"Spartans were a Greek warrior society."

"Were they like the Kra-ell?"

"In some respects. Any baby judged weak or deformed was left at Mount Taygetus to die because the Spartan society was no place for those who could not fend for themselves. But like most human societies of the time, they were patriarchal, and women had very few rights compared to the men."

Aliya shivered. "That's so bad. Even Jade would have never left a baby to die. She would have given them away to humans."

Vrog chuckled. "It's sad and funny at the same time. I guess there are many shades of monsters out there, and we should be thankful that Jade wasn't the darkest of them."

"I feared and respected Jade, but I didn't hate her." Aliya looked out the window again. "I think that she did her best to run the compound." She turned back to Vrog. "Vlad should be glad that he has you in his life, and he shouldn't blame you for not being there for him when you didn't even know where he and Stella were."

"Vlad is not the problem." Vrog smiled. "Richard is resentful enough for the two of them."

"Richard should mind his own business. And if he's still mad about you attacking his mate, he can challenge you to a duel."

"He won't. I'm much stronger than he is, and he knows it."

That was obvious. If she was stronger than two immortal warriors, then Vrog should not have been defeated by Stella's mate. Perhaps Richard had a gun? Had he taken Vrog by surprise?

Aliya had wanted to ask about that for days, but to do so in front of the others would have embarrassed Vrog.

Leaning closer to his ear, she whispered, "How did Stella's mate overpower you? Is he a compeller?"

"He's not," Vrog answered out loud, seemingly not embarrassed at all. "Richard had vials of sleeping potion that the clan doctor had concocted for them. They were just a safety measure in case they encountered humans who were immune to thralling and needed to be knocked out. It wasn't supposed to affect the immortals at all, but it worked on me. I don't know if that's because my human half is stronger, or if the Kra-ell are not immune to what was in the potion. It didn't knock me out like it would a human, but it disoriented me and weakened my muscle control enough for Richard to finish the job with his fists. He gave me quite a beating."

Surprisingly, Vrog didn't seem shamed by his defeat, which was atypical for a Kra-ell, even a hybrid. When one of the purebloods was defeated by another, the one who'd lost would be ridiculed by all the other purebloods. Even the hybrids had been allowed to poke fun at him.

"Wasn't Vlad mad at you for attacking his mother?"

"Vlad is a good man." Vrog smiled. "Maybe not by Kra-ell standards, but by human and immortal ones. He's nonviolent and nonaggressive. He's a graphic artist, for Mother's sake. A pureblooded father would have disowned him for engaging in such unmanly activities."

Aliya twirled the end of her braid around her fingers. "Then who created artful things in Jade's quarters? If it was dishonorable for the males to engage in, then it was even more so for the females."

"That's a good question. I think that only humans engaged in creative endeavors, but I might be mistaken. Hybrids weren't allowed access to the purebloods' inner sanctum."

"Except for me. Jade allowed me to hang around the females."

"I've been thinking about that." Kalugal swiveled his seat around to face them. "Maybe your mind holds a treasure trove of forgotten conversations that you overheard as a child. I should hypnotize you and try to retrieve them. Maybe we could learn a few more clues about Kra-ell history."

MIA

"Thanks for coming to help me." Mia hooked up her laptop to the big screen monitor on her desk. "This questionnaire is crazy. I scrolled through it, and it has like five hundred questions per section, and there are several of them. It will take me days to answer all of them." She turned to her friends. "Maybe we could divide them between us? It's not like cheating on a test. No one cares who actually supplies the answers, and you two know what I like."

Squinting at the screen, Margo pulled her glasses out of her purse and plunked them on her nose. "Many of them are just yes or no boxes to check off, so it's not so bad. But I suggest that we start with what matters most." She took her glasses off and smiled at Mia. "What do you want your dream guy to look like?"

"That's not what matters most," Mia protested.

"That depends on what you want to get out of it," Margo said. "If you're looking for your Mister Right, then of course personality and character are the most important. But since you are only interested in a hookup, you shouldn't waste time on that and focus on looks."

Mia disagreed. If she got paired with a sleaze-ball, a bully, or just an ignoramus, the virtual hookup wouldn't be enjoyable.

"Buff," Frankie said. "Since it's Mia's fantasy, he can have Thor's amazing body and Loki's cunning mind."

"I like Thor's personality more than Loki's," Mia said. "He's a nice guy. Loki is a self-serving jerk."

Frankie folded her arms over her chest and stuck out her chin. "Loki has redeeming qualities. Just when you think he's the worst kind of scum, he saves the day."

Mia shook her head. "I would never trust a guy like that, and if I can't trust him, I can't get romantic with him either. He has to be nice."

"Define nice." Margo pulled out her tablet. "I'm going to take notes because the next section is probably about his character."

"Let me check." Mia scrolled down the page and then down another one. "Look at this. This section has almost seven hundred questions. I didn't even know you could describe physical attributes in so many details. Perhaps I will draw them a picture instead."

"Not a bad idea." Margo waved her stylus up and down in a nodding gesture. "They say that a picture is worth a thousand words, right?"

Mia scrolled down another page. "Here it is. Character attributes. The first one is a good sense of humor. I'm going to mark it as a definite yes."

Margo lifted her stylus. "Hold on. If you check funny, you might get a clown. They are amusing, but not very sexy, and we want sexy."

"Funny can be sexy," Frankie protested.

"On a scale of one to ten, how important is a good sense of humor?" Mia leaned away from the screen so her friends could see it. "I can mark it as seven."

Frankie gave her the thumbs up. "Go for it. What's next?"

"Chivalrous. I'll mark it as a ten."

"Don't," Margo protested. "Chivalrous can be a euphemism for chauvinist."

Mia rolled her eyes. "My grandpa is chivalrous. Does that make him a chauvinist?"

"Of course it does, but he's eighty-nine, so he's allowed. Besides, I love your grandpa. He's a sweetheart."

Everyone loved her grandfather because he was a great guy who was always ready to help, whether it was with a kind word or with his toolbox. If she could find a man like that to call her own, Mia would consider herself lucky. But as her grandma liked to say, they just didn't make them like that anymore.

"Why do you think that my granddaddy is a chauvinist?"

Margo rolled her eyes. "If a man treats women differently than he treats men, it means that he's a closet misogynist."

"I disagree." Mia marked chivalrous as a ten. "And even if you're right, I still want that."

Margo shrugged. "It's your fantasy. You can do whatever you want."

"Intelligence," Mia read the next item. "That's a ten as well, and so is emotional intelligence."

"Good luck with that," Frankie murmured under her breath. "Are you looking for a hookup or a best friend?"

"Now you're being a misandrist." Mia cast her friend a mock glare. "Men can be emotionally intelligent and still be manly."

"Not in my experience." Frankie scribbled a note on the tablet. "So you want a smart, empathetic guy with a good sense of humor, who looks like Thor. Do you also want him to have a single horn on his forehead? Because you are describing a unicorn."

"Why not? It's my fantasy. Besides, he can look like a marshmallow in real life, and just use a beautiful avatar in the virtual world. That's why personality and character are more important. He can't fake that."

"You're right." Margo wrapped her arm around Mia's shoulders. "I'm glad that we solved the problem of the physical description. Just draw a picture of Thor."

Mia scrunched her nose. "I prefer men with dark hair."

"So give him black hair. What do you want your own avatar to look like?"

That had been the first thing Mia had visualized.

Smiling, she lifted her sketchbook, flipped it to the page she'd been working on the entire morning, and handed it to Margo. "Like this."

"Oh, Mia." Her friend's eyes brightened. "That's adorable, and she looks a lot like you, just with pointy ears and slightly slanted eyes."

Mia chuckled. "I wish I was that pretty."

"You are." Margo held up the sketch next to Mia's face. "What do you think, Frankie?"

Mia could count on Frankie to be truthful even when the truth was painful.

"If you cut your hair short and color it black with purple streaks, you will look like this. We can also do your makeup to match the picture."

"I say we take you to the hair salon today." Margo swiveled Mia's chair around. "We can all get new hairstyles."

Mia sighed. "By the time we finish the questionnaire, everything will be closed, and before you offer, I'm not letting you cut my hair."

Margo laughed. "The last time I gave you a haircut we were eight, and I haven't dared touch yours, or anyone else's hair since. I think you cried for a week after your grandma took you to the salon to fix what I'd done, and they cut it short."

"That's about right." Mia swiveled her chair back to face the screen to hide her eyes from her friends.

To her eight-year-old self, losing her long hair had seemed like the end of the world. If she'd known what was still in store for her, Mia would have shrugged off that episode and not wasted even one tear on her missing braid. Then again, if she'd known that she was living with a ticking bomb in her chest, she would have missed out on much more. She would have been living as she did now—leading a very cautious and boring life.

RONJA

"Mom!" Lisa called from the kitchen. "It's David. He wants to talk to you."

Ronja took out her earphones. "Why didn't he call my mobile?"

"He called me." Lisa walked into the living room and handed Ronja her phone. "He's mad," she mouthed. "You didn't tell him."

Ronja put her finger over the mic. "Didn't tell him what?"

"That you are going for the transition."

"I thought it was self-explanatory when Merlin moved in." She'd told David about that but hadn't volunteered more information. Her sex life wasn't a subject she wanted to discuss with her children.

Ronja moved her finger off the mic and lifted the phone to her ear. "Hello, David. How is your book coming along?"

That usually got him talking for an hour, telling her about the newest plot twists in the novel he was working on, and asking her advice about this or that character.

"Splendidly, thanks for asking. But what I want to

59

know is why I had to hear from Lisa that you are attempting to transition. You should have told me."

Her ploy hadn't worked. Evidently, David was too upset to talk about his novel, which was a shame since she really enjoyed their literary conversations. It was a much more interesting topic of conversation than her love life.

"You know that Merlin moved in with Lisa and me. The rest shouldn't come as a big surprise to you."

"One does not automatically mean the other. I thought that you would let me know when you started. I need to be there when you transition for Lisa and for myself. She will need my support."

Sighing, Ronja switched the phone to her other ear. "It might take weeks until I start to transition, and then the transition itself might take a long time. I was told that Turner was in a coma for over two weeks."

"That's irrelevant. You are my mother, and I want to be by your side at a critical time like that. I'm flying over."

She rolled her eyes. "I would love to have you here, but it doesn't make sense for you to come now. Sari can't take such a long vacation, and as a newly mated immortal, you can't stand to be away from her for more than a day. Wait until I start to transition and then come. After all, I will be under a doctor's supervision the entire time, and you have nothing to worry about."

"That's not true, and you know it. I'm glad that Merlin is your mate and that he will watch over you, but I need to be there not as a doctor but as your son and Lisa's brother."

"I agree, but you shouldn't come prematurely. Will Sari accompany you?"

"She'd better. As you said, I can't stand being without her for more than a few hours, and the same is true for her." He chuckled. "We had another desk brought into her office so I could work on my novel and be with her at the same time."

"How do you manage to concentrate? She's constantly on the phone or talking with people who stop by her office."

"I have my noise-canceling headphones on, but they are not much help. I can still hear everything that's going on around me, just muted. But since I can't concentrate without her near me anyway, I have to train myself to ignore the sounds of conversations while I'm working."

Pushing to her feet, Ronja walked over to the kitchen. "What are you planning to do once your sabbatical is over? Are you going to submit your resignation?"

"I don't have a choice. Sari can't leave her post, but even if she could, I would never ask it of her."

Ronja didn't like the idea of David giving up his career to be with Sari. He'd worked very hard to get his professorial position in Stanford, and he loved his work.

"She could if she transferred her people to the village. Sari and Kian could take turns managing things. I also think that Annani should move here together with the clan members from Alaska."

David chuckled. "Perhaps you should ask to join the council, so you could influence clan policy."

Ronja laughed. "I don't think that they have any seats open, or that they hold democratic elections for those seats."

"I don't think it's fair that the humans living in the village are not represented in the council."

He sounded serious, but that was David's brand of dry humor, and she knew that he was teasing. "Since the only humans in the village are Lisa and me, I don't think your argument would fly."

"You have a point, but you could represent all the non-immortals. That's you, Lisa, and the three hybrid Kra-ell. It could also be argued that the Odus are non-immortals in need of representation, but since they deserve a separate classification, they need their own representative."

Now she really wasn't sure whether David was serious or not. "You are being silly. You know that, right?" Ronja activated the speakerphone and pulled a bottle of water out of the fridge.

"What did he say?" Lisa asked.

"He wants me to run for a position on the council, but since it's not elected democratically, he's just teasing."

"If it's not, it should be, and I meant everything I said. Five people might not be that many, but given that the entire clan numbers less than a thousand, it's not such an outrageous proposition for them to seek representation."

"You can't lump together hybrid Kra-ell and humans. Besides, there are only two of them and neither is in the village right now. Emmett will return at some point, but I doubt Vrog will. He has a school to run."

"I have news for you, Mother. Not only is Vrog coming back, but they also have a hybrid Kra-ell female with them, who Kian offered a place in the village."

Lisa's eyes widened. "Awesome! Is she as horrible as the other Kra-ell females?"

"What did you hear?" Ronja asked Lisa.

"That they are cruel and bitchy."

"Alena told Sari that Aliya is very nice," David said. "And I'm sure she will need a friend. So instead of prejudging her, how about befriending her?"

"How old is she?" Lisa asked.

"She's thirty, but she lived in isolation for the past fourteen years, so emotionally she's like a sixteen-year-old."

"Yeah, but she's not going to go to school with Parker and me, right?"

"Not likely."

"Then I'm not the best girl for the job because I'm not in the village most of the day. Ella could be her friend, though, and also Wonder. Wonder is ancient, but according to your logic, she's nineteen emotionally because she was in stasis for most her life."

David chuckled. "Wonder is in a category of her own, but maybe you are right. Sari says that I should leave it up to Alena to take care of Aliya, so don't worry about it. What I need you to do is contact me the moment Mom starts transitioning."

"I will. I don't want to face this alone." She turned a pair of worried eyes at Ronja. "Maybe it's not such a bad idea for David to come now instead of waiting for me to call him."

"Oh, sweetie." Ronja pulled her daughter into her arms. "David and Sari can be here the next day, but you will not be alone until they arrive. Merlin is here for both of us, and so are Bowen and Margaret, Parker and his family, and all the other friends we've made in the village. We have an entire community ready to support us."

13

KIAN

*K*ian shifted his gaze from the new furniture occupying the center of the entry pavilion to the balloons tied to Allegra's stroller and shook his head at Amanda. "You overdid it with the welcome wagon this time."

Amanda shrugged. "I wanted to do this for the longest time and kept postponing it, which is not like me. I should have done it the day it occurred to me that welcoming guests down in the parking garage was ridiculous."

Kian very much doubted that the idea to furnish the entry pavilion with a sitting area was older than a day or two.

Amanda, who wanted to welcome their sister right as she arrived at the village, was in no condition to stand for even several minutes. Naturally, that hadn't deterred her, and since she'd had a couple of days to prepare, she'd gone all out, turning the glass pavilion from a mere entryway into a lobby.

Yesterday, she'd sent Ingrid shopping with Onidu, and today the pavilion had two couches that were covered in some sort of dark gray fabric that looked like leather but wasn't and had shiny chrome legs. Four matching armchairs, three occasional tables, an area rug, and several decorative pillows and other pieces completed the ensemble.

Since there were ten of them in the welcome wagon, Amanda must have planned the number of seats accordingly. Geraldine, Shai, Onegus, and Cassandra were there to welcome Orion and Alena, while Vlad and Wendy had come to welcome Vrog and Aliya.

Darlene had stayed at Roni's to help Sylvia and him to prepare for the barbecue later today, which was good because Kian had planned on seeing her there and not before.

Allegra cooed at the balloons, her eyes wide and bright as she gazed at the colorful display overhead.

"Your daughter likes them." Amanda's expression was smug.

"Of course, she does. She's a baby."

"No one is too old for balloons, except for you, old goat."

Kian laughed. "I haven't heard that one in a while. You must be in a good mood."

"I hear the elevator," Syssi said. "It must be them."

"Give me a hand." Amanda heaved herself up with Dalhu's help. "When the elevator doors open, I want everyone to yell 'congratulations, Alena and Orion!'"

Kian had no such intentions. A regent didn't yell unless it was, 'engage!'

But as Alena stepped out of the elevator and everyone yelled 'congratulations,' he joined in, just not as loudly.

Alena looked so happy, and Orion seemed to have grown a couple of inches.

When his sisters embraced, Kian clapped Orion on the back. "Who would have thought that we would be celebrating such a happy occasion so soon. When is the wedding?"

Normally he wouldn't have asked, but Annani had told him that the subject had been brought up and that Alena and Orion wanted a clan-wide celebration.

"As soon as it can be arranged. With your permission, I would like to invite the entire clan."

"So I heard, and I have no problem with that." Kian cast a glance at Amanda. "But if you want the queen of parties to organize it, you will need to wait until Amanda's baby is born and she has recuperated enough to resume her command post."

"Naturally."

As the other elevator door opened, Orion stepped aside. "Let me introduce Aliya."

The female was tall, nearly Kian's height, very slim, and looked like a deer caught in headlights, her huge eyes blazing turquoise one moment and red the next. According to Emmett, Kra-ell eyes blazed different colors corresponding to their emotions, but Kian couldn't remember which one indicated what. Turquoise was probably the color of excitement, while red was most likely the color of aggression or fear.

Alena pulled out from Syssi's arms and walked over to Aliya. "Everything is okay. The screeching, yelling, and the balloons are just my family's way of expressing their happiness for Orion and me."

Aliya forced a smile, which was a sorry attempt at one. It seemed like the female wasn't used to smiling.

"Welcome to the village, Aliya." Kian offered her his hand. "I'm Kian."

Instead of taking it, she bowed, bending nearly in half. "Thank you for inviting me. I vow to become a useful member of your community for as long as I enjoy your hospitality."

From Vrog's story, Kian knew that the Kra-ell took their vows very seriously, so Aliya's was as good as binding.

Emmett had found a way to circumvent the vows he'd been forced to pledge to Jade, but Kian was starting to realize that Emmett wasn't a typical Kra-ell.

"I have no doubt that you will. I want you to feel at home here." He motioned for Onegus to come forward. "I'm very diligent about my clan's safety, which is why you will have to wear a cuff around your wrist until you prove yourself."

Aliya took a step back, partially hiding behind Alena. "You didn't say anything about handcuffs. You said that I would be a guest, not a prisoner."

Alena put a reassuring hand on Aliya's back. "I didn't know that my brother would want to put a cuff on you, but it's not a restraining device, it's just a location tracker." She glared at Kian. "Is that really necessary? Who is she going to run to? Besides, we promised to let Aliya go if she's not happy here."

"I'm well aware of that. But when she leaves, she does so sans her memories of us and the village. As long as she keeps her memories, I need to keep an eye on her." He turned to Aliya. "You have my word that as soon as you tell me that you want to leave, your memories of us will be erased, the cuff removed, and you'll be on the next flight to China."

Aliya was still hiding behind Alena, which was ridiculous since she was taller than his sister.

"I mean no offense, but I need you to vow it."

"I vow that you will not be kept here against your will."

Her eyes turning nearly black, Aliya inclined her head. "If I vow not to leave without having my memories of you and your people erased first, can I come to your village without a cuff?"

"Please," Alena mouthed. "For me."

"Fine." He motioned for Onegus to put the cuff away. "But one wrong move and the cuff goes on."

"Thank you." Aliya stepped in front of Alena to offer him her hand. "You won't regret it."

He already did.

"I hope I won't." He shook what she offered.

14

ALIYA

*H*er suitcase handle clutched in one hand, Aliya extended the other to Vlad. "I'm honored to meet you."

He smiled. "You probably mean pleased, and the feeling is mutual."

She frowned. "Is it wrong to say honored?"

"It's not, but you usually say it to someone important, or someone you admire."

"Then I meant honored. Your father told me a lot about you, and you sounded like someone I would like as a member of my tribe. Therefore, I'm honored to meet you."

Vlad looked embarrassed. "I'm no one special."

"He's so modest." His mate offered her hand to Aliya. "I'm Wendy, and I'm so happy that you'll be staying with us."

Aliya took Wendy's hand and dipped her head. "Thank you for inviting me to your home."

She wasn't sure what protocol they followed, and whose hand she should have shaken first, Wendy's or Vlad's.

The girl smiled and cast a quick glance at Vrog. "I hope

you don't mind sharing a room. We have only one extra bedroom. If you do, we can ask Ingrid to open up one of the vacant houses for you or for Aliya, but I think that it will be more fun if both of you stay with us. I work in the café during the days, and Vlad is in the bakery early in the morning and then goes to school, so you'll have the house to yourselves."

Aliya didn't know what to say.

"I'll sleep on the living room couch," Vrog said. "Aliya and I are still at the courtship stage." He gave her a tight smile.

"Oh." Wendy's face fell. "Well, that's also an option." She smiled at Aliya. "I hope you are not too tired after the flight. I organized a little get-together for you and Vrog and invited my mother and her mate and Vlad's mother and hers."

"It is your house. I'm just a guest." Aliya followed Wendy out of the pavilion.

The others had already left, and only their little group had lingered behind. Phinas had cast her an unreadable glance before following Kalugal and Jacki out, and she'd smiled at him with what she'd hoped had been a reassuring expression.

Aliya was going home with Vrog, but Phinas wasn't out of the race. She hadn't decided yet who she wanted to invite to her bed first and lose her virginity to. For some reason, every time she thought about inviting Phinas she got excited, while the same thoughts regarding Vrog made her anxious.

Perhaps it was because Phinas had no expectations, so she couldn't disappoint him. She would, however, disappoint Vrog if he expected her to be anything like the pure-blooded females.

"I want you to be comfortable," Wendy said. "It's your first day at the village, and it must be overwhelming."

Aliya glanced in the direction of an outdoor café that was crowded with people. It seemed that they would be passing by it, and she dreaded the looks she would no doubt get. "It's very pretty here. Is there a way to get to your house without going through there?" She pointed.

"I'm afraid not." Wendy threaded her arm through Aliya's. "Just smile, wave, and keep going." She patted her arm. "Not too long ago, I was new to this place as well, and I came with nasty baggage."

Aliya turned her head to look at the suitcase she was rolling behind her. "Is my luggage okay?"

For some reason, her question had everyone in their group either laughing or chuckling.

"You have no baggage," Wendy finally said after her laughter died out. "Well, I heard that you beat up Arwel and Phinas, but they don't seem to be holding it against you."

"I was just defending myself." Aliya looked at her suitcase again. "My English is not so good. I thought that baggage and luggage mean the same thing."

"Your English is excellent, and you are right. They do. But baggage can also be used to describe your past deeds, or your obligations, or even your emotional state. Everything that weighs you down can be called baggage."

"So if I'm sad, I can say that I have baggage?"

"No, that wouldn't work." Wendy turned to Vrog. "You are the teacher. Can you explain?"

"Certainly." Vrog fell in step with Aliya. "The beliefs and feelings that influence how we think and behave and sometimes how others perceive us can be called emotional baggage. Using your example, the sadness itself is not the baggage, but what caused you to be sad might be. For example, you might be sad because you miss someone you lost, or you might be sad because you heard something that upset you."

She still didn't understand the difference but was embarrassed to keep asking. In time she would understand. "This really is a village. You have no roads here and no cars. It's nice."

"We have souped-up golf carts," Wendy said.

Aliya stifled a groan. She didn't know what a golf cart was, but she assumed it was some kind of a small vehicle. Could the immortals have invented something that ran on soup?

"Oh, boy." Wendy chuckled. "I've just used another phrase that you don't understand. You're probably wondering what soup has to do with golf carts."

Aliya nodded.

"It means improved or supercharged," Vrog said. "Like you and me. Compared to the immortals, we are souped-up. We are stronger, faster, and we have sharper senses."

"True, but they live longer."

Vrog smiled. "Can't have everything, I suppose."

15

MIA

"We are done for today." Frankie dropped back on Mia's bed. "It took hours."

They'd had tons of fun, teasing and making jokes and laughing until their bellies hurt. Perhaps they would have accomplished more if they hadn't horsed around so much, but they'd still completed the most difficult parts, and the rest Mia could do on her own later.

"I couldn't have done it without you. You were awesome." Mia glanced at her watch. "We can still make it to the hair salon. Now I'm super motivated to look like my avatar. My dream guy awaits."

"Let me check with Rick." Frankie typed a message to their stylist.

The three of them had been going to Ricardo since he'd opened his first salon over ten years ago. It had been just a room in his rented apartment, and he hadn't had the required licenses, so his customers were people he knew and friends of friends. Now, he had a fancy salon on Breyer Street with twelve other stylists working for him.

"First, we eat. I'm hungry." Margo pushed to her feet

and opened the bedroom door. "I'm going to help your grandma set up the lunch table."

"Thanks, Margo. I promise to help you fill out your questionnaire when I get you a digital token for your birthday."

"I'm counting on it." Margo winked before closing the door behind her.

Frankie's phone pinged with an incoming message. "It's Ricardo. He says that he can see us at five. He'll keep the salon open for us."

"Tell him that he's the best." Mia examined her shoulder-length hair in the monitor's reflective screen.

Cutting it short and dying it black was a big departure from her regular style, but Mia felt that it was time for a change. Besides, her hair would grow back in no time, and changing back to her natural color wasn't a big deal either.

"He knows." Frankie typed up a message back and then turned on her stomach. Propping her elbows on the mattress, she put her chin on her hands. "It was fun. I felt like we were building characters for a story. You could use the same steps when you write your children's books."

"I didn't think of that, but you are right. We all learned something today."

"Yeah." Frankie smirked. "I learned that you dream of a fae prince with interesting sexual proclivities."

Blushing, Mia rolled her eyes. "I had limited choices. I couldn't go for anything too taxing because my body wouldn't have known that I'm not actually moving, and my heart might have been unable to tolerate all that excitement. So instead of a fast-paced adventure, I chose one that happens in one place, doesn't involve chases, explosions, or gunfire but is still complex enough to attract the kind of men I'm interested in."

"You don't have to apologize." Frankie gave her a smile. "I applaud your courage and honesty." Her smile wilted.

"Speaking of which, did you let the Perfect Match people know about your limitations?"

"I told them about the implant. That's the only thing they should be concerned with. The rest is none of their business."

"You're absolutely right. What did they say?"

"That I will be supervised by one of their doctors. The technician I spoke to said that the inventors of the virtual machine originally designed it for people with disabilities, so it has many safeguards built into it, but since I have a heart problem, they want to be extra careful. Naturally, I had to sign a waiver that I'm aware of the risks and will not hold them responsible if my heart gives out."

Frankie grimaced. "That's not very reassuring."

"Can you blame them? I'm happy that they let me go on the adventure at all."

"When I bought the token, I asked if you'd be able to use the virtual machine. They told me that you could, but if you decided not to use the token for medical reasons, they would refund the cost."

"I want to do it." Mia looked at the sketch she'd made of her avatar. "I can't wait to become her."

"What's her name?"

"Azul."

Frankie arched a brow. "Blue?"

"Why not? I like blue. I even thought to color Azul's hair blue, but she looked too pretty with her black hair and purple highlights."

"Did you tell your grandparents?"

Mia nodded.

"What did they say?"

"They freaked out. I spent hours promising them that I would choose the mildest, least exciting adventure. But what finally got them to relax was letting them speak with the technician who promised that a doctor would supervise my experience."

They'd already lost their only daughter, and they'd nearly lost their only granddaughter four years ago. The last thing Mia wanted to do was cause them to worry, but she really needed that virtual adventure. Her life was so limited, there was so little she could do, and this was her chance to be all that she'd dreamt of being and had been denied because of faulty genetics. As a girl imagining her future, Mia hadn't envisioned herself still living with her grandparents at twenty-seven. She'd thought she would be married by now, or living with a boyfriend, partying at night and working hard on her career during the day.

Thankfully, she'd been able to accomplish the career part despite the difficulties, and she had her childhood friends who had stuck by her through thick and thin.

Her counselor had told her to count her blessings instead of focusing on her misfortune, and Mia had been doing her best to follow that advice. She was grateful for her grandparents, for her friends, and for the talent she'd been born with, which allowed her to earn a living from home while doing what she enjoyed.

Mia wasn't as courageous as some of the others she'd gotten to know in the rehabilitation center, though. They had helped her get on her feet, literally.

They were her heroes, the ones she looked up to, the ones she measured herself against and found herself lacking.

16

ANNANI

*A*nnani had not joined the welcoming party for Alena and Orion. She had wanted to, but as a goddess and the head of the clan, she had certain standards to maintain. People came to her, not the other way around, and that included her daughters and son.

She could not wait to hold Alena in her arms, though, and have a good joyful cry with her eldest daughter.

The news of Alena's pregnancy had been so wonderfully surprising.

Annani's gut, which usually foretold when something big was going to happen, had not foreseen that. But perhaps the uneasy feeling that had been plaguing her the entire time Alena had been gone had been her gut trying to tell her to expect big news.

Hopefully, the uneasiness was not about trouble with the pregnancy or Alena's relationship with Orion. Most likely, it had nothing to do with the pregnancy but was about separation anxiety.

With a sigh, Annani turned away from the window and walked over to the dining table that had been set up for a light lunch.

Over ten minutes had passed since Kian had texted her that Alena and Orion had arrived at the village, and since they were heading straight to her house, she was expecting them at any moment.

Only her children and their mates were coming over to her place for brunch. Later tonight, Kalugal and Jacki would join them for a big family dinner at Syssi and Kian's.

Ogidu cut her a worried glance as he came out of the kitchen with a platter of sliced bread in his hands. "Is anything wrong with the table setting, Clan Mother?"

"Everything is perfect, Ogidu. Thank you."

A smile bloomed on his face. "I am pleased, Clan Mother."

The Odus had always been good at mimicking human expressions, either tonal or facial, but lately, it had seemed to her that they had gotten more genuine. Perhaps she was imagining it, or perhaps Okidu and Onidu's reboot had affected the other Odus as well.

When the Odus were in proximity to each other, they shared information as if they were connected through something like Bluetooth technology. It was not a far-fetched idea to imagine that they could also share information about activating dormant circuitry.

She should mention it to Kian.

"I shall get the door, Clan Mother." Oshidu walked up to the front door, opened it, and bowed. "Welcome back, Mistress Alena, Master Orion. Good afternoon, Mistress Syssi, Master Kian, Mistress Amanda, Master Dalhu."

Well, some things did not change. The Odus still followed a rigid greeting protocol.

Annani smiled at her eldest daughter a moment before they flew into each other's arms and the tears started flowing freely.

"I am overjoyed." Annani wiped the moisture away with her hand and turned to Orion. "Congratulations, Daddy."

He bowed. "Thank you."

"Can I sit down?" Amanda waddled to the table.

"Of course." Annani motioned for everyone to take their seats. "The Odus have prepared a repast sure to please weary travelers."

"They had food on Kalugal's jet, Mother." Kian leaned to kiss her cheek.

"Yeah, but it wasn't very good." Amanda unfurled her napkin and put it over her belly, which made sense since anything that fell off her fork would land there and not on her knees. "Atzil prepared meals ahead of time, and they were kept frozen in the jet's freezer. Shamash reheated them for us, but I don't like eating reheated food. It just doesn't taste good. If Kalugal really wanted to treat us to luxury, he should have brought Atzil with him on the trip to cook for us right on the jet."

"Atzil has been busy." Annani lifted her coffee cup for Ogidu to refill. "He is courting Ingrid."

Amanda put her fork down. "Those two are perfect for each other. Why didn't I think of that?"

"It's better that they found each other on their own," Syssi said. "People don't like matchmaking."

"I agree," Orion said. "And I told my sister so, but naturally, she didn't listen. Roni, Cassandra, and Geraldine are planning on introducing William to Darlene at the barbecue later this afternoon."

"That's not the same as matchmaking," Syssi said. "That's what supportive family and friends should do. They create an opportunity for a couple to get to know each other without any pressure. I think it's a great idea."

Orion shook his head. "Darlene is not going to like it, and she'll likely reject William on principle rather than give him a fair chance. Besides, it's too soon. She's still married."

Kian put his fork down. "Divorce is a lengthy process,

and Darlene is already late to the game. She shouldn't wait that long."

"Is there any way to expedite it?" Alena asked. "Orion could *convince* Leo to sign the papers right away. I know it's not a hundred percent legit according to clan law, but it will save Darlene a lot of heartache and headache."

"It is a hundred percent legitimate when a clan member's life is on the line," Annani said. "Since Darlene's family belongs to the clan, so does Darlene, and the longer she waits to transition the riskier it gets. It could be argued that compelling or thralling her husband to expedite their divorce is being done to save her life."

17

DARLENE

As Roni walked over with a tall, bespectacled guy, Darlene smoothed her hand over her skirt and forced her face to relax.

This was no doubt William, the genius programmer everyone had been telling her about. He was a little pudgy, and the unfashionable Hawaiian shirt he wore was too big even for his large frame, billowing around him like a tent. He must have lost weight recently and hadn't updated his wardrobe, or perhaps he just liked being comfortable and didn't care about appearances.

William was handsome nonetheless, tall with broad shoulders, and he had kind eyes. But he looked no more than a few years older than her son. She knew that appearances were misleading, and that he could be hundreds of years old, but even if she were already divorced, she couldn't date a guy who looked like he could be her son.

Had they told him about her? Did he know why Roni was dragging him over to meet her?

Hopefully, he had no idea, so she wouldn't have to turn him down. She didn't miss Leo, but she wasn't ready to meet anyone new either.

"Mom, I want you to meet William. We work together." Roni turned to his friend. "This is Darlene, my mother."

"Nice to meet you." The guy offered her his hand. "Welcome to the village."

"Nice to meet you too." She shook what he offered. "I've heard so much about you that I feel like I know you already."

"Good things, I hope."

The man sounded unsure, which was kind of endearing.

"The word genius was uttered once or twice or a dozen times."

William actually blushed. "I'm good at what I do because I'm obsessed with it, and I spend nearly all of my waking hours working." He put a hand over his belly. "Or eating, but more often than not, I do both at the same time." He laughed nervously.

She knew all about insecurities, had enough of them to spare, but if even a smart guy like William whom everyone thought so highly of had body image issues, what chance did she have to overcome hers?

Darlene used to tell herself that life was too short to obsess about a few extra pounds, or even more than a few, but apparently immortality didn't have all the answers, and if she turned immortal, she would just have a lot more time to obsess.

Darlene cast William a reassuring smile. "I eat when I'm stressed." She lifted her plate, which was stacked with two steaks, two ribs, corn on the cob, and a small serving of potato salad. "That's my usual excuse for overeating. But today, I have a better one. I'm sampling my son's exceptional barbecuing skills."

William eyed her plate hungrily. "Roni is the best. If you'll excuse me, I'm going to load up and be right back."

"Take your time."

As William and Roni walked away, Geraldine leaned to whisper in her ear, "So, what do you think? He's cute, right?"

"Adorable, but I'm not interested."

"Why not? William is not only a genius, he's also one of the clan's leaders. He's a council member."

Darlene put her plate down and turned fully toward Geraldine. She still couldn't think of her as her mother, and probably never would. Sabina was dead, and Geraldine was a different woman with the same face. "I'm not going to start dating anyone until I divorce Leo. He's not cheating on me, so I'm not going to be disloyal to him either. I want to end our marriage honorably."

Geraldine pushed a lock of hair behind her ear. "He was disloyal, just not with another woman."

"I know." Darlene snatched the corn cob off her plate and attacked it with renewed gusto even though she couldn't taste it.

Yesterday, Roni had invited Andrew and his wife and daughter to dinner at his and Sylvia's house, specifically so Andrew could tell her about Leo's betrayal of Roni.

She no longer had the luxury of entertaining doubt.

Her husband had sold out her son for the reward money, and that was a deal-breaker. Even if Leo was a fabulous husband, which he wasn't and never had been, she couldn't stay with him after what he had done.

"What are you going to do?" Geraldine asked.

"File for a divorce."

"You can stay here while you do that. Shai told me that Edna, the clan's judge, has a legal practice in the city, and she can handle the divorce for you. She did that for another Dormant who was married to an abusive jerk."

"Leo wasn't abusive."

Geraldine arched a brow. "Maybe not physically, but I've seen how he treated you. You deserve better."

"Do I?" Darlene dropped the half-eaten corn cob on her plate. "I'm no one special. I haven't done anything selfless or charitable. Why do I deserve better?"

Perhaps that was why she'd stayed with Leo for all those years. Deep down, she believed that he was what she deserved. Or maybe it had been just fear of being left alone.

"Not everyone is born a hero," Geraldine said. "I didn't do anything special either, and I'm riddled with guilt for abandoning you even though I didn't know any better. And yet the Fates gave me Shai. Maybe just going through life and doing the best we can with what we have is enough?"

Closing her eyes, Darlene let her head drop back. "I know that I didn't do the best I could. I'm smarter and more capable than what I put forward. I'm ashamed of the life I've lived, and I'm full of regrets. I should have been a better mother to Roni, and perhaps I could have been a better wife to Leo as well. Maybe if I'd tried harder, he wouldn't have grown resentful toward Roni and me." She groaned. "I feel like such a failure."

Geraldine put a comforting hand on her shoulder. "We all have days like that, sweetie, when all we can see is what's behind us and hate ourselves for it. But we also have good days when we look into the future and decide to do better. When you are immortal, there are many more good days ahead than bad ones behind."

Darlene opened her eyes and looked at her mother. "You don't have to convince me. I've already decided that I'm going to attempt immortality. I just need a little more time to grieve the death of my marriage."

Geraldine's eyes shone with excitement. "You've made the right decision. Are you going to stay here with us from now on?"

"I haven't decided yet."

She had until the end of the day to make up her mind,

but no longer than that. If she decided to go back tomorrow morning, Onegus would erase her memories of the village, and Cassandra would take her home.

The problem was that Darlene didn't want to forget the village or the people she'd met so far. What she wanted to forget were the years she'd been married to Leo, but then she would also forget having Roni, so that was not possible. She would have to live with the memories of her imperfect marriage and her imperfect life.

"Stay," Geraldine said. "You can grieve your marriage right here, where you have people who love and support you. Why do that alone in an empty house? You'll just let yourself spiral down into depression, drink too much, or engage in some other self-destructive behaviors."

Darlene cast Geraldine a sidelong glance. "And how would you know that? You haven't grieved any of your relationships. You didn't even remember the men you had relationships with. Not my father and not any of the others."

Geraldine lifted her hand and rubbed her temple. "Orion did that for me. He made me forget them to save me heartache."

"Oh, yes, dear Uncle Orion." Darlene shifted her gaze to Alena and Orion, who were talking with Roni and William. "So full of good intentions. I can practically see the horns sticking out from the top of his unnaturally lush black hair."

The guy was too handsome to be her uncle. Why did everyone in her family have to look like damn gods except for her?

She was a freaking god's granddaughter. She should be stunning.

Maybe they were all mistaken, and she wasn't Geraldine's daughter after all? Or maybe even gods sometimes produced ugly ducklings.

Geraldine patted her thigh. "You are in a strange mood today."

"I know." Darlene sighed. "I'm cranky, and I can't even blame it on my period, since I don't get them anymore. It would seem that surliness is a family trait. I have it in common with my sister and my son." She eyed Geraldine. "When you were still Sabina, you were moody too, so we probably got it from you. But you are so cheerful now. Did your accident change your personality?"

"I regrew a big chunk of my brain." Geraldine rubbed her temple. "I used to think that the accident had messed up my internal wiring, but maybe it fixed it instead." She smiled. "It seems that after the accident, I became more pleasant to be around."

18

GERALDINE

*G*eraldine still hoped that Darlene would warm to William, but it seemed like it wasn't meant to be. There was no chemistry between them.

Then again, given Darlene's sour mood, she probably would have found any guy they introduced to her not to her liking.

"Don't look so glum," Shai whispered into her ear. "We can't expect her to fall for the first available immortal she meets. We will need to introduce her to many more."

"Make a list of prospects." Geraldine leaned on his arm. "I'll start inviting men for dinner."

"We need something more covert than that. I think Darlene doesn't appreciate us trying to find her a guy."

She looked up at him. "What do you suggest we do?"

"I spoke with Merlin earlier today, and he told me that he put Ronja on a special diet and exercise routine to improve her physical condition in preparation for the transition. I think Darlene needs to do the same, and she will need either a coach or a buddy to do it with. I can ask Onegus to assign a different Guardian to be her trainer every two or three days."

"I thought that there was a shortage of Guardians."

"There is." Shai rubbed the back of his head. "Maybe I should talk to Kalugal and see if any of his men are available and willing."

Geraldine nodded. "I think it's a great idea to put Darlene on the same regimen as Ronja. In fact, we should introduce them to each other. They are in a similar situation, and Darlene could use a friend."

"Did she decide if she's staying yet?" Shai wrapped his arm around her waist.

"She said that she's still thinking about it."

"Let's help her decide." Shai headed to where Darlene was talking with Orion and William.

"Paris, how exciting," Darlene said to Orion. "Can I come too?"

She was holding an empty wine glass, her third or fourth of the afternoon, and given her ruddy cheeks, she was a little tipsy. That wasn't good. If Darlene was drunk, how was she going to make an informed decision about staying in the village or going back home?

Orion smiled apologetically. "If you turn immortal by the time we go, Kian might allow it. But as long as you are still human, I don't think that will work."

Darlene pouted. "I haven't been to Paris in years, and I want to help search for my naughty grandfather."

"We are probably not going to find any clues there," Alena said. "It's a very long shot."

Darlene snorted. "So is me transitioning, and yet I'm still going for it. Sometimes a long shot is all you get. Right, William?"

The guy lifted his wine glass. "Let's make a toast to long shots and their success."

Darlene looked at her empty glass. "I need a refill."

"I think you've had enough." Cassandra took the glass from her hand. "I'll get you coffee."

"Only if it comes with a cake," Darlene called after her.

Cassandra looked at Darlene over her shoulder. "I'll see what I can find. Are cookies okay?"

"Bring 'em."

"Maybe you should sit down." William put a gentle hand on Darlene's arm.

"Yeah, I should." She let him lead her to a chair. "You're a really nice guy."

"Thank you." He sat next to her. "I heard that you are leaving us tomorrow morning. Is that true?"

"Nope. I'm staying." Darlene reached for his shirt. "Ha, I knew it was silk."

Geraldine let out a relieved breath. "Thank the merciful Fates. I just hope she won't change her mind tomorrow morning."

"I won't." Darlene hiccuped. "Tomorrow morning, I want to see Judge Edna. I need to file for a divorce."

"Hallelujah," Roni said. "That's music to my ears."

"Bye, bye, Leo." Darlene waved a hand. "I'm not going to miss him." She leaned on William's shoulder. "I need to find an immortal guy to induce me, but not you. You're too nice."

She was definitely drunk.

William chuckled. "So it's true then. Nice guys finish last."

Darlene waved a hand. "You don't want me, so don't pretend like you do. You want a pretty young thing with long blond hair and big fleshy lips."

William laughed. "That's very specific, and just so you know, I prefer brunettes, and I like older, more mature ladies."

Darlene was a brunette, and she was older. Was that William's way of letting her know that he was interested?

"Well, tough, because you are getting a very young blond."

"Are you clairvoyant?" William asked.

Darlene had never said anything to that effect.

"I'm not. But sometimes I get very strong hunches, and this is one of those times."

"Perhaps that's Darlene's special talent," Shai said quietly into Geraldine's ear. Out loud, he asked, "What other strong hunches have you gotten that turned true?"

"I always know who's going to win *The Voice.*"

Cassandra rolled her eyes. "That's no proof of clairvoyance." She laughed. "It's the wine. You've had a little too much."

"It's not the wine, but it could have been my ear. Maybe I should be a talent scout. I know who will make it and who will not." Darlene worried her lower lip. "There have been other little things over the years. You have no idea how many times I said the words *I knew it.* But since I never foresaw that my mother was alive, or that I had a sister, or that my grandfather was a god, I'm likely not a seer."

19

TOVEN

*T*oven went over his answers, read again the comments he'd added, and re-examined the sketches he'd made, scanned, and attached to the document.

He hadn't expected to be spending so much time on the questionnaire, or to be so indecisive about the kind of adventure he wanted, or even who he wanted his avatar to be. He must have gone through four or five different story-boards before deciding on the final version, and the end product was very different than the one he'd started with.

The fantasy still didn't meet all of his objectives, but it was ridiculous to keep tinkering with it when he could have as many virtual adventures as his money could buy. If he wanted to, he could have one every day for the next two thousand years and still not empty his coffers.

Maybe that was the answer to his millennia-old existential crisis?

Each day he could live in a different world, be a different person, and make love to a different female. He could design an adventure with a goddess as his lover and relive happier days. He could even recreate his wife, who'd been gone for over five thousand years.

Anat and he hadn't been a truelove match, but they'd loved each other, and he'd mourned her death for many years. Eventually, though, his memory of her had faded, and he'd laid that to rest as well.

Sometimes he felt guilty for not remembering her as vividly as he should, and when the melancholy and guilt became overwhelming, he attempted to sketch her portrait to remind himself of her. Somehow, though, he'd never finished any of them. He had a sketchbook full of Anat's partial depictions, but he could never bring himself to finish even one.

Perhaps his subconscious mind refused to resurrect her for a good reason. Maybe she'd been reborn and was having a wonderful time on some alien planet, and by completing a sketch of her image, he would call to her spirit and interrupt the good time she was having in her new life.

Closing his eyes, Toven leaned back in his swivel chair and lifted his feet onto the desk. He should just click send and be done with it. If the fantasy didn't live up to his expectations, he could make a thousand iterations until he got it right.

Should he give Brian a call first, though?

Did the guy work on Sundays?

Toven opened his eyes, dropped his feet to the floor, and looked through the many burner phones scattered over his desk. He had ten of them, each with a different name printed on a label attached to its back. The one with Brian's phone number on it had Perfect Match printed on its label, and it contained two phone numbers in its contacts application along with two email addresses. One belonged to Brian and the other to the Manhattan branch of the Perfect Match Virtual Fantasy Studios.

The phone didn't even ring once before Brian answered it. "Mr. Navón. I've been anxiously awaiting your completed questionnaire, and I started to get worried when it failed to arrive. What happened?"

"Indecision, my dear Brian. Creativity comes at a price. I wrote and rewrote my fantasy too many times for me to admit without shaming myself."

"There is no shame in striving for perfection, Mr. Navón."

"Please, call me Tobias, Brian. Very soon, you are going to become privy to my most secret desires. We should at least be on a first name basis."

"Can I call you Toby? My best friend in high school was named Toby."

Toven chuckled. "I prefer Tobias. Toby sounds like a boy's name, and I'm much too old to be called a boy."

"You can choose one of the childhood fantasies and be a boy once again."

Toven's only fond memories from his childhood had been the long hours he'd spent with his father tinkering with Ekin's inventions and listening to him explaining how they worked. A virtual fantasy couldn't recreate that.

"Perhaps one day I will, but right now, I have other goals to fulfill through my virtual adventure. I know it's Sunday afternoon, and you are probably not in the office, but I'm ready to submit my questionnaire, and if you could take a look at it first thing tomorrow morning, I would greatly appreciate it. I need to know whether your customization can handle it, or will I have to order it made from scratch."

"First, let me congratulate you on completing the questionnaire. I will take a look as soon as I get it and call you back."

"Don't tell me that you're at work right now."

Brian chuckled. "What can I say? I'm obsessed with

finding people their perfect matches. You could say that I live for it."

The guy was strange, but Toven liked him. Brian's passion for what he did was so palpable that it was infectious. Toven was actually starting to get excited, and he hadn't felt that in a long time for anything other than new ideas for his novels.

"Thank you, Brian. If you ever need a testimonial from a satisfied customer, I would be more than happy to write you one. The service you're providing me with is above and beyond anything I could have ever expected."

"It is my pleasure, but don't sing my praises yet. Let's wait with that until after your adventure. I'll run your input through our servers and see what they spit out, and I'll let you know to what degree the AI can match the adventure to your fantasy, based on your parameters."

"Very well. I am awaiting your verdict." Toven ended the call and leaned back in his chair.

If the AI achieved even eighty percent of what he'd envisioned, that would be satisfactory.

20

ALENA

*A*lena pushed salad greens around her plate. "I can't take another bite. I wasn't hungry when we went to Roni's, but I felt bad about refusing his famous ribs when he handed me a plate, so I had some with some fries on the side, and then Ruth brought out her chocolate soufflé, and I couldn't say no to that either."

"That's okay." Amanda patted her arm. "You don't have to eat if you don't want to. Ogidu and Oshidu won't get offended."

Alena wasn't sure about that. The Odus were becoming more and more human by the day, but a quick glance at Oshidu proved that Amanda had been right. He looked just as stupidly happy as he had when he'd opened the door for them and ushered them to the dinner table. The question was whether he was truly glad to prepare and serve dinner for Annani's family, or was he reflecting their mother's happiness over having three out of her four children and her nephew over for dinner.

"I hope Aliya is okay." Alena pushed her plate away and reached for a glass of water. "I feel like I abandoned her at the pavilion."

"Why wouldn't she be okay?" Kalugal asked. "Wendy has taken her under her wing." He held his wine glass between his thumb and forefinger. "I wouldn't be surprised if I saw her working in the café tomorrow."

"That might be the best thing for her," Syssi said. "Full immersion in the clan's central hub from day one. How are things between her and Vrog?"

"Hopefully, great," Alena said. "They are both staying with Vlad and Wendy."

"Vrog seems taken with Aliya." Syssi glanced at Allegra, who was sleeping in her stroller unperturbed by the sounds of conversation going on right next to her. "But I caught her sneaking glances at Phinas." She turned her gaze to Alena. "What's the deal with that?"

"Let's not slide into gossip territory." Kian put his hand on his wife's shoulder. "Aliya is a big girl, and she's free to explore and choose whoever catches her fancy."

"I'm betting on Phinas." Amanda ignored their brother's comment. "Who's with me?" She raised her hand.

When no one followed, Amanda pouted. "Oh, well. If you don't want to talk about Aliya's love life, then let's talk about Alena and Orion's wedding. Where and when?"

Alena shifted her eyes to their mother. "Do you have a preference?"

"I would have loved to host everyone at the sanctuary, but we do not have enough beds even if everyone agreed to host a person or even two in their rooms."

Alena would have loved that as well.

The sanctuary was still her home, and it was beautiful. She couldn't have asked for a better setting for her wedding. They could put up a platform in front of the waterfall in the central chamber and put chairs and tables on the grassy lawn. If they could solve the sleeping arrangements problem, the central open area of the dome was big enough for a party with the entire clan present.

"Maybe we could have everyone stay in Anchorage and fly them over just for the ceremony?" she suggested.

When Kian didn't immediately shoot down the idea, Alena turned to Orion. "What do you think?"

"I've never been there, but if that's what you want, that's what you'll get."

"That's not going to work," Kian said. "Our largest plane can carry no more than twenty-eight passengers at a time. We couldn't transport everyone on the same day even if we combined all of our jets, including Kalugal's. The wedding will have to be either here or in Scotland."

"I can't go anywhere." Amanda rubbed her hand over her belly. "If you want to get married before my baby comes, you will have to do it in the village. My due date is in three weeks, and after the baby arrives, I will need at least two more weeks to recuperate."

"We shouldn't take a two-week-old baby out of the house," Dalhu said. "Our daughter will still be human and vulnerable to human diseases."

"No worries." Under the table, Orion clasped Alena's hand. "I want to meet all of Alena's children at least once before our wedding, which means a trip to Scotland. Alena and I talked about combining that visit with a sojourn in Paris, but since we are not going anywhere until your daughter is born, the wedding will have to wait for a couple of months."

Amanda let out a relieved breath. "Thank you. That takes care of half of my stress. Alena told me that you wanted to take Mey to the place Toven rented when you met him in Paris. I think that's an excellent idea. I just wish I could come with you. Any chance you can postpone the trip to Paris by several months?"

"That depends." Orion looked at Kian. "Did Edna finish translating Toven's journal?"

"She did, but she wasn't happy with her translation.

Edna said that she was too rusty to translate the stylistic nuances and told me that she needed to go over it again. Turner's guy in Russia didn't find a book titled *An Angel in Moscow*, so that's a dead end. Since we only have the journal for stylistic comparison, I agree with Edna that it needs a more thorough translation job."

"How long is it going to take her?" Alena asked.

"A week, give or take."

"I hope she'll have time to handle Darlene's divorce." Orion reached for the coffee carafe.

Kian pushed it toward him. "Edna is not dedicating all of her time to the translation. She has a busy practice, and she does much more than take care of the clan's legal matters. The journal is a side project for her."

Amanda waved a hand to get Orion's attention. "Back to Paris. Can you or can't you postpone the trip by a few months?"

Orion looked conflicted. "Frankly, I harbor an absurd hope that my father will attend my wedding, but that's not the only reason I don't want to wait too long before investigating that apartment. I would like our wedding to take place before Alena starts feeling uncomfortable."

Jacki chuckled quietly. "You're lucky that you found out about your pregnancy right as it happened. Even if you wait a couple of months, you will not start showing yet."

"I don't mind if I do." Alena squeezed Orion's hand. "A marriage ceremony is not a prerequisite for having babies together, but I am looking forward to having a partner to share this pregnancy and raise a child with. It will be a novel experience for me."

"Are you going to move to the village?" Jacki asked. "Our children will be very close in age, and if you do, they could grow up together."

"That would be amazing." Alena cast a sidelong glance at Kian. "Finally, the playground you've built will be put to good use, and the sounds of children playing will fill the village square."

"That is such a lovely vision," Annani said.

"Someone needs to convince Vrog to stay in the village and open a school for our kids." Jacki put her hand on the side of her belly. "The playground years will be over in a blink of an eye, and then we will need a school. Callie is opening a restaurant, so she's no longer a candidate for the job. Vrog is our only option."

"Vrog runs an international high school for high achieving students." Kian put down his empty coffee cup and reached for the carafe. "He's not going to settle for kindergarten and elementary school education."

"It doesn't hurt to ask." Syssi looked at their sleeping daughter. "Maybe he can help us set things up."

21

TOVEN

*A*fter ending the call with Brian, Toven had gone for a walk, eaten dinner in an Italian restaurant, walked back to his building, and watched a documentary about bird migration and a romantic comedy about enemies turned lovers.

That had killed over five hours, and Brian hadn't called back yet, but Toven knew that he would. By now, the guy felt like an old friend, which was beyond bizarre since Toven didn't make friends with humans. He could be friends with a dog, but given his nomadic lifestyle, having a pet was not in the cards.

But then Brian wasn't a human. He was a voice on the other end of the line, an extension of the sophisticated AI that powered the virtual fantasy studios.

Now, that was an interesting thought. What if Brian wasn't a human male working late at the office? What if he *was* the AI?

Transposing two letters turned Brian into brain—a computer brain.

An AI with a sense of humor was difficult to imagine— the computational power would need to be enormous to mimic the biological brain's ability to make such connections—but it wasn't impossible.

That would explain why Brian was always available to take Toven's calls, and why he was in the company's headquarters on a Sunday evening.

Except, even the best computerized voices couldn't fool Toven.

But then, he had never encountered an AI as sophisticated as the one running the virtual worlds of Perfect Match Studios. Was it possible that it had mimicked human interaction so perfectly that even Toven's superhearing couldn't detect it?

He had to find out.

Once Brian called back, he would ask him point-blank whether he was human. Could artificial intelligence lie? If it could make jokes, it could also lie.

When Toven's phone rang nearly an hour later, he snatched it from the side table. "Hello, Brian. Do you have a verdict for me?"

"First, I want to congratulate you on one of the most unique and imaginative ideas I've seen. You gave me the inspiration for a new line of adventures."

Toven smiled and leaned back in his chair. "Does that mean that you are going to create mine for free?"

"Yes and no. Do you want the good news first or the bad?"

"I always prefer to hear the bad first so I get to enjoy the good news without dread. But before you do that, I need to ask you a question that has been nagging me all morning. Are you human, or are you the artificial intelligence running the Perfect Match Virtual Fantasy Studios?"

The guy chuckled. "If I were the AI, it wouldn't have taken me six hours to get back to you. I would have had the answers in minutes."

"You could have delayed your response to make me believe that I was dealing with a human."

"As I said before, you have a very creative imagination, Tobias."

"And you are being evasive. A simple yes or no will suffice."

"No. I'm not the AI."

"Are you human?"

Brian snorted. "Some of my friends and coworkers call me a god."

The hairs on the back of Toven's neck prickled in warning. This was the second time Brian had referred to himself as a god. Was it a coincidence? Or had Toven made a big mistake by naming his avatar Tobias Navón and hinting at his real identity?

And then he had gone even further and made it even more obvious by including gods in his fantasy.

But to think that Brian was a god or worked for one was an absurd thought. None of the other gods had survived, and even if any had, there had been none who had a score to settle with Toven. No one had blamed him for his brother's insane behavior. In fact, the other gods had been sympathetic to Ekin and Toven for having to sentence their own to entombment.

"Have you been influenced by my fantasy, Brian?"

The guy laughed. "I wasn't influenced by your fantasy. I was inspired by it. But my god complex has nothing to do with that. It's nothing new."

"So you are not a god, and you are not artificial intelligence. That leaves only two possibilities. You are either a human or an alien."

"I could also be a ghost, the voice of your conscience, or your alter ego. Do you want me to switch to video so you can see for yourself that I'm just an average-looking human? My avatar is much more handsome, and I would prefer you to see him rather than old out-of-shape me, but that wouldn't satisfy you, now, would it?"

Toven was curious about both. He would have loved to see what Brian looked like in real life, but switching to video would expose him as well, and he preferred to keep his face anonymous for now. Eventually, he would have to show himself to the technician who would hook him up to the device and monitor him throughout his adventure. After all, he couldn't shroud himself while his mind was inside the virtual world. Once it was over, though, Toven planned to thrall the tech to erase every trace of his bio input and then forget that they had done it.

"Let's leave our real appearances a mystery."

"You've got it." Brian let out an exaggerated relieved breath. "I much prefer that. By the way, your artistic skill or that of the person who drew your avatar is extraordinary. Tobias is so handsome that I'm tempted to copy some of his features and make them my own. I hope that's okay with you."

Even if Brian used his avatar in its entirety, Toven would have probably never found out. But since he was a decent enough guy to ask for permission, Toven decided to grant it.

"Tobias is my creation, and you're welcome to use any part of him."

"Thank you. That will probably increase my match rate by at least fifteen percent, which brings me to the afore-mentioned bad news. You indicated that you would accept an eighty percent match for your imagined fantasy and an eighty-five percent match for your desired partner. First of all, I strongly advise against such a high level of matching, and secondly, the software could only match sixty-seven percent of your storyline, which is below the seventy percent I would normally like to see. It will take me about a week to tweak it, but since I'm already working on it, I can get it as high as the eighty percent you indicated you were comfortable with."

"Why not a hundred? If you are already working on it, why not go all the way?"

Brian chuckled. "Because for one, your fantasy will have to be modified to match your partner's wishes and desires, and secondly, it won't be exciting to you without some element of surprise. Your adventure is not going to be enjoyable if it's predictable."

"But if I don't remember who I am, I will not remember creating the fantasy either. I will think that it's my reality."

That was why he'd included gods in his fantasy. If they had a way of injecting a different backstory into his head, they could also do the opposite. In the Q&A section of the online brochure, someone had asked that question, and the answer was that it was impossible to siphon out memories and that the virtual feed went only in one direction, which was in, not out. The analogy given was of a movie projected directly into the brain, overriding the regular sensory input channels. But Toven wasn't the trusting sort.

"That's not how it works," Brian said. "When you are the creator of your own story, it lives in your subconscious even if you don't remember it consciously. You will expect things to happen a certain way, and nothing will surprise or challenge you. Talk about déjà vu. Every moment will feel like you lived it before."

"Got it. So this was your bad news along with the good? My adventure cannot be customized by the AI, but you can do that for me for a fee?"

"The good news gets even better. In exchange for you giving me permission to use your ideas to create similar environments and storylines for our customers, I will not charge you for the customization."

"That's indeed a nice surprise. Thank you."

There was another advantage to Brian using his ideas.

The more popular they became, the less his adventure would stand out.

"You're welcome. The other good news is that the program found a ninety-three percent match for you, which is truly unprecedented. Anything over seventy percent is considered a perfect match. I'm almost afraid that the match is too good. It's like she was created for you."

MIA

*M*ia turned her daylight desk lamp off, closed her sketchbook, and glanced at her computer screen to take another look at her new hairstyle.

She was so glad that she'd followed Margo's advice and taken the sketch to Ricardo. He'd laughed when she'd shown him her avatar, but he'd copied the hair color and style nonetheless, and it had come out even better than she'd expected.

Her grandparents hadn't looked too happy about the black hair with purple streaks, but they'd still smiled and said that she looked pretty.

"At least she didn't get a tattoo," her grandfather had murmured under his breath.

Her grandmother had nodded in agreement.

In Mia's opinion, it looked amazing, especially with the makeup job Frankie had done. It was a shame that she would have to take it off before going to bed, but she didn't want to leave eyeshadow and mascara smears on her white pillowcases.

Looking at the screen again, she moved her mouse to wake it up and opened her inbox. Unsurprisingly, she had no new emails. It was too early to hope for an answer from Perfect Match.

She'd submitted the questionnaire right before leaving for the hair salon, about six hours ago, and since it was the weekend, she doubted anyone had taken a look at it. Only freelancers like her worked weekdays and weekends and into the night, or those who had no life outside of their occupation.

Well, that was also like her.

"Stop complaining," she said out loud, and swiveled her chair around.

Her bed was messy from her friends rolling around on it earlier, a reminder of the wonderful day they'd spent together.

Frankie and Margo were the best. Filling out the questionnaire had taken the entire morning and afternoon, and after submitting it, they'd celebrated in the hair salon.

After Margo had dropped her at home, Mia had been so hyped up from the day that she'd needed to sketch to relax. While she worked, immersing herself in the story she was telling through her illustrations, the real world receded into the background, and everything calmed down. Even though her books were about kids' adventures, she had no problem living inside the story.

But that was nothing compared to what awaited her in the Perfect Match virtual world. That would really be living within a story, but it wouldn't be entirely her own. Her partner would add other dimensions to it, enriching it in unexpected ways. She had checked the recommended seventy percent match ratio, and thirty percent variation left a lot of room for surprises.

As for the excitement factor, she had chosen the minimal setting, which might limit her matches, but with her condition, that was her only option, and it was non-negotiable. She'd spoken with someone from the studios about her condition and why she couldn't get overly excited, but just to be safe, she'd explained it again in the comment section.

Per her doctor, sexual excitement was fine, and even pregnancy was okay, as long as she was under medical supervision. What she needed to stay away from was stress and strenuous activity.

But wasn't sex considered strenuous?

Mia chuckled sadly.

The most she had tried since that fateful day was a little self-play just to make sure that everything still worked down there. She indulged from time to time, but the orgasms that had previously been so easily attained eluded her.

Despite all the progress she'd made and all the hard work she'd put into her rehabilitation, Mia still couldn't think of herself as sexy or desirable, and without that, it was difficult to get excited.

When her phone rang, she knew it was Frankie even before looking at the screen.

"Hi, girlfriend. What's up?"

"That's what I want to know. Did you get an answer yet?"

"The earliest I should expect an answer is on Monday, and that's being optimistic. The brochure says that, on average, it takes two weeks to find a match, not because the computer needs that long, but because it depends on who else is filling out questionnaires at the same time and whether a match can be found among them."

"On average means that some matches can be found within an hour and others can take a month. Check your email, Mia."

"I did."

"Then check again."

"Fine." She rolled her chair closer to the desk, opened

her laptop, and clicked on the mail application. "Oh. My God!"

"What?" Frankie screeched on the other end of the line. "Tell me!"

"It's probably just a confirmation email that they received my questionnaire." Mia clicked on the provided link, entered her digital token, which she'd had memorized by now, and read the message. "They found a match, but our adventure is only going to be ready in about a week because it needs more customization than the AI can handle. There is another link to find out more about my partner."

"Click it!"

"I am." Her hand shook as she moved the mouse and clicked on the link. "Oh, wow." She leaned back and gazed at the screen. "His avatar is absolutely gorgeous."

"Does he look anything like your drawing?"

"He has dark hair and blue eyes, and that's where the resemblance ends. He looks nothing like Thor."

"I want to see him. Can you send me the picture?"

For a brief moment, Mia considered refusing. She didn't want to share her guy with anyone, not even with her best friends.

But that was stupid.

It was just an illustration, and despite being very realistic, it wasn't a picture of a real person. It was a picture of a wet fantasy.

"Give me a moment. I don't think I'm allowed to download it or share it, but I can take a screenshot."

"Why wouldn't you be allowed to download it?"

"It's a drawing. It might be copyright protected." She leaned closer to read the fine print. "It was supplied by the guy I matched with. Do you know what it means?"

"What?"

"That he's an artist like me. No wonder we've gotten

matched." Mia activated the speakerphone and put the device face up on the desk.

"You didn't ask for an artist."

She hadn't. All she'd marked as desirable was an appreciation for art.

"Maybe it was just a stroke of luck, or maybe he requested an artist." She made a screenshot and sent it to Frankie. "Did you get it?"

"Yeah, I did, and I must say that you were very smart to give them plenty of room to improvise. This guy is much hotter than the one you requested."

"He is."

He was exquisite.

Mia had a feeling that tonight she was going to revisit her self-pleasuring activities, and that this time, a climax wouldn't be difficult to reach.

"Does the email say anything about him?" Frankie asked.

"His avatar's name is Tobias Navón, and it says that I will get more information about him once our adventure is ready."

23

VROG

*T*he couch was too short, but that wasn't what had kept Vrog awake despite being bone tired.

Dinner had been a slightly awkward affair, with Stella and Wendy doing most of the talking and trying to pull Aliya into the conversation. Wendy's mother hadn't said much, but her eyes had been full of compassion for Aliya. At some point Margaret's mate, who was a Guardian, had taken over the conversation, telling Aliya about the Guardian training program, and why it took decades to graduate from it.

Replaying the events of the past few days in his head, Vrog still didn't know where he stood with her. She'd been acting friendly toward him, and on a few occasions, he'd sensed the awakening of her sexual interest, but she hadn't made a single move to indicate that she was romantically interested in him.

Perhaps that was the Kra-ell way.

The purebloaded females hadn't been very lustful. They would become very active when they were in their fertile cycle, but the rest of the time, they were markedly less interested in male company than the average human female, let alone an immortal.

In that regard, an immortal female was every male's dream, whether he was Kra-ell, human, or immortal. That reminded him that he still had a virtual hookup with a clan female that he felt obligated to take part in.

Vrog had planned on postponing it even further if possible, and even better finding a way to wiggle out of the obligation, but perhaps that would be a mistake.

Aliya seemed determined to remain uncommitted, and he couldn't wait forever for her to make up her mind. Besides, if he thought about it objectively, a clan female would make a much better mate for him than Aliya.

Come to think of it, clan females would be invaluable to the Kra-ell males, and if they ever found out about them, they would hunt them to the ends of the earth.

There would be no place for them to hide.

It was imperative that they never find out. Kian had taken a big risk by allowing three hybrids into his hidden village. He had nothing to fear from Vrog or Aliya, but what about Emmett?

The guy was mated to a clan female, which in Kian's eyes meant that they were bonded, and that Emmett would never betray his mate or her people. But the Kra-ell didn't bond with their partners, and although betrayal of any kind was dishonorable, there was no guarantee that the male was honorable.

Something about him bothered Vrog. The guy was too smooth, too cunning, and too damn good of an actor.

With a groan, Vrog turned on his back and stretched his legs over the armrest.

Was Aliya trustworthy? What did he know about her?

Next to nothing, but his gut said that she was an honorable female, and she would never betray her benefactors.

The more he thought about Kalugal's generosity

toward her, the more Vrog realized how brilliant the guy's move had been.

No wonder Kalugal was so successful.

He was not only a good judge of character, but he also knew how to use that knowledge to his advantage. Realizing that Aliya's honor was all she had, he ensured her loyalty by obligating her to him. After he had bought her a place to live, ensuring that she would never be homeless or destitute again, she would never knowingly do anything to endanger him or his family, and she would do everything in her power to protect them.

The problem was that Aliya had very little real-life experience of dealing with people, and she might unintentionally disclose things she wasn't supposed to.

When the door to Vlad and Wendy's room opened, Vrog glanced at his watch. It was three in the morning, and Vlad would be leaving for his shift in the bakery shortly.

His son didn't turn the light on as he padded to the kitchen and loaded the coffeemaker.

"Want some company for that coffee?" Vrog asked.

"Sorry for waking you up." Vlad turned the light on in the kitchen.

"I wasn't asleep." Vrog swung his legs over the side of the sofa and pushed to his feet. "The couch is too short."

"I can get you a cot from the underground storage on my way back from the bakery. They are not as comfy as the couch, but at least they are long enough."

"That would be great. Thank you."

As Vrog sat down at the kitchen counter, Vlad stuck two mugs under the coffeemaker spouts. A few moments later they were both sipping on black coffee in quiet companionship.

"It must be difficult to rise so early every day," Vrog said to start a conversation.

"I only work four days a week, but yeah. It's not fun

leaving the warm bed with Wendy in it in the middle of the night."

"Do you have to do that? From what I understand, your share in the clan's profits should cover all of your expenses."

"It does, but I prefer to invest my share and live on what I make. Besides, the bakery is a temporary gig. Once I'm done with college, I plan to open my own graphic design business and advertise my services on the internet. I already have a website where I display my better works. When I make enough money from that, the only baking I'll do will be for my family and friends."

"Sounds like a solid plan." Vrog took another sip of the coffee. "What about Wendy? Does she plan to keep working in the café?"

Over dinner, Wendy had said that Aliya should come with her to the café and spend the day with her. That was the fastest way to get to know nearly everyone who lived in the village. Some, she'd told them, were recluses who never stopped by the café, but there was only a handful of them.

"For now." Vrog emptied the rest of his mug and took it to the sink. "She's enrolled in a nearby community college for the fall semester."

"That's wonderful. What does she want to study?"

"She's undecided. Wendy wants to take courses in various subjects and then decide." Vlad slung his backpack over one shoulder. "What are your plans for today? Are you going to hang out with Wendy and Aliya at the café?"

Vrog shook his head. "I need to speak with William about the virtual adventure."

"Right. I forgot about that. Do you still want to go for it?"

"I'm not sure. On the one hand, I shouldn't do it if I'm

courting Aliya, but on the other hand, I can't drop my obligation to the female who matched with me."

"I'm sure she'd understand once William explains the situation."

"That's what I want to speak with him about. Obviously, he knows who the female is, so he might have a better feel for how I should handle it."

"Makes sense." Vlad headed for the front door. "Good luck, and try to get some sleep."

"Thank you. I will."

24

ALIYA

*S*urprisingly, Aliya had slept like the dead, and when the morning sun woke her up early the next day, she felt refreshed and ready for a day at the café.

Her first real day in the village.

The day before had passed like a blur, but despite the jet lag and her exhaustion from having to interact with people for so long, she'd survived the introductions to Vlad and Wendy and their families.

She'd managed to have cordial conversations with them during dinner, and after they had left, she hadn't been overly upset when she'd lost the argument with Vrog over who was going to take the bedroom and who was going to sleep on the couch.

They were both too tall for the sofa, and she was used to sleeping in odd places, while he wasn't, but he'd insisted, and she'd been too tired to argue.

The truth was that she'd been glad he'd given her the bedroom.

Having her own room was such an incredible luxury. She'd never felt safer, more relaxed, or more enthusiastic about starting a new day.

When she emerged from the bedroom fifteen minutes later, Wendy was already in the kitchen preparing breakfast with Vrog's help.

"Good morning." Aliya stood next to the kitchen counter. "Can I do anything?"

"Yeah. Take a seat." Wendy waved with a spatula. "The eggs are ready."

"Good morning." Vrog put a mug of coffee in front of her. "How did you sleep?"

"Excellent. Thank you." She stirred in sugar and took a sip. "I love coffee."

He chuckled. "So I've noticed."

"Did you sleep well?" she asked him, hoping he would say yes.

"Can't say that I did. Vlad promised to bring a cot for me on his way back from the bakery."

"You should sleep in the bedroom," she offered half-heartedly. "For me, even the couch is a luxury."

"I wouldn't dream of it." He gave her a charming smile.

"*Bon appétit.*" Wendy placed a plate of scrambled eggs and toast in front of her. "Usually, I don't eat breakfast and just grab something at the café, so tomorrow morning you'll need to make your own if you want to eat." She put two more plates on the counter for her and Vrog.

"Thank you." Vrog pulled out a barstool next to Aliya. "Now that I know where everything is, it would be my pleasure to prepare breakfast for everyone."

"Or you can come with Aliya and me to the café and grab something there. What are you going to do here alone all day?"

"I have work that I need to do for the school, but I need a laptop with an internet connection that works in the village. After breakfast, I plan to pay William a visit and ask if he has one he can loan me."

"Good idea." Wendy gave him a look that Aliya couldn't

decipher. "You also need to talk to him about the other thing."

"I will." He lifted his fork and stuffed his mouth full of eggs.

Whatever his reason was for not accompanying them was, Aliya was glad of having a break from him.

Vrog was nice, and she liked him, but she couldn't give him what he wanted from her. He expected her to commit to him when she wasn't ready to commit to anyone or anything yet.

She'd lived in isolation for fourteen years, which was more about existing than living, and suddenly she was thrust into a new life, in a new community, with seemingly endless choices. She was overwhelmed, confused, unsure of her next step, and he expected her to have the rest of her life figured out?

It would be foolish of her to do so without exploring her new world first.

The challenge would be to keep him interested in her without leading him on, which would require a delicate dance Aliya didn't know the steps to. It would be dishonest to pretend that she wanted a life with him when she wasn't sure about anything, but she didn't want to reject him either.

Perhaps the best thing to do was to just tell him what was going on in her head?

But what if that pushed him away for good? He might think that she was immature, or irresponsible, and unsuitable for a man like him, and maybe he would be right.

Aliya needed advice, and once she was alone with Wendy, she could ask her opinion. The girl was several years younger than her, but she'd lived in the human and immortal worlds and knew how to navigate them. Wendy was also going to introduce her to Wonder, who had an interesting story of her own.

Wonder was over five thousand years old, but she'd actually lived only twenty of them. The rest of the time she'd been in stasis, which was a state similar to hibernation and could apparently keep an immortal's body alive for thousands of years.

The Kra-ell had used a similar method to traverse space, but Alena and the others speculated that they'd been kept in stasis in something they called pods. Did that mean that unlike the immortals the Kra-ell couldn't enter stasis without technology's aid?

She had so many questions, and so many things that she needed to learn that just thinking about it made her head spin. Vrog had promised to tutor her, but he expected her to go back with him to his school, and she had no intentions of doing that.

In the immortals' village she didn't need to hide, and people seemed to accept her odd features, the occasional flare of red light from her eyes, and her elongating fangs. She could be herself here and have as normal a life as a hybrid Kra-ell could have. In Vrog's school, she would have to hide or wear glasses and a face mask.

It would be just like living in the tunnels, and she was never going back to that.

VROG

"*I* can hook you up with a laptop." William opened the bottom drawer of his desk and pulled out a brand-new device.

"What make is it?" Vrog asked.

The cover was smooth metallic gray with no logo on it.

"Ours. We buy most of the components and assemble them in-house, but some of it is our own technology that we are not yet ready to share with the public."

Vrog smiled. "I'm not even going to ask. My education is well-rounded, but I'm not an engineer, and technical terms confuse me."

"They do most people." William flipped the top open and started clicking away. "It connects to our own Wi-Fi network, so it's not totally private. We monitor communications from the village. It's mostly done by bots, but if you use certain terms, the bots alert the people in security and your communication gets checked."

"Even if it's in Chinese?" Vrog lifted a hand. "I'm just asking out of curiosity. I'm not going to mention immortals in emails to my staff or anyone else."

"The bots do what bots are designed to do, and they are

programmed with all major languages—" William stopped mid-sentence. "Which gives me an idea. You are fluent in Kra-ell, correct?"

"Yes."

"How about the new girl? Aliya?"

"She can speak it, but she can't write or read it."

"Then I'll have to use your services for the written part and hers for the spoken. I want to program the bots to recognize the Kra-ell language."

"Why? Do you suspect Emmett of something?"

William took his glasses off. "I don't suspect anyone. Do you?"

Vrog shrugged. "He's an interesting fellow, and I can't get a read on him. He's much more human than Kra-ell, and he's as smooth as an eel."

William wiped his glasses with the corner of his shirt and put them back on his nose. "You're right. But Eleanor is much easier to read, and I've made it a habit to check her responses to everything Emmett says. She knows him better than anyone else, and when he starts bullshitting or exaggerating, she either rolls her eyes or presses her lips together." William leaned back. "The guy is not trustworthy, but he has nothing to gain and everything to lose by selling us out."

"I'm not sure about that." Vrog hesitated before continuing. "Emmett is a smart guy, and it's probably occurred to him that clan females would be invaluable to the Kra-ell. They hold the key not only to your people's continued existence but also to mine. I would never sell you out to the monsters who slaughtered my tribe, but I don't know Emmett well enough to be sure that he wouldn't either."

"First, he needs to find them, which is not likely to happen. But I'm not dismissing your worry. We need to keep an eye on him."

Vrog smiled. "In your mind, you have probably added

Aliya and me to the watchlist, but that's okay. I would have done the same."

"You have a son in the village, and you're an honorable guy. In your case, I only worry about your loyalty to your former mistress. I have a feeling that you would do just about anything to free her if you could."

"I'm bound by an unbreakable vow to her, but I would never sacrifice my son or his people to save her. I can't break one vow to uphold another. Vows don't work that way. The only one I'm allowed to sacrifice for Jade is myself."

"Have you vowed to keep Vlad and his mother safe?" William pushed the laptop over to Vrog.

"I did." He flipped the top open and was relieved to see the familiar search engine logo. "Does it work like any other laptop?"

William smirked. "Better."

"Thank you." Vrog closed it. "I also wanted to talk to you about my virtual adventure. I would like to postpone it if possible, or even cancel it, if the lady agrees." He pulled the device down to his lap. "I want to give a relationship with Aliya a chance."

"Naturally." William nodded. "I can let the lady know."

The guy looked as if he would prefer to chew on glass shards rather than communicate Vrog's request to the clan female.

"Maybe it would be better just to postpone it. As things stand between Aliya and me right now, there is no relationship." Vrog's lips twisted in a grimace. "It would appear that Aliya wants to keep her options open."

William's eyes brightened. "Then why not go for the adventure? If she's exploring her options, so should you."

"Indeed." Vrog rubbed the back of his neck. "But I'm working hard on changing Aliya's mind, and if I go on the virtual adventure, she'll think that I'm not serious about her, and that will give her even more license to explore other options. Besides, this is a small community, and the clan female who matched with me knows who I am. She might be bothered by my pursuit of Aliya while enjoying her company as well."

"I don't think she'd mind." William's cheeks reddened. "This adventure is about a virtual hookup, not about finding a true-love mate."

Vrog sighed. "As a Kra-ell, I should be perfectly okay with that, but I'm not. I guess my human side is stronger, or maybe the many years I've spent among humans have influenced my morals. I want a female who will be exclusively mine, and I exclusively hers, but I don't think Aliya is that woman because she's more Kra-ell in nature than I am. That being said, I'm not ready to give up on her just yet."

For a brief moment, William just looked at Vrog as if he was trying to get a read on him. "Let me check with the lady if she's willing to wait." He pulled his keyboard toward him and started typing.

Vrog pushed to his feet. "Would you let me know her answer?"

"Yes." William didn't turn to look at him. "She says it's fine. She's not in a rush."

Vrog let out a relieved breath. "I'm glad to have this off my chest. Did she say anything else?" Like asking William to find her another partner?

"That's privileged information." William shifted his gaze to Vrog. "Good luck with Aliya. I hope things work out for you two."

"Thank you. I hope so too."

ALIYA

"You need to watch the temperature readout." Wonder pointed to the little dial on top of the frothing thermometer wand she'd put inside the pitcher. "It needs to be between a hundred and forty to one hundred and fifty degrees. The frothing helps the milk taste sweeter, but if the temperature gets too high, it will lose its sweetness and start to taste flat or even burned."

"Got it." Aliya admired the velvety texture of the froth. "It looks tasty."

Wonder gave her a smile. "Would you like to try it?"

"Am I allowed? I don't have any dollars." She didn't have any yuan either, but that was beside the point.

"That's okay. You can have as many cappuccinos, pastries, and sandwiches as you like. It's a perk of the job." She turned to Wendy. "We need to ask Jackson to put Aliya on the payroll."

She liked that suggestion very much. Working in the café for free would fulfill the usefulness to the clan requirement, but getting paid would be even better.

"Who is Jackson?" Aliya asked. "Does he own the café?"

"He runs it," Wendy said. "The place and the equipment

inside of the café belong to the clan, but the vending machines belong to Jackson."

Wonder poured the frothed milk into the coffee cup. "The guy is Vlad's age, and he's already a big-time entrepreneur."

"They are childhood friends," Wendy said. "Jackson started out managing one coffee shop, but then he opened a commercial bakery, the one where Vlad works, and he also invested in several other coffee shops. The bakery supplies pastries and sandwiches to the cafés he owns and it also makes lunch deliveries to offices."

Wonder put a pastry next to the cappuccino she'd just made and handed the tray to Aliya. "Take it to table five. In the meantime, I'll start on your cappuccino."

Which one was that?

Wendy and Wonder had drilled her on the layout throughout the morning, but she was so nervous that she kept forgetting which table was what number.

Wendy took pity on her. "That's the one on the left under the willow tree. Remember, number one is the closest to the counter, and you count from there."

"Got it." She took in a deep breath and headed toward the table and its lone customer.

His back was to her, but those broad shoulders looked familiar.

Could it be Phinas? She hadn't seen him ordering at the counter, but he might have placed his order during her bathroom break. She'd only been gone for a couple of minutes, though.

When she got closer, he turned around and grinned. "Good morning, Aliya."

"I thought it was you." She put the tray down. "I didn't see you order."

"I had one of my men place it. Sit with for a moment." He motioned to the chair across from him.

"I can't. I'm working." She narrowed her eyes at him. "Aren't you supposed to be at work as well? Wendy told me that you work in an office building in the city."

His grin got even wider. "I see that you were asking about me. What else did you learn?"

"Nothing that I didn't already know. Wendy only knows that you are Kalugal's second- or third-in-command, and that you are not much of a conversationalist. I told her that she must have you mistaken for someone else because you talked plenty in China."

He hadn't, but she felt like teasing him back.

"You must be very intuitive." He motioned to the chair again.

"Why do you think that?"

"Because you must have heard all the things I wanted to say to you but didn't."

It was on the tip of her tongue to ask what those things were, but even a novice like her knew it was a well-placed trap. If she fell for it, she might give him license to say much more than she was willing to hear.

Still, curiosity got the better of her. "Maybe I heard your unspoken words, but they were so unclear that I didn't understand any of them."

Phinas laughed, his deep male voice sending shivers up and down her spine.

"Your cappuccino was getting cold." Wonder placed a cup on the table. "Enjoy."

She had been so absorbed by Phinas that she hadn't even noticed Wonder walking up to them.

"I was just leaving." Aliya reached for the cup.

"No, stay." Wonder put a hand on her shoulder. "Cappuccinos are meant to be enjoyed sitting down."

"Thank you," Phinas said. "Put it on my tab."

"It's on the house." Wonder winked and turned on her heel.

"Now, you no longer have an excuse." Phinas pushed to his feet and pulled the chair out for her. "Your boss told you to enjoy your cappuccino."

Playing along, Aliya shrugged and sat down. "So, why aren't you at your city office today?"

"Kalugal needed me to stay in the village today. What about you? How do you like it so far?"

"I like it here. People are still gawking at me, but at least it's just curiosity and not fear. So far, everyone I met was friendly."

He leaned closer. "That's because you are an attractive female, and they don't think of you as the enemy. My men and I were greeted with suspicion by most of the males, and outward hostility by some of the others. The ladies, on the other hand, were mostly happy to see us."

"I bet." She gave him an appreciative look. "Alena told me a little about your history and that you used to be part of the DOOM brotherhood. I'm glad that you got away."

"Thank you." He smiled. "I owe my freedom to Kalugal."

Aliya nodded. "He's a good man."

"He is. But I don't want to talk about him. Don't you want to know what I was thinking so loudly about you that you thought you heard me talking?"

Her lips twitched with a smile she was trying to stifle. "I have a feeling that you will tell me whether I want to hear it or not."

He looked at her from under lowered lashes. "Admit it, Aliya. You are dying to know."

Sexy male.

"Okay, I admit it."

"Remember my offer to take you dancing in a club?"

She nodded. "We ended up not going because Kalugal and Arwel forbade it."

"They didn't forbid it. They just said that it was a bad idea. Anyway, I still want to take you dancing."

"I'm not allowed to leave the village."

"We can dance in my living room." His smile was lascivious. "I have a house all to myself. No roommates."

Aliya swallowed. "If you want to dance with me, you will have to invite many people because there is no way I'm going to be alone with you."

"Why not? We both know that you can overpower me with ease, and frankly, that's one hell of a turn-on."

Aliya's good mood soured.

Like the boys in the Mosuo village, Phinas also thought that she was a freak, but unlike those boys who had feared her, he was turned on by it.

"You're sick." She pushed to her feet.

"What did I say?" He followed her up. "Please, Aliya." He caught her elbow. "I didn't mean to offend you. You must tell me why you're upset."

"You think that I'm a freak, but you are one of those twisted guys who are turned on by it instead of being afraid or repulsed."

"That's not it at all." He motioned toward the chair. "Please. Give me a moment to explain."

He sounded so sincere, and she really wanted to be wrong.

"Okay. You've got a minute."

"Your physical strength is not what I'm attracted to. I just wanted to communicate that I'm not intimidated by it. I'm attracted to you because you are beautiful, smart, kind, resourceful, honorable, and you can kick ass."

She blew out a breath. "You could've started with that."

"I'm not good at flirting," he admitted. "I've never had to put much effort into it. If a female liked what she saw, that was good enough, and if she didn't, that was fine as well. I just moved to the next one. But you are special, and I'm inclined to work harder for you."

She wasn't sure, but that sounded like a compliment.

"You'll have to be patient because I'm not ready to have a relationship with anyone. This is all new to me, and I need time to learn the rules of this community. I don't want to make mistakes."

"If you want me to back off because you want to be with Vrog, I will. But I have a feeling that you are not sure about him either."

"I'm not. Before I choose a partner, I need to find my way in this new world. Besides, I'm a Kra-ell, and we usually don't limit ourselves. I might choose more than one partner to be with. Would you be okay with that?"

Phinas grimaced. "Usually, I would say yes, but that's with females I just want to entertain myself with, those I regard as casual lovers, which so far, was all of them. You are different, and I might want to have more with you. If that happens, I would not want to share you."

"That was an honest answer." She leaned back and crossed her arms over her chest. "So, are you going to throw a dance party for me?"

"Let me get back to you on that."

Was the door closing? Had she pushed him too far?

That hadn't been her goal. She just needed him to back off a little, but not give up on her completely.

"Okay." She pushed to her feet and lifted her cappuccino cup. "It was nice talking with you, Phinas. I would like to do it again."

"You can bet on it." He followed her up. "Are you going to be working in the café every day now?"

She nodded. "Wendy said that it was the best way to get to know everyone, and I also need to be useful and earn my keep. Do you know anyone who needs their house cleaned and is willing to pay for it?"

Phinas's grin was back. "I could use a housekeeper."

She glared at him. "Other than you. I don't work for potential suitors."

"So that's what I am to you now? A potential suitor?"

"Do you want to be something else?"

Grinning, he leaned to whisper in her ear. "I want to be your lover, and I'm not a patient man."

A blush creeping up her cheeks, she leaned away from him. "Behave, Phinas. If you want a chance of ever becoming my lover, you will need to learn to obey my wishes."

He dipped his head. "I'm at your command, mistress."

"My command is for you to be patient and wait for me to make the first move."

"As you wish." He took her hand, lifted it to his hot lips, and kissed the back of it. "I'm your devoted servant."

KIAN

*K*ian opened his office door and let William in. "Given your sour expression, you don't have good news for me."

"If you are referring to Toven's journal, then you are correct, but other than that, life is good."

Kian arched a brow. "Does that mean that things are going well with you and Darlene?"

Shrugging, William put his briefcase on the conference table and pulled out a chair. "It's not romantic between us." He sat down.

"You are spending a lot of time together."

"Yeah, we are, but that's only because she tricked me into taking Merlin's challenge and joining her and Ronja on their health quest. But after this month is over, I'm out. I don't have time for an hour-long morning jog, an afternoon hour-long session in the gym, and an hour-long lunch break to eat a healthy meal with Darlene." He patted his somewhat flatter stomach. "I've lost some weight over the week and a half since I started following the regimen, and I feel good about that, but I also lost valuable time that I could have dedicated to making progress on everything

I'm working on, and I don't feel good about that. In fact, it stresses me out. And when I'm stressed, I eat. It's a vicious cycle."

"I get it." Kian walked over to the fridge and pulled out two bottles of water. "I'm also an overachiever, and finding balance is difficult for me. But Syssi taught me that sometimes I need to put myself and my family first. I still struggle with leaving the office at five and not taking work home with me like I used to, but I count it as a victory every day that I overcome the urge to finish just one more thing or take a file to work on at night." He handed one bottle to William and twisted the cap off the other. "Now when I get home, I give Allegra and Syssi my undivided attention." He took a sip from the water. "Or at least I try to. Sometimes my head is still in the office."

"My head is always in the lab." William opened his briefcase and pulled out the well-thumbed copy of Toven's journal that Edna had been working on. "I even dream about work at night, and that's when I manage to fall asleep. Most nights, I lie awake in bed and think about the problems I still need to solve."

Kian pulled out a chair and sat next to William. "So, no luck with the journal?"

William shook his head. "Edna did an admirable job trying to emulate Toven's writing style in her translation, but it wasn't enough. I don't know whether it's the translation or the size of the sample, but I didn't find any stylistic matches to Toven's writing."

"It can also be that he's as good as he claims, and he changes his style between one book and the next enough to avoid detection by the software. Or his books haven't been published in electronic format."

"Right." William leaned back in his chair. "So, what's next? Mey goes to Paris?"

"I'm not holding my breath for that. They probably

won't find anything, but it would be a nice vacation for Alena and Orion. The Lugu Lake one turned out not very relaxing."

They'd gotten pregnant, so they would remember Lugu Lake fondly, but Alena said that she would probably never go back there.

"So I've heard," William said, "but I also heard that they'd enjoyed themselves."

"Evidently, they did, because Kalugal and Jacki want to join the trip as well. Vrog will no doubt be overjoyed if Kalugal takes Phinas with him to Paris."

"Are they still competing for Aliya's attention?"

"She's turned out to be quite the player, and she's not committing to either of them."

William pushed his glasses up his nose. "She's a Kra-ell hybrid, and monogamy is not their thing. I've been to the café a few times this past week, and she seemed perfectly happy working there and flirting with all the single males. That's why I thought that Vrog and Phinas were no longer in the picture."

Kian smiled. "I'm glad that she's acclimating well, but enough about her." He twisted the cap back on the bottle and pushed it aside. "Let's move to the next item on our agenda. How is your hunt for bioinformaticians going?"

William grimaced. "Almost as well as finding Toven. If they are any good, they are happily employed and are not interested in a secret project that mandates months of isolation from their friends and families. So far, I have only one potential candidate, and she seems too good to be true, which means that she's not going to work out either."

"Why's that?"

"First of all, she's only nineteen, a prodigy who got a full-ride scholarship to Caltech at sixteen and graduated this year at the top of her class. She doesn't have any experience outside of academia, but she's really good."

"So offer her a deal she can't refuse and get her."

"That's easier said than done. Because she's so young, I will need to meet not only with her but also with her parents, and without thralling them, I'm not going to convince them to let their daughter work on a secret project in complete isolation without them being able to keep an eye on her. Would you let Allegra take a job like that?"

"Never." Kian felt his fangs twitching in response to the mere idea.

"Neither would I. That's why it would be a waste of time to even try. Besides, I need a team, not just one nineteen-year-old greenhorn with an excellent academic record." William groaned. "I hope we find Toven. As Ekin's son, he might have some of the gods' scientific knowledge and understand what the symbols in Okidu's journals stand for. Maybe he even has some knowledge of genetics."

"I doubt that." Kian folded his arms over his chest. "According to Annani, Ekin was an engineer, while his and Ahn's sister was the geneticist. That's why his tablet doesn't contain anything about biology or genetics."

"But Annani also said that Ekin had worked with Athor." William took a sip from his water. "He might have learned about genetics from her."

"He did." Kian unfolded his arms. "But it wasn't his field of expertise, and I doubt that he imparted that knowledge to Toven. According to Annani, Toven was more an explorer and an anthropologist than a scientist."

"He was known as the God of Wisdom and Knowledge. That implies that he was smart and educated."

"The question is in what. He could have been a linguist or a philosopher. Both are valuable fields of study but not useful for deciphering Okidu's schematics."

2 8

TOVEN

*N*ew York was starting to grate on Toven's nerves, or maybe it was just his new noisy neighbors and their nightly parties. Usually, he didn't mind staying in one place for a month or two, but he needed to get out of that apartment. The other option was to compel his neighbors to keep quiet and destroy their sound system.

Toven sighed.

It wasn't their fault that he had super-sensitive hearing. The other neighbors probably weren't bothered by the parties because they only heard muted echoes of what was going on inside.

There were two reasons why Toven hadn't left yet. He really liked the apartment and the view it offered of Manhattan, and he was waiting for his virtual adventure to be ready.

Then again, Perfect Match had studios all over the United States and in all the major European cities. He didn't need to have his adventure at the same place he'd purchased his token, and he could get hooked up at any of the others.

Or maybe not. Since his adventure was custom-made, or rather custom tweaked, it might need Brian's supervision. The guy hadn't mentioned it, but it was always better to ask.

Sifting through his array of phones, Toven picked the correct one and dialed the guy's private number.

"Tobias," Brian exclaimed as if he were getting a call from his best friend. "You must be a mind reader. I was planning to call you later today."

"Is my adventure ready?"

"I'm running final tests on it, but it should be ready in the next couple of days. But that's not why I wanted to call you. I was going over your questionnaire earlier, and when I saw that you haven't logged in since the last time we spoke, I realized that I forgot to email you that your partner's avatar picture was available for you to download. It's totally my fault. Because I've taken over your file, it didn't go through the regular channels."

"I'm going to log in right now." Toven walked over to his desk and opened his laptop. "I'm putting in my digital token." He punched in the sequence of numbers and letters. "Okay, I'm in. Where can I find her picture?"

"Go to resources, scroll down to additional information, and click on it."

"Got it." Toven looked at the illustration. "She's very pretty, but that's not the drawing I uploaded."

"Of course it isn't. This is what she chose to look like. Do you approve?"

"I do. It took me a moment to switch gears in my brain and push aside the picture I had created, but she's lovely. I wouldn't change a thing about her."

He hadn't asked for sweet, or innocent, or vulnerable, and yet the woman looking at him from the picture with big green eyes tugged at heartstrings he'd thought had completely atrophied.

"I'm glad. I want to book your time slot, so we don't waste any more time. Do you have a preference for a particular day in the week?"

"No. I'm a freelancer. I can arrange my schedule as I please."

"Perfect. Do you prefer mornings or afternoons?"

"Any time is good. I don't sleep much."

"Awesome. I'll check with the lady and let you know."

Toven enlarged the picture and looked at his match's avatar. "I have two questions. First, what's the name she chose for her avatar?

"Her chosen name is Azul."

"Blue. I wonder whether it's a preference for the color blue or a reflection of her mood."

"I'm not free to discuss her with you. You will discover everything you need to know about her during your adventure. What's your second question?"

He could have compelled Brian to tell him anything he wanted, but that would spoil the mystery and the anticipation.

"Do I have to do it in the same location I purchased the token from?"

"Normally, you would have your experience at the branch you bought your token, but if you prefer a different branch, I can arrange that for you."

"I have no problem with the New York branch as long as it's in the next couple of days. Otherwise, I might opt to use your Milan location."

"I can't promise anything until I hear from the lady. She might not be available. But Milan is a no-go in any case."

"Why not? Aren't all of your branches connected to the same servers?"

"Normally, they are, but since this is a new storyline, I'd rather keep it in the States. It's too complicated to explain why, but it's better for everyone involved to stay local."

Toven smiled. "Now I know that my match is an American. You've just revealed something about her."

"Oops." Brian didn't sound concerned about the slight breach in anonymity. "It's a big country, Tobias. She could be anyone."

Toven grimaced. "That doesn't sound reassuring. I don't want my match to be an old man pretending to be a young woman."

"Why not? The soul is beautiful no matter what body it occupies. That's the beauty of using avatars."

"So you're not going to tell me whether she's a she or a he?"

Brian chuckled. "Do you remember checking the box that asked whether the true gender of your partner is important to you?"

"Oh, yes. I did check it off."

"Originally, we didn't want to add the option because the whole idea was to free people from the constraints of their bodies, but many of our customers were concerned about that, so we decided to add the option."

Well, great. Now he was being shamed by a snooty human for being a dedicated heterosexual.

"Don't you mind whom you are paired with?"

"As long as they are good people, I don't, and since I haven't found my perfect match yet, I keep experimenting. But that's me. Everyone should be free to choose their own perfect fantasy."

"I thought that finding a perfect match was guaranteed."

"You should read the fine print, Tobias. A perfect match only means that from everyone who is available in our database, the person chosen for you is your best match, and usually, that's better than anyone you could have found using regular methods. But we can't claim that there isn't someone even better for you out there in the entire world."

Toven hadn't read the fine print.

"Yes, of course. I knew that. Thank you for being so candid with me."

"You're welcome. I'll email you as soon as I get an answer from the lady. Have a great rest of your day."

"You too, Brian."

As Toven ended the call and dropped the device on the desk, he was struck by a strange thought. He would have liked to meet Brian, maybe share a drink with him and discuss philosophy. That hadn't happened to him in ages.

Most people bored him, and he had no patience with them, but he'd enjoyed talking to Brian.

With a few clicks of the mouse, Toven added the girl's picture to his photos and enlarged it. He found her very appealing, but would his avatar feel the same?

How similar was he to his alter ego?

Toven had made very small changes to his own appearance. After all, he was a god, and there was not much to improve upon. On the contrary, his avatar was a toned-down version, a little less perfect than what Toven saw in the bathroom mirror every morning.

Azul was probably not as pretty in real life, but he didn't really care if she was beautiful or not because he valued character and intelligence more than outer beauty. However, he didn't want her to be vastly different than her avatar. If Azul stirred anything at all in his stagnant soul, he would like to meet her in person, and he didn't want to be disappointed.

Fates knew he'd had enough of that in his long life.

MIA

"*T*hanks for taking me." Mia clutched Margo's hand. "Can you stay until I'm inside the virtual fantasy?"

Margo looked at the tech. "Can I?"

The woman shook her head. "I'm sorry, but that's against company policy. The doctor should be here shortly, and she will stay with Mia the entire time. You can either wait outside or come later to pick her up."

"Can I at least stay until the doctor gets here?"

"Of course." The tech, whose name was Deja, smiled. "Have you ever been on a virtual adventure before?"

Margo shook her head. "And I don't think I ever will. This contraption looks like something from a horror movie."

It was. The chair was the type found in a dentist's office, and it had arm, leg, and torso straps. The helmet thing that was supposed to go over Mia's head was enormous, and she had at least twenty sticky pads with wires and tubes attached to her body.

It didn't bring back good memories, and neither did the annoying hum and soft whizzing sounds of the medical equipment behind the chair. But the worst thing was the tech's Android phone when it received notifications. For some reason, medical professionals favored Androids, and that diabolical sound triggered her PTSD flashbacks, especially when it was muted as the technician's was. That's what Mia had heard all around her when she'd been hospitalized.

The tech eyed her readouts with a frown. "I don't like how stressed you are. I would have given you a relaxant, but given your medical history, I'd rather wait for the doctor to do that."

When the door opened, and a tall woman with a mop of curly blond hair walked in, Mia immediately knew she was a doctor even though she wore jeans and a button-down blouse, and there was no stethoscope hanging around her neck.

It was the confidence, the authority, and the technician's deference to her.

"Sorry I'm late." She walked over to Mia and offered her hand. "I'm Doctor Brenna Hutchinson, and I will be supervising you during the entire three hours of your experience."

Just then, it occurred to Mia that the doctor and the technician would be privy to all of her bodily responses, which would hopefully include arousal and a couple of orgasms.

At least they were both females, so it wouldn't be as embarrassing as if either one was a guy.

"Thank you. I'm surprised I'm not getting charged extra for this."

"No way." The doctor pulled out a stool and sat next to Mia. "You are providing us with valuable data. We encourage people with disabilities to take advantage of our studios. Helping people with limited mobility was the founders' original goal when they came up with the idea of enabling them to have adventures inside a virtual world as participants and not just as observers."

The thing about doctors was that they didn't shy away from calling anything by its name. Evidently, they weren't taught political correctness in medical school.

Everyone else tried to act as if there was nothing wrong with her, which Mia appreciated even though it was a white lie, so hearing what the doctor said made her cringe.

"Mia needs a relaxant, doc," the tech said. "But I didn't want to administer anything without you approving it first."

Doctor Brenna glanced at the readouts and nodded. "In a moment. Sometimes just talking things through helps." She looked at Margo. "I hate to kick you out, but once we start, no one aside from the client and the staff is allowed in here."

Margo gave Mia's hand a reassuring squeeze before letting go. "I will be right outside in the waiting room. I'm not going anywhere."

Despite her valiant efforts, the stinging in the back of her eyes resulted in tears. It was mainly the stress and fear of the unknown, but also gratitude to Margo for taking time off work to be with her.

"Thank you." Mia wiped the tears. "You are the best."

"Yeah, yeah. I know." Margo gave a little wave and walked out of the room.

When the door closed behind her, the doctor took Mia's hand. "Is there anything I can do to make you more comfortable? Would you like a glass of water? Maybe some orange juice?"

Mia shook her head. "I don't want to have a full bladder."

The doctor smiled. "Do you need to go to the bathroom?"

"No. I'm fine." When the tech's phone sounded with yet

another notification, Mia's readouts spiked again. "Can I ask you a big favor? Can you turn the sound off on your phone? It triggers my PTSD. When I woke up in the hospital after my heart failure, I kept hearing the incoming notification sound from the nurses' phones, and I thought it was coming from the medical equipment. I had nightmares about it for years."

"I'm so sorry." The tech pulled her phone out of her scrubs and turned it off.

"Thank you."

"Feel better?" Doctor Brenna asked.

Nodding, Mia gave her a tight smile.

"What else can we do to make you more comfortable?"

What she was really asking was what would help Mia relax. "My regular doctor tells me that my condition is well-managed with the implanted cardioverter defibrillator and the beta-blockers. I'm not supposed to engage in strenuous activities, and I should avoid extremely stressful situations, but other than that, she says I can do anything I please. She says that I should live my life without fear, but sometimes I can't help but be afraid. This machine scares me, and these restraints even more so."

Brenna's expression was full of understanding and compassion. "Don't worry about them. I will not strap you in until you are in the virtual world, so you won't feel me putting them on you. The reason they are needed is to prevent involuntary movements. The virtual experience works similar to dreaming, and your body will most likely switch into sleep paralysis, and you won't move. But in case you do, it's important to prevent you from pulling out wires and tubes. While awake, you would have no problem pulling your wrists out of the restraints, but during sleep, you will be too uncoordinated to manage it."

That was a huge relief. If she could get free whenever

she wanted, she didn't mind the restraints. "Okay. That makes sense. What if I get overexcited in the fantasy?"

"That's why I'm here. I will be monitoring you closely, and the moment you show distress, I will stop the experience."

"Isn't it dangerous?"

Brenna shook her head. "It will be like waking up from a dream. You might feel disoriented and maybe even get a headache, but there are no risks involved."

Mia nodded. "Okay. Let's do it."

"Not so fast. Tell me the name you chose for your avatar first."

"Azul."

"How old is Azul?"

"She's twenty-one."

"And how old are you?"

"Twenty-seven."

"What's Azul's occupation?"

"She's a student, or rather about to become one. She's about to be tested to enter the fae academy."

Doctor Brenna smiled. "Is she going to learn how to use fae magic?"

"Of course."

"I love it. I'm a Harry Potter fan myself." She winked at Mia.

Brenna continued asking questions as if Mia hadn't filled out the questionnaire, and when she was done, she cast Mia a grin. "You are good to go, and you didn't even need relaxants." She turned to the tech. "Let the fun begin."

TOVEN

"*H*ello, Mr. Navón." The tech led Toven to what looked like a dentist's chair.

His name tag identified him as Ruben.

How disappointing.

"I hoped that Brian would be here." Toven sat down.

"Brian?" Ruben asked.

"The guy from headquarters who designed my custom adventure." Toven lifted his legs and got comfortable on the chair. "I was under the impression that he wanted to supervise it personally."

"He might be doing it from there." Ruben rolled his stool next to Toven's chair. "I need to open your shirt a little to attach the wires. Is that okay?"

Toven didn't like anyone touching him other than the ladies he engaged with, but it was unavoidable. "I watched the instructional video. I know what to expect."

"Excellent. But I'm going to explain everything I'm doing anyway. Would you like to use the bathroom before we begin?"

"No, I'm fine. Please, proceed."

"Very well. I understand that you want to use your

avatar's name exclusively." The tech attached a sticky pad to Toven's chest.

"That's correct."

"Not a problem, but I recommend that you repeat your real name in your head several times. When you emerge from the virtual experience, you might be disoriented and not remember who you really are. It would help if I knew your real name so I could help you reorient yourself, but since you prefer to remain entirely anonymous, you can tell me something personal about yourself instead. Your mother's first name, or the name of your first crush. The city you were born in is also a good one. Anything that will help you remember who you are."

He could tell the tech none of that. The names of his mother and father could be found in mythology, and the city he was born in no longer existed. But there was one name that would be meaningless to Ruben but meant a lot to Toven.

"Orlando. That's my son's name."

"Perfect." Ruben attached the sixth pad to Toven's chest. "How old is he?"

"Twenty-nine." Orlando was over five centuries old, but the one time Toven had seen him, that was what he'd looked like.

Ruben laughed. "One of those kids, eh? My son is five, but hearing him talk, you would think that he was a twenty-five-year-old with a squeaky voice."

Sometimes, Toven found it difficult to remember that he didn't look as old as he felt. As someone who looked like he was in his early thirties, he couldn't possibly have a twenty-nine-year-old son.

"Yes, indeed. Orlando is nine, but he's very mature for his age." That would seem more acceptable to the tech.

"Are you recently divorced? I see a lot of fresh divorcees here. After realizing that they married the wrong person, people don't trust their own judgment and prefer to rely on science to find them their perfect match."

"I'm a widower."

Ruben blanched. "I'm so sorry for your loss. It must be difficult to raise a son by yourself."

"Orlando is in boarding school." Toven said the first lie that popped into his head and then looked into Ruben's sorrowful eyes. "Let's focus on the here and now. Do you have any other instructions for me?"

The tech glanced at the readouts. "You are doing very well. Calm as could be. Have you participated in a virtual adventure before?"

"Other than the ones I create in my mind, no."

Ruben nodded sagely. "Having a vivid imagination will make your adventure more interesting. The AI adapts the environment to how you respond to it, and the more imaginative you are, the more it will throw at you."

"Good to know." Toven looked at the straps attached to the chair armrests.

The instructional video he'd watched explained about involuntary movement and the risks of wiring detaching. If that happened, the program would immediately shut down as a safety precaution.

Toven didn't like the idea of being strapped down, but he wasn't overly worried about the restraints. If need be, he could easily break free.

"Are these necessary?" Toven asked as Ruben wrapped one around his right wrist.

The guy stopped. "If that bothers you, I can wait until you are inside the virtual world to strap you down. That way, you won't feel it."

Toven hated the idea of that being done to him while he wasn't aware of it, even more than having it done while he was awake. "Go ahead. I'd rather you follow the protocol to the letter." He focused his gaze on the guy's eyes. "You will do precisely what was promised in the advertising material and keep my experience completely confidential. You will not tell your wife or anyone else a single thing about it."

Not wanting to impair Ruben's mind even in the slightest, Toven had used just a smidgen of compulsion on him. For the next three hours, he was in the guy's hands, and it was imperative that those hands remained capable and in full control.

"No worries, Tobias. What happens in this room stays in this room."

MIA/AZUL

"*G*ood morning, sleepyhead." The melodic voice of Azul's mother was followed by the brush of her soft lips on her forehead.

Why did it feel like a miracle even though her mother woke her up the same way every morning?

A smile lifting her lips, Azul opened her eyes and wound her arms around her mother's neck. "I love you."

"I love you too." Her mother kissed her cheek. "Time to get up. The best harvest is early in the morning."

"You say the same thing every day."

"Because it is true." Her mother pushed to her feet. "Your father is waiting to eat breakfast with you. So don't take long to get ready."

"I won't." Azul threw the blanket off and lowered her feet to the floor.

As she padded to the corner of the room that served as her washroom, the cold stone felt delicious against her toes. People took small things like that for granted, and usually she did too, but this morning everything felt a little more intense. What had she dreamt about that hugging her mother felt like a gift, and so did walking on a cold stone floor?

She couldn't remember, and a splash of water on her face didn't help bring the dream memory back either. A quick brush of her teeth and a comb through her short hair was the extent of her morning routine. With a full day of manual work ahead of her, showering was best done at night.

Thankfully, their home still had running water, and the fact that it was cold didn't bother her as much as the fear that the pipes were going to quit any day now. They were falling apart, and there were no replacement parts to be found.

Whatever was still made or could be salvaged was used to maintain the gods' temples.

Azul's temper flared. Why should they live in luxury while humans lived in squalor?

If they were as powerful as they claimed to be and had humanity's best interests at heart, why hadn't they revived manufacturing?

Stomping her feet into her boots, she walked into their home's main room and plastered a smile on her face as she approached her father. "Good morning, Daddy," she said as she kissed his scruffy cheek.

He tilted his head. "What got you upset this time?"

She could never hide anything from him. "I was wondering how much longer we will have running water in the house. Why aren't the gods doing something about rebuilding factories and manufacturing the things that are so badly needed?"

"You know why. I explained it to you many times before." He pushed a plate of steaming potatoes her way. "Eat, drink, and your mood will improve."

With a huff, she pulled out a chair and sat down. "I

don't accept your explanations." She stabbed her fork into the potatoes. "Not all of it anyway."

The story was that when birth rates started to decline five centuries ago, humanity had been too busy worrying about other perceived risks to its future to pay attention to the insidious decline that proved to be the worst of them all.

As it turned out, humanity's end wouldn't be the result of an atmosphere too polluted to breathe, or even a global nuclear war. The end had been creeping up as a small but steady, one-percent annual decline in global birth rates.

The compound effect was devastating.

Over the past five centuries, the world's population had shrunk from nearly eight billion people to fewer than fifty million, and it was still declining despite the gods' return and their misguided attempts at saving humanity from vanishing.

People didn't want to make more babies because that meant feeding and clothing them, a tall order when everything was scarce. And even though contraceptives had been banned a century before the gods' return, humans were resourceful and found other ways to prevent pregnancies.

She and her mother were breaking the law by brewing contraceptive potions. They did that not just because it provided their household with extra income that was much needed, but also because it was no one's right to force people to have babies when they didn't want them and couldn't feed them.

Besides, no one really enforced the law, so there was very little risk involved. The gods used genetically enhanced winged warriors to police their municipalities, but there weren't many of them, and they had their hands full with bandits and hoodlums.

No one in her village had ever been arrested for

conducting illegal activities, and there were others besides her mother and her who engaged in unreported trade or sold hallucinogens that were also illegal.

That didn't mean that arrests weren't made elsewhere. From time to time, the winged warriors caught lawbreakers, and the punishments the gods meted out were horrible enough to sow fear in the hearts of mortals. The suffering inflicted was terrible and excruciating, but it was nonetheless an illusion that only impacted the mind and left the flesh unmarred.

There was no death penalty, there were no jails, and if the worst happened and they got caught, Azul and her mother figured that their brains were strong enough to withstand the torture.

"If you feel so strongly about it," her mother said. "You should go to the temple and ask for an audience with our municipal god."

Azul grimaced. "I might do that just to let off some steam. That new pretty face they put in charge of our municipality is as worthless as the rest of them. The gods are just a burden on humanity's meager resources and contribute nothing."

"That's not true," her father said. "Without the genetic modifications they introduced, what was left of humanity would have perished by now. The hospitals fell apart, there was no one to make medications, and there were no universities to teach medicine to new doctors. People thought that machines could replace human workers, even doctors, and they were right, but what they didn't realize was that the entire chain of manufacturing would eventually collapse without humans to run it. Someone needed to make the parts for the robots, and before that, someone else needed to make the materials those parts were made from, and so on. It's not the gods' fault that humans let everything fall apart."

"It's true that what happened to us is not the gods' fault, and it's also true that they gave us a fighting chance at survival by altering our genetics and making our bodies self-repairing and longer-lasting. But they could have done so much more."

Human life expectancy was supposed to have been extended to three hundred years on average, but since the gods had started their genome rescue mission only seventy-two years ago, whether that was true still remained to be seen.

The gods had done and were still doing other modifications as well, some for their own whimsical needs, and others upon special request.

For some reason, pointy ears had been all the craze when her mother had been conceived, and her grandparents had requested them for their daughter. The trait was hereditary, so Azul had pointy ears as well. They were cute, and guys were into them, but she didn't like having modified features. Most of the time, she hid the pointy parts under her hair, but sometimes, when she was in a flirty mood, she tucked her hair behind her ears and flaunted them.

Wings were so much more impressive and useful, though. If she had them, the trip to the temple would take a fraction of the time it took on horseback.

The thing was, the gods didn't do anything for free, and there was a price tag on special requests. It was either volunteering for more modifications at the gods' discretion or providing goods and services to the spoiled beings.

Wings were the costliest and required either a large contribution to the temple or conscription of the enhanced child to the gods' service upon their twentieth birthday.

Her grandparents couldn't have afforded them without either submitting their daughter to gods knew what other heinous modifications or conscripting her into the gods' service.

Besides, the wings were probably a pain to live with. How did the winged ones sleep? On their bellies?

She'd only seen one, and he was magnificent, soaring over their village like a huge bird of prey, the black membrane reflecting the sunlight like a mirror.

"Life spans and appearances were not the only things that the gods altered." Her mother gave her father a meaningful look.

"Oh, please." Azul laughed. "Save it for when I'm not in the room."

A popular conspiracy theory claimed that the gods had secretly increased human sexual appetite to boost birth rates, but if they had, it wasn't working.

Most of the families in their village had only one child, the Leehs had two, and the Smiths had three. If other villages were like theirs, then humanity was going to disappear in a generation or two despite the gods' best efforts. According to statistics, to preserve current numbers each female had to birth 2.2 children on average. Anything below that meant a continued decline.

32

TOVEN/TOBIAS

*T*obias stood to the left of the god's throne, looking appropriately menacing and trying not to yawn. To the god's right, Percy was doing the same, and Tobias wondered if his friend's wings itched as badly as his did. They weren't statues, and those wings needed to be flared from time to time, but that would have to wait until the day was over and the doors to the temple were closed.

Their job was to look good flanking Had-dar's chair, Tobias with his black leathery wings and Percy with his feathered white ones. After all, it was all about appearances, and they were there more for decoration than protection. Having a guard of winged warriors elevated Had-dar's grandeur in the eyes of his subjects and was supposed to intimidate them into obeying the law.

The god patron of the sixth region didn't need the guard for protection.

He might be a young and an inexperienced god, but he could still seize the minds of any would-be attackers and have them screaming in agony, engulfed in an all-consuming fire that existed only in their heads.

Had-dar was a decent god, but he'd been given the post

not because he earned it, and not because he'd been apprenticed for many years and was ready to govern, but because his mother had petitioned the other gods to give it to him. Eshkada, the goddess of the fourth region, was influential, and when the god who'd held the position before had mated the goddess patroness of the first region and moved in with her, Eshkada seized the opportunity for her young son to fill the vacancy.

Whatever.

Tobias didn't care much for the gods' politicking, and he didn't care for the endless line of petitioners and their petty requests either.

All he wanted was for the day to be over so he could retire to his room and enjoy his solitude.

His parents should never have made the bargain with Eshkada, enlisting their unborn son for thirty years of service in exchange for her giving him wings.

Five years ago, on his twentieth birthday, he'd said goodbye to his parents and enlisted in Eshkada's guard. He had twenty-five more to go before he was free to soar through the sky whenever he pleased without having to answer to anyone.

Twenty-five years might be a long time to serve, but then he would have his wings for the remainder of his days, which supposedly would last two hundred and seventy years after he gained his freedom.

Was it worth it?

Tobias wasn't sure.

Spending twenty-five more years standing behind some god's throne or flying through the sky to catch humans breaking the law seemed just as depressing today as it had five years ago. He'd thought that he would get used to it, that he would find camaraderie and maybe even friendship with the other guards, but he just wasn't the type.

Tobias was a loner.

He didn't care for the way the men amused themselves with booze and women, preferring to spend his time off reading or sketching or painting. One of the perks of working for a god was access to art supplies. Those were so scarce that they were nearly impossible to get for mere mortals, even those who could afford them. Sculpting presented less of a problem since stone was abundant, and before he'd been conscripted, it had been his chosen medium of artistic expression. It had even gotten him accepted into the gods' academy.

Today, though, he was in a particularly sour mood, making him bad company for himself. Going out with the other winged guards to the town's tavern and medicating his bad mood with alcohol and sex seemed more appealing than spending the night brooding.

One of the perks of having wings was that females loved them, and getting a partner for the night was as easy as crooking a finger.

When the guards at the doors finally started pushing them closed, Tobias let out a relieved breath. There were only twelve more petitioners in line, and since Had-dar allowed them only ten minutes to state their case, the torture would be over in a couple of hours. But just as the doors were closing, a girl pushed through the crack, and when Gavoh tried to push her out, she glared at him.

To Tobias's great surprise, Gavoh relented and let her in.

Amused, Tobias waited for her to turn toward him so he could see the fierce harridan that had given a seasoned warrior like Gavoh pause.

But when she turned and looked right at him, his smile vanished, and his heart skipped a beat.

He'd seen goddesses so perfect and beautiful that it had been difficult not to stare, and he'd also seen his share of beautiful human females, but the little pixie looking at him with defiance in her green eyes took his breath away.

The genetic modification that had given him wings had also given him an eagle's eyesight, and he could see every freckle on her slightly ruddy nose and alabaster cheeks, and even on her eyelids. She was small and slim, but her breasts were ample, straining the brown leather vest that cinched her white blouse to her body. Tight riding pants and knee-high boots hugged her toned, long legs, showing off the slight flare of her hips.

Tobias wondered where she'd ridden from.

He hadn't seen her in town, so she must be from one of the surrounding villages. Who knew a rare diamond like her was hiding among the fields of wheat and barley? Since he also hadn't seen her offering tribute to the temple, someone else from her household must have done it.

Tobias hoped it was her mother or father and not a husband.

He couldn't wait for her to turn around once more so he could ogle her backside, which he was sure was just as toned and shapely as her legs, but then he didn't want to miss out on looking at her gorgeous, freckled face either.

As an image of a sexual position that would allow him to see both at the same time had him hardening in his leather pants, he moved a few inches to the right to hide his reaction behind Had-dar's throne.

33

MIA/AZUL

*A*zul had never been to the municipal temple court before. The one time she'd seen the new god in charge of their region was when he'd arrived in a procession that had passed through their village.

She'd been more fascinated by the hover platform that Had-dar and his entourage had traveled by than the god himself.

You've seen one god, you've seen them all. Perfect, luminous, and stuck-up. Supposedly, Had-dar was a young god, but who could tell the difference with creatures that didn't age? His predecessor had looked the same and was rumored to be ancient.

Azul had found the hover platform much more interesting.

Humans once had automobiles and planes and even spaceships, but now they traveled by horse and carriage the way their ancestors had a thousand years ago.

The roads had fallen into disrepair, so even carriages and carts couldn't go most places, and the only way to travel and transport goods was by horse or by donkey.

Those who had been genetically modified to have wings could go anywhere they damn pleased. Maybe that was the answer to their problems. If everyone could fly, they wouldn't need roads.

Except, goods could not be transported like that, so roads would still be needed, unless the damn gods brought more flying machines and hover platforms with them from wherever their home planet was.

They hadn't shared that information with humanity.

Figures. They'd returned only when human technology had fallen apart, and there was no way to track their origins. But the people still remembered the past, and they were not the ignorant primitives the gods had encountered during their previous sojourns to Earth. Well, the gods claimed that they created humanity, which was why they deserved to be worshipped and called gods even though they were just aliens from a more advanced society somewhere else in the universe.

"I'm sorry." The winged warrior at the door tried to push her out. "You are late, and we are closing the doors."

"They are not closed yet." She glared at him. "It took me three hours to get here, and I'm tired and cranky. Don't you dare throw me out."

Something in his expression softened, and he relented. "Fine." He let her inside and then leaned to whisper in her ear. "But you owe me. How about you and I have a drink at the tavern after you are done with your petition?"

He was handsome, and she was curious about his wings, but she had a long ride home and no intentions of doing it in the dark. "I'll have to take a raincheck. I want to get home before nightfall." She cast him another glare. "The roads are not safe for earthbound creatures like me and my horse."

He nodded. "I can't argue with that."

Casting him a quick smile, she turned around, and as

she looked at the god sitting on top of the dais, her breath caught in her throat.

But it wasn't because of Had-dar's godly grandeur. Standing to the left of the god's throne was the dark-winged warrior she'd seen soaring above her village, and he was just as magnificent up close as he had been from afar.

Even from where she stood, which was a hundred feet or more from him, she could see his piercing blue eyes, and those eyes were trained on her.

A shadow of a smile lifted one corner of his mouth, softening his fierce expression just a fraction.

Her heart galloping like a pair of frantic horses, she forced back a small smile. Azul never allowed anyone the satisfaction of knowing that they intimidated her, or in the winged warrior's case, captured her interest.

With women flocking to the winged ones like moths to a flame, the guy probably had one hell of an ego on him, and she had no intention of boosting it even more.

The twelve people in line ahead of her took forever to present their cases, and she listened to their petitions not because she found them interesting, but as a way to force her attention away from the dark warrior.

Azul had to grudgingly admit that Had-dar treated them with respect and tried to solve their problems the best he could, but not surprisingly, his best wasn't much.

As she'd told her father, the gods' help was limited to genetic manipulation. Other than that, they were a drain on the limited resources humans still had.

When her turn finally arrived, she approached the dais and did her best to look only at the god and not the warrior standing behind him.

"Thank you for granting me this audience, my lord." She dipped her head in a perfunctory bow.

"What's your name?" the god asked.

"My name is Azul, and I came here to ask what the gods are planning to do about reviving manufacturing. If humanity is to survive, we need to start making things again. You want us to have more babies, but you don't give us the means to feed and clothe them."

Had-dar sighed. "I hoped you would have a simple request like asking for my blessing on your betrothal."

"I'm not getting married. I just wanted to officially petition you to bring my inquiry before the gods' council the next time it convenes."

The god gawked at her for a long moment before turning to the dark-winged warrior standing behind him. "Can you take Azul to my study so she can pen an official address to the council?"

"Of course, my lord." The winged warrior bowed his head.

She hadn't expected that, and there was no way she was going to the god's study. "If your guard brings me writing implements, I can pen an official letter right here."

"What's the matter, brazen Azul?" Had-dar leaned his elbow on his thigh and his chin on his fist. "Lost your nerve? Are you suddenly scared of being alone with a god?"

Damn right, she was scared. It was one thing to be alone with the warrior and another to be alone with a god. She'd trained in hand-to-hand combat all her life, and if need be, she could hold off an attack by a human male. But she would be like a puppet in a god's hands. The gods strived to keep up their benevolent façade in front of people, but if he had her cornered alone, Had-dar could command her to do anything he wanted, and she would have no choice but to obey.

Still, what could she do? Turn around and walk out like a coward?

That wasn't her style.

"I don't want to impose, my lord." She bowed her head. "But if you prefer that I make use of your study, I'd be delighted for the opportunity to see where you work."

TOVEN/TOBIAS

"Follow me," Tobias said in the most amicable tone he could muster.

Despite her outward bravado, he could sense that the spitfire was apprehensive, and he couldn't blame her. Being alone with a male, whether human or god, was not safe for a young, gorgeous female.

More so with a human male than a god.

Had she noticed his interest in her?

His hip-long tunic should have covered the evidence, and a quick inconspicuous glance down proved that it did. Tobias stifled a relieved breath and strode forward, leaving Azul to catch up.

The gods had strict rules about obtaining consent, which most of them followed. Naturally, they were so otherworldly beautiful and finely cultured that it was rare for them to be denied, but as in every society, there were deviants who got a kick out of bullying others.

Had-dar's dear mother walked a thin line between coercion and consent. When Tobias had ignored her innuendoes, she'd shipped him off together with her son to one of the poorest municipalities.

Eshkada couldn't fathom a mere human could be uninterested in her amorous advances, but Tobias had seen her when she wasn't performing for public consumption, and the goddess wasn't a nice person. Beneath the veneer of her otherworldly beauty, she was a scheming, manipulative, selfish creature, who sneered at the other gods' lofty ideals.

Gods and humans weren't all that different, and the gods expected humans to follow the same rules and obey the same laws that were supposed to govern all equally. But with the sparse law enforcement at the gods' disposal, compliance was basically voluntary.

Keeping a step behind him, Azul asked quietly, "Is he coming?"

"Do you mean Had-dar?" Tobias slowed down so she could fall in step with him.

"No, Santa Claus." She rolled her eyes. "Of course, Had-dar. We are going to his study. Isn't he going to join us?"

He'd implied that he would, probably to scare Azul into leaving, but Tobias knew he wouldn't.

"It's not likely." The first thing Had-dar did at the end of each day was to lock himself in his private quarters and drink himself into a stupor.

Tobias cast her a sidelong glance, noting the cute, upturned nose and the smattering of freckles covering it. "Does anyone still celebrate Christmas?"

She shrugged. "My father used to tell me bedtime stories about Santa Claus that he made up."

"What does your father do?" He stopped next to Had-dar's study and opened the door.

"He's a hunter."

"And your mother?"

"My mother is a teacher."

Tobias didn't have Had-dar's ability to smell lies, but he was pretty sure that Azul had lied about her mother's occupation. There was a slight delay in her answer, and she said *teacher* with much less conviction than she'd said hunter.

"What else does your mother do?" He motioned for her to take a seat at the round table that Had-dar used for his chess games.

"It's a full-time job. She teaches hand-to-hand combat, staff fighting, archery, swordsmanship, and so on. Everyone in our village trains with her at least twice a week."

That had been delivered with much more conviction than the word teacher and with no small amount of pride.

Perhaps her mother was one of the early winged warriors?

The trait wasn't hereditary, so Azul wouldn't have them.

"Did your mother serve in a god's guard?" Tobias moved the chessboard to Had-dar's desk and pulled out a block of white paper and a pen from the desk drawer.

Azul chuckled. "The only genetic enhancement my mother got was fae ears." She pushed her short black hair behind one ear. "These are hereditary."

"Adorable." He had the sudden and inexplicable urge to nibble on those pointy tips.

He'd never been with a lover who had that enhancement, but he'd heard from others that they were highly sensitive to stimulation and that a female could orgasm just from having her ears kissed and licked.

"Ugh. You're giving me that look." She covered her ear.

"What look?" He pretended innocence.

"The kind that speculates whether the rumors are true and the fae ears are as sensitive as other erogenous zones on a female's body."

"Are they?"

She batted her eyelashes. "You'll have to find out for yourself."

As his shaft turned into a hard club, Tobias was never more grateful for the tunic covering it up.

"When you're playing with fire, pixie girl, don't be surprised when you get burned."

She blushed. "I didn't mean with me. There are plenty of girls with fae ears for you to sample." She waved a dismissive hand. "You can probably find several in the town's tavern who would be more than happy to let you play with theirs."

Her innocence was endearing. She didn't even realize all the openings she was handing him on a silver platter.

Luckily for her, he was a decent male, and he decided to ease up on the sexual banter. If they kept at it, she would end up going home without writing a single word.

"I'll pass." He placed the pen and paper in front of her. "So, how did your mother acquire her combat skills?"

Azul's shoulders lost some of their tension. "She learned her combat skills from her father, who also taught his entire village how to defend themselves. The gods are not doing enough to protect us from bandits. We have to fend for ourselves."

"I applaud your grandfather's and mother's initiative." Tobias flipped the other chair so he could straddle it. Haddar didn't have backless chairs in his study. "The gods are not as powerful as they want us to believe they are. They can only control those around them, and they can't be everywhere at the same time."

Azul took the pen but didn't start writing. "That's why humans need to get organized and take care of the lawbreakers themselves. But the gods don't allow us to have weapons other than what we can make ourselves, and that's limited."

Smiling, he folded his arms over the chair back and

rested his chin on them. "You seem to have given a lot of thought to solving the problems facing humanity. I suggest that you start writing if you want to finish putting down everything you want to say. I don't want to be here all night."

That was a lie. He would love to spend the night with her, even if it was only to look at her freckled face.

Nodding, Azul put pen to paper, wrote a heading, and then lifted her head to look at him. "Are you going to sit there and stare at me the entire time?"

He smirked. "Does it bother you?"

"I can't concentrate when I feel your eyes on me."

Tobias would have loved to have Had-dar's ability to sniff her arousal right now, but even with his limited human senses, he knew that Azul was into him.

Good. He was very much into her as well.

"Then I'll close my eyes and take a nap. How's that?"

"Can't you leave and come back later?"

He shook his head. "I can't leave you alone in Had-dar's study."

"Why?" She narrowed her eyes at him. "Are you afraid that I'm going to steal his precious white paper?"

It was indeed precious and difficult to find, but she didn't strike him as a thief.

"Are you tempted?" he teased.

"Of course I am." She smoothed her hand over the page in front of her. "I love to draw, but with how difficult and expensive it is to get supplies, it's a hobby I can't afford to pursue."

"If you're very good, you could apply to the gods' academy. You'd be given all the supplies you can dream of."

35

MIA/AZUL

*T*hat was a very nice thing for Tobias to say, and also unexpected. It seemed that the intense warrior who had flirted with her so unabashedly had a gentler side to him.

"I don't know if I'm any good."

He waved a hand at the nearly blank page in front of her. "Sketch something for me, and I'll tell you whether you are good enough for the academy or not."

"And how would you know how to evaluate my skill? What do you know about art?"

"I know enough to get accepted."

Her eyes widened. "No way. So, what are you doing here?"

He winced. "Serving a sentence."

"What do you mean? Is serving the god punishment for a crime?"

"No, and Had-dar is not so bad as gods go. But I was conscripted into the service even before I was born, and I had no say in it. My father thought that he was giving me a leg up in life, or a wing as it was." He smiled, and the dimple that formed in his cheek was sexy as hell. "He was probably right, but I would rather be sculpting than guarding a god and catching lawbreakers for the next twenty-five years. That's a very long time."

Azul swallowed. She was one of those lawbreakers, and Tobias monitored their municipality. She would need to be extra careful not to say anything incriminating, which meant saying very little about herself. Sticking to generalities was the safest way to go.

"If you think about it as a sentence, then that's what it will feel like. Change the story you're telling yourself in your head, and instead of suffering for the next twenty-five years, you might enjoy your service. It's all in the attitude."

"How very astute of you. How old are you, Azul?"

"I'm twenty-one."

"Do you have a boyfriend?"

She shook her head.

"Why not? You are beautiful and sexy and smart. The young men of your village must swarm around you."

"Well, they don't. Can we change the subject?"

For three long years, she'd dated a guy who everyone, including her, thought she would marry. Then one day he'd informed her that he was sick of life in a small village and was going to explore the world.

Tobias smiled again, but this time, both of his cheeks dimpled. "I have a better way of changing my attitude. We could escape together and find the hidden free city."

He was such a gorgeous male, but he was also a terrible tease, and what he'd said sounded eerily similar to what Nathan had told her before dumping her. Except, Nathan hadn't offered to take her along.

"The hidden city is a myth, and I have nothing to escape from. I happen to enjoy my life."

He tilted his head, and his wings flared out a little. "Do you? What's the name of your village?"

"Patagonia," she reluctantly told him. "It's about three

hours on horseback from here, and I'd better start writing this petition, or I'll be riding home in the dark."

"Why did you wait until the end of the day to get here?"

"Because I wanted to be the last petitioner. I figured that the god could give me more time if there was no one else in line." She shook her head. "Please stop distracting me and let me concentrate on this thing."

"I don't want to. I like talking to you."

She enjoyed talking to him too, and she also liked looking at him and flirting with him.

In fact, Azul had never felt as alive and as wired as she did with this magnificent creature, but she had a mission to complete, and even though it might be naive of her to think that her petition would change anything, she had to try.

Letting out an exasperated breath, she put the pen down. "Since I can't talk and write at the same time, let's make it quick. What else do you want to talk about?"

He pinned her with his incredible blue eyes. "I want to do much more than talking. Is there a chance that you will allow me to kiss you?"

Talk about blunt.

Many guys had flirted with her before, especially after Nathan had left, but no one had been that brazen.

"I don't know you, and I don't kiss strangers."

"So let's get to know each other. Don't worry about getting home in the dark. I'll escort you all the way back." He flared his black wings. "No bandits will bother you with me flying overhead."

Her mother would have a panic attack if she saw a winged warrior escorting her daughter home.

"If I don't get back by nightfall, my parents will be frantic with worry. I can't do that to them."

"Fine," he relented. "I wouldn't want them to worry either. I'll tell you what we will do. I'll keep my mouth shut so you can write down your petition, and when you are done, I'll escort you home." He smirked. "We will have three hours to get to know each other, and by the time we part at your doorstep, I will no longer be a stranger, so you can kiss me goodnight."

36

TOVEN/TOBIAS

For nearly two hours, Tobias had not only watched Azul write her petition, but he'd also read each page as she was done with it.

Her handwriting was neat, her mind was sharp and well organized, and he couldn't find fault with any of her suggestions. How could a twenty-one-year-old villager see things so clearly when gods thousands of years old couldn't?

Or maybe they could but didn't want to?

The gods needed humans to remain dependent on them. That was why they hadn't returned until humanity was in the pits, its technology lost, its people few and scattered. If humanity regained its prior splendor and went back to being a technologically advanced society, there would be no need for the gods other than their secret of immortality.

They would have to flee, and he wasn't sure they had the means to. Supposedly, their spaceship was orbiting around the planet, but since there was no way to check if it did, they might be lying about it.

What if they had been dumped on Earth as punishment?

What if they couldn't go back?

He knew better than most how vulnerable the gods really were. Their power was all in their minds, and to use it, they needed to be conscious. But even gods needed to sleep to keep their bodies and minds going. That was when they could be easily killed.

Well, not easily, but it could be done.

Had-dar slept in a room that had been carved out of stone and was twenty feet underground. It had no windows, only slim shafts to allow air in, and it had a heavy iron door that was locked from the inside. If anyone tried to break in, the god would wake up and seize their minds.

It wasn't that Tobias was plotting to kill Had-dar, but to protect him, he needed to think of all the ways he could be killed. Sneaking up on the god unawares could accomplish that, provided that the assassin was swift enough.

When Azul handed him the last page, her face was flushed from the long hours of concentration. "What do you think?"

"I think that you're brilliant. Why don't you sketch something for me while I read through your summary page?"

She looked at the stack of white pages. "Do you think the god would mind if I took this paper?"

"He wouldn't even notice. Go ahead, take everything that's left."

"Are you sure? Won't you get in trouble for letting me take it?"

"I won't."

The sweet girl was worried for him. He liked it more than he cared to admit.

Tobias spent much longer than he needed to read

through the last page and then pretended to leaf through the previous ones. While he read, Azul sketched, and he didn't want her to stop before she was done.

When she put down the pen, he lifted his head. "Is it ready?"

With a nod, she lifted the page and handed it to him. "It's you."

He would have easily recognized himself flying through the sky without her telling him. No one else in Had-dar's guard had black wings, but that wasn't the only thing that made it uniquely him. What bothered him about it, though, was that she had somehow drawn him luminous like a god.

"This is very good, but I'm not shiny like the gods." He handed her the page back.

She looked at the drawing and frowned. "Only your wings are shiny, and that's because they reflect the sunlight. Your skin is not luminous. I mean the rest of the skin on your body, that is, not your wings." She lifted her eyes to him and smiled. "Besides, most people would have taken it as a huge compliment to be depicted as a god."

"Not me." Tobias flared his wings. "They don't have these." He frowned. "I wonder why. They could have easily given themselves the ability to fly."

"Maybe not." She eyed him from under lowered lashes. "Maybe to have wings, they would have to give up something else."

"Like what?"

Azul shrugged. "How should I know? It's not like they tell us how they manipulate genes. Still, you have something the gods do not." Her smile turned into a smirk. "Good-looking young men like you usually have a god complex. They think that they were created by the gods to the benefit of womankind."

Something about her words sounded very familiar, as if he had heard them in a dream, or maybe a premonition.

Tobias pushed to his feet and stretched his wings. "Having these, I might feel like a god from time to time. But then I remind myself how flawed the real gods are, and I don't want to be compared to them."

She arched a brow. "Flawed? In what way? And are you allowed to talk like that in your boss's study?

He handed her a large envelope to put her petition in and took out another one for the sketch that he intended to keep. "Physically, the gods are perfect, and they have the power to play with our minds. But they are just as manipulative, greedy, selfish, and power-hungry as their human counterparts. Had-dar agrees with me, so it's not like I'm mouthing off behind his back. He happens to be one of the good guys, but he's powerless."

"He shouldn't be any more or less powerful than the other gods. Don't they all vote on every major decision?"

Tobias smiled. "Don't be naive, Azul. They form power cliques, they campaign and promise favors in exchange for votes, and they gang up against decisions that they don't want passed."

MIA/AZUL

$\mathcal{T}$obias was proof that appearances were often misleading. At first glance, he looked like a cocky young warrior, confident, sexy, flirty, but there was depth to him that didn't match his years. In that, he was like the gods, who he seemed to dislike at least as much as she did.

His seemingly young body housed a very old soul, and he vacillated between acting his age and sounding like a wizened old man, weary and disillusioned.

Her mother used to comment about some people having old souls with others having fresh ones. Azul was supposed to be a brand-new soul with no prior baggage, while her mother claimed to possess an ancient soul that had seen a lot during its many reincarnations.

Not much surprised her mother, and she was good at predicting things, so maybe there was something to her claim.

"What's your last name?" Tobias asked as he wrote her first name on the envelope he'd put her petition in.

"Talisman, and please don't tease me about it. I had enough of it growing up."

He stifled a smile. "I wouldn't dream of it. It suits you. Azul Talisman. A magical pixie girl, with wee pointy ears, a wee pointy nose, and the sweetest curves."

She snorted. "Can you be more creative?"

On the inside, though, she was preening.

"What would you like me to call you?" He offered her a hand up.

"Just call me Azul." Without thinking, she put her hand in his and was zapped with an electrical current that could have lit up her house if they had electricity. "That's my name." She pulled her hand out of his.

For a moment, he seemed just as shocked as she'd been, but he recovered quickly.

"Come on. Let's get you home before your parents send out a search party for you."

She wanted to decline his offer to escort her home, but as they stepped out of the temple, the sun was already setting, and she didn't dare make the three-hour-long journey alone at night.

"I hope that you're as fierce as you look," she told him as she entered the stable and paid the stable hand for taking care of her horse.

Bolt trotted over to her and nudged her with his muzzle, asking for a pat.

Tobias grinned. "I'm much fiercer. Not many know that, but the wings enhancement comes with several more perks."

She wanted to ask about those perks when another stable hand walked over with a huge black horse in tow.

Azul arched a brow. "I didn't know that the winged guard rode horses. I thought that you only traveled by air."

"Usually, we do. But not when escorting beautiful young ladies home." He waited to see if she needed help getting up on her horse but didn't offer her his hand. "If you had come on foot, I could have flown you back, but I

178

can't carry you and your horse, and I'm sure you don't want to leave him behind."

"I wouldn't dream of it." She effortlessly mounted Bolt. "Bolt is not only my means of transportation. He's also my friend." She patted his neck.

"I get it." He mounted his enormous horse. "So is Thunder."

Azul laughed. "Thunder and Bolt. Our horses match."

"So do we." He winked at her.

Tobias was a relentless flirt, but he managed to be charming and confident without being obnoxious. It was a skill that she would have expected from a much older man, one who had flirted with hundreds of women and had perfected the craft. Tobias was young, but he was very different than the young guys she usually interacted with. Maybe it had something to do with serving a god. It exposed him to politics and taught him to deal with people.

He also hadn't assumed that just because she was a small female, she couldn't handle getting up on her horse without aid, which was a huge pet peeve of hers with most guys. Azul prided herself on her independence and on being able to do most things without having to ask for help. She didn't like to be offered assistance when she didn't need it.

Unfortunately, most men didn't know the difference between gallant and overbearing, but Tobias seemed to have it mastered.

Azul enjoyed the friendly yet respectful way he treated her, and given that he was also sexier than sin, she was looking forward to the kiss that he expected to get when they parted at her door.

Tobias glanced at the staff tied to the back of her saddle. "How good are you with that thing?"

"I'm very good. How about you?"

"The Guard doesn't train with staves. We only train with swords."

"What about bows and arrows?"

He shook his head. "Just swords, knives, and the perks I've mentioned before."

"Yeah, I was wondering about that. What are those perks?"

He lifted his hand, and as he wiggled his fingers, claws shot out from his fingertips. "These are very useful. I also have fangs." He smiled, and his canines elongated.

Azul swallowed. "Are those the same as the ones the gods have?"

Male gods had elongating fangs and venom glands, while goddesses had small, stationary fangs and no venom.

"They function similarly." Tobias cast her a lascivious look.

"Oh." Feeling her cheeks get hot, she shifted her eyes away from him.

Supposedly, the male gods could deliver unimaginable pleasure with their venom bite, giving their partners multiple explosive orgasms.

Azul would settle for one that wasn't delivered by her own hand. Nathan had been the only man she'd been with, and he'd never succeeded in bringing her to a climax, and not for lack of effort.

He'd done his best, but she just couldn't orgasm for him, which was an endless source of strife and friction between them.

Maybe he'd left her because he'd given up on her?

Hell, who was she kidding. That wasn't a maybe.

That was precisely why he'd left.

She'd made him feel like a failure, and he wanted to prove to himself that he wasn't.

TOVEN/TOBIAS

"You ou asked me if I had a boyfriend," Azul said after they'd been riding for a few minutes. "What about you?"

He chuckled. "I don't have a boyfriend either."

"Very funny. Are you seeing anyone? And please, don't make another joke about seeing people all day."

"I thought that you liked my jokes."

A small smile lifted the corners of her lush lips. He'd been salivating to have a taste of those puffy, pink pillows, and he had a feeling she wouldn't deny him the kiss he expected on her doorstep.

"I like it when you are lighthearted because I don't think you get to be like that often, but I want you to answer me seriously." She cut him a sidelong glance. "I'm not going to kiss you if you have a girl you're currently seeing."

Azul was not only beautiful, smart, and talented, she was also insightful.

Tobias was surprising himself with the lighthearted banter he'd engaged in with her. He realized that Azul's youthful optimism and zest for life had lifted his spirits.

"I'm not seeing anyone, but I also haven't been living like a monk."

She sighed. "I have. Ever since Nathan left, I've been all work and no play. I grew up with all the single guys in my village, and they are like family to me. I can't think of them as potential boyfriends, and since I haven't attended any of the festivals lately, I haven't had a chance to meet guys from other villages either."

"Why haven't you?"

She shrugged. "I don't know. I guess I just wasn't in the mood after Nathan dumped me."

That was a surprise. Tobias had been sure that she'd dumped her boyfriend, or that he'd had to leave for other reasons. He couldn't imagine any guy dumb enough to dump Azul.

"He's an idiot who didn't deserve you."

She smiled. "Thank you. I needed to hear that. What about you? Why haven't you gotten yourself a steady girl? Fear of commitment?"

"I haven't met anyone who piqued my interest. Until today, that is."

She rolled her eyes. "Do you use that line on all the girls?"

"I don't use lines. I'm brutally honest."

"Right. So how do you engage with women? Do you just ask them if they want to hop into your bed?"

"Usually, I don't even have to ask. They come to me. I'm not boasting. It's just the way it is. I guess it's the wings. Women find them alluring."

She eyed him from under her eyelashes. "And unusually?"

"Unusually, I meet a fascinating girl who is a little prickly, and a lot of cautious, and I have to beg for a kiss."

"Don't tell me that I'm the only one you ever had to work for."

She was, and maybe that was part of the appeal. He liked that Azul was a challenge and that she demanded he prove himself worthy of her.

Unexpectedly, it made him feel better about himself than if she'd taken him for a romp in the hay without asking anything, without attempting to find out more about him, without wanting to know the man behind the wings.

Since he'd been old enough to satisfy a female, he'd been coveted for his wings and his handsome face, and when he joined the goddess's guard, he was coveted for his flashy uniform and the status that came with it. To the women, he'd been a commodity, a piece of flesh, not a person worth getting to know.

"Okay, I won't tell you that."

Azul laughed. "I don't know what to think of that response. Does it mean that you are so full of yourself that you think all women want you, or that you are actually telling me the truth as it is, and you have females chasing you as if you were a god."

"It's mostly the wings."

She laughed. "Was that your attempt at modesty?"

"Yeah, it was. It's the face too."

"You have a very handsome face."

"Thank you." He inclined his head. "Is that what you like about me the most?"

"Tobias, are you fishing for compliments?"

"I just want to know where I stand with you and if I have a chance."

"That depends on what kind of a chance you are after. I'm not into casual flings."

"Neither am I, but that's what I've been given, and it was okay. But I want more with you."

"How do you know that? You haven't even kissed me yet. What if I'm a terrible kisser?"

"I'm sure that you are exquisite, and I'm dying to be proven right."

He looked up at the darkening sky. They had no more than one more hour to go before they reached her village.

Soon, he would get his kiss and perhaps an invitation for another date.

MIA/AZUL

*A*zul hadn't planned on returning home at night, and her clothing was more appropriate for the day's mild weather than the night's chill.

Riding a little ahead of her to look out for potholes, Tobias didn't seem to be bothered, even though his tunic was sleeveless and opened at the sides. The garment was designed to accommodate wings, with a thin swath of fabric running between them in the back and a wide belt holding it together. It left Tobias's muscular arms exposed to her ogling eyes, and when he leaned forward, she'd even gotten a peek at his sculpted pectorals.

But even her simmering arousal wasn't enough to keep her warm, and she wondered whether Tobias's wings sheltered him from the cold. They were slightly flared, their bottoms draping over his horse's flanks like a cape.

"Do your wings keep you warm?" she asked.

He slowed down and looked at her with hooded eyes. "Are you cold?"

"A little. I didn't plan on returning home so late."

"I can help with that."

Before she knew what was happening, he plucked her

off her horse and put her in front of him on his. She was about to protest, when his wings wrapped around her, cocooning her in warmth.

Letting out a breath, she slumped against his warm chest, but as she felt his erection pressing against her bottom, she straightened up quickly and tried to shift forward.

"Relax," he said against her ear. "I don't bite." He chuckled. "Well, not without an invitation."

At that moment, she was more worried about the other part of his anatomy than about his fangs, but the heady mix of fear and thrill that his comment had evoked made her squirm on the saddle, which made the situation even worse.

Or better, a small voice whispered in the back of her head.

No, it wasn't better. The rational part of her mind raised its head from the ashes left by her raging desire.

Tobias was a law enforcer, and she was a lawbreaker. After the one kiss she'd promised him, she would do her best to never see him again.

She'd better make that kiss count.

Scooting a fraction of an inch forward, she kept her back ramrod straight and her shoulders square.

"Are you scared of me?" he murmured against her ear.

"No."

"Then why are you so tense?"

She couldn't state the obvious, and no clever comment came to her.

Why did she feel so frazzled because of his hard-on? It was a natural thing for a healthy male, and she should be flattered being the cause of it. She wasn't a virgin, and she was attracted to him, so why was she suddenly such a prude?

"You're hard, and I don't mean your chest."

He laughed. "Is that what has gotten your panties in a wad? I didn't keep it a secret that I lust after you. I've been hard from the moment you entered the petitioner's hall."

Her eyes widened at his admission.

"Well, it's one thing to talk about it, and quite another to be pressed against the physical evidence. We met only a few hours ago."

"And yet, I don't remember ever talking to anyone for so long, male or female, and enjoying it so much that I don't want it to end. Do you think your parents would mind if I stayed the night to talk to you?"

"Just talk?"

"If that's all you'll allow, then yes. I'm at your mercy, sweet Azul. You can do with me as you please."

She smiled. Having him at her mercy gave her all sorts of ideas that he would probably like very much, but there was no way she was bringing him home, let alone letting him stay the night.

"My parents will mind very much. In fact, we better say goodbye at the village's outskirts."

"What about my kiss? You promised me a kiss goodnight."

She hadn't, but it had been implied, and she wanted it.

Heck, she wanted much more than just a kiss, but she would settle for that.

Why? The same insidious voice whispered in her ear. *You can never see Tobias again, so why not have your fill of him right here, right now?*

Azul had no doubt that sex with Tobias would be spectacular, and not just because he was a winged warrior with a venom bite that was rumored to bring a woman unimaginable pleasure.

He was unlike any of the men she'd met before, and if he wasn't a law enforcer, she would have let herself fall for him hard and fast.

But her family couldn't afford to stop selling the contraceptive tonics, financially as well as morally.

Azul could entertain the idea of having sex with this magnificent male, only because she knew she was protected from unwanted pregnancy. Even though Nathan had left nearly a year ago, and there had been no others, she was still drinking the tonic once a week because it minimized her monthly to three days instead of seven.

"I didn't promise you a kiss, but I didn't say no either, so you are getting your kiss, just not on the doorstep. My father might come out with a club or a nocked arrow."

"Why? Aren't you allowed to have male suitors? You are an adult."

"I'm allowed to do as I please, but since it is not my custom to kiss strangers on the doorstep, he will assume I'm being accosted."

"Then introduce me, and then come out with me and kiss me."

Right. One look at his wings, and her parents would be sure that he was there to arrest their entire family. They might even say something incriminating in a misguided effort to save her hide.

Turning her head around to look at him, she was struck again by how beautiful he was. "Why are you so interested in meeting my parents?"

"Because I want to get to know you, Azul from Patagonia, and I want your parents to approve of my suit. Isn't that what a serious contender for your affections is supposed to do?"

Damn. How was she going to get out of that?

As much as she desired Tobias, she would never endanger her family to satisfy her cravings. Her mother and father would always come first.

"It's too early for that. First, I need to decide whether

you are boyfriend material, and when I do, or rather if I do, I'll introduce you to my parents."

"Fair enough. So how are we going to play this?"

The relief that washed over her was a good indicator of how much the idea of him insisting on coming to her house had stressed her. She would do anything to protect her parents, including faking disinterest in the first male to capture her interest and fuel her desire since her breakup with Nathan.

Heck, she'd never felt such a strong attraction to Nathan. Maybe that was why she'd never climaxed for him?

"You'll have to wait for me on the village outskirts. I'll go home, so my parents know that I've returned safely. I'll tell them that I was escorted by a kind guard, and that I want to thank him with provisions for the road."

Her parents would most likely demand that she invite him into their home, but once she told them who he was, they would sing a different tune.

Their brewing equipment was all over the place, and it didn't require detective skills to figure out what they were brewing in their home.

TOVEN/TOBIAS

*A*s Tobias waited for Azul's return, rain started drizzling, and as the minutes ticked off, his patience began wearing thin.

Had she ditched him?

Could he have been such a bad judge of character?

He'd been sure that Azul would never go back on her word. If she said she was coming back to give him a kiss, she would.

The girl wasn't a coward either, so if she didn't want anything to do with him, she would have told him to get lost instead of having him wait for her.

Perhaps her parents were giving her grief about leaving the house again?

It wasn't safe for a woman alone at night, not even outside her own home. There were no sentries guarding the village, no wall to keep its inhabitants safe, and bandits were a real problem.

Except, he hadn't spotted any on the way, and he'd been as vigilant as always despite Azul's distracting presence.

Most of the land was farmed, and visibility even from horseback was good. The few islands of trees that were scattered in between the fields were not dense enough to provide cover for a band of hoodlums.

A lone hoodlum, however, could make his way into the village undetected, either to steal supplies, or horses, or to accost an unprotected woman.

When he finally saw Azul approach on foot, a weight rolled off his chest. She was wearing a heavy cloak and carried a basket that he assumed contained the provisions she'd mentioned.

He dismounted and walked over to her. "I was worried about you." He took the basket from her. "Did your parents object to you leaving the house again?"

"They wanted to invite you to supper, but when I told them that you were in a hurry to get back and didn't have time for a social visit, my mother insisted on preparing a basket of food for you. That's what took so long. They send their gratitude for escorting their daughter safely home."

He executed a sweeping bow. "It was and still is my pleasure."

Smiling, she started walking, and he fell in step with her.

"Where are you taking me?"

Thunder followed behind them, his hooves making very little noise on the wet soil.

"I thought that we could have a picnic in the village square, but then it started raining, so the grass was out. But then it occurred to me that we could hide out from the rain in the amphitheater. It's open on three sides, but it has a roof."

"A delightful idea." He lifted one wing and spread it over her head. "How is that?"

She looked up and smiled. "You are very useful to have around, Tobias. First you were my blanket, and now you are my umbrella."

Her words thawed a chunk of his heart that he hadn't

known had been frozen. "I'm glad to be of service, my lady Azul, and I hope to become much more than a blanket and an umbrella to you."

"You are very persistent."

He chuckled. "You have no idea."

As they reached the village square, he was glad to see that it was deserted. It wasn't late, and there were lights in many of the windows they'd passed, but people were not going to venture out of their homes in the rain.

The amphitheater was small, but it was probably big enough to accommodate village assemblies and maybe even host traveling performers. It had a wooden stage with a wall behind it, and although its three other sides were open to the elements, the trees and bushes surrounding it provided plenty of privacy. Once they were seated inside, no one would see them there unless they walked right in.

"Nice and dry." She led him to the stage. "We can sit here on the floor or on the benches. What's your preference?"

"Here is good." He put the basket down. "I hope you told your parents that you planned to dine with me so they wouldn't get worried about you."

What he really wanted to know was whether they would come looking for her.

"I told them my plan, so they know that I'm with a fierce warrior who will protect me."

"Good."

Hopefully, they wouldn't come to check on their daughter because he had seduction on his mind.

"I'll get us a blanket." He walked back to the grassy area where he'd left Thunder.

When he returned a moment later, she looked at him with accusation in her eyes. "You had a blanket this entire time and didn't tell me? You could have given it to me instead of cocooning me inside your wings."

He laughed. "And miss an opportunity to hold you in my arms? I don't think so."

Azul's lips twitched with a barely suppressed smile. "You're a scoundrel."

"On the contrary." Tobias spread the blanket on the wooden stage. "I'm brutally honest." He put the basket on the blanket. "If you don't mind, I'm going to take my boots off. I don't want to get mud on it."

"Good idea. I'll take mine off as well."

That was a good start.

Tobias stifled a smile as he tugged his left boot off along with the woolen sock. If all he got out of it was to see Azul's toes, it would be good enough. But perhaps he would get much more than that.

41

MIA/AZUL

There was no graceful way to take off boots, so Azul sat on the edge of the blanket with her back to Tobias and tried not to grunt as she pulled the first one off. The other one came off more easily, but to her horror, there was a hole in her sock, and she quickly removed both.

The cold air on her feet felt good, as did the solidity of the wooden planks under them. Turning toward Tobias, she stretched her toes and wiggled them, happy that she kept her toenails neatly trimmed. Her feet looked nice if she said so herself. They weren't small and dainty, but they weren't huge either, and all her toes were straight.

Those were small things that might not matter to others, but Azul took pleasure in them.

"I hope my feet don't smell." Tobias lifted his leg and, in a show of impressive flexibility, brought his bare foot next to his nose. He sniffed. "All good. I can still smell the soap I used this morning."

Azul laughed. "You are nothing like I expected a winged warrior to be."

"What did you expect?"

"A gruff, grumpy, humorless, macho guy who looked down his nose at everyone." She gave her own foot an inconspicuous sniff.

"And what do you think of me now?"

Gods, if she waxed poetic about how sexy and handsome and charming he was, he would think that she'd fallen in love with him like some silly goose.

"I think that you're charming and funny, and you are also surprisingly down to earth considering that you have wings and soar through the sky."

"Thank you." He rewarded her with a panty-melting dimpled grin.

Forcing her eyes away from those dimples, Azul turned to the basket her mother had prepared. "Let's eat before it gets cold." She opened the lid and started pulling out everything that her mother had so carefully packed.

He eyed the fare with a frown. "That's too much. I know how hard it is for farmers to put food on the table."

"We are not farmers." She handed him a plate piled high with smoked venison and cooked root vegetables. "My father is a hunter, and he's very good at it. We also grow vegetables and fruit in our garden, and we never lack for food. We even have enough to share with our neighbors."

That wasn't entirely her father's doing, but that was the story she was going to stick with.

"I'm glad that you are well taken care of."

He made it sound as if she wasn't an equal contributor to her household's resources, and it rankled even though she couldn't tell him what her contribution was.

"We take care of each other. Don't mistake my love for my parents for dependence. I'm not a child they have to take care of. They need me as much as I need them."

He inclined his head. "I meant no offense, my lady Azul. Forgive me. I was glad that you lack for nothing." He smirked. "Well, you did lack me, but now that I'm here, you truly lack for nothing."

She shook her head. "Why do I find your cockiness amusing instead of infuriating?"

"Because I'm charming and funny?" Tobias took the fork and knife she handed him.

"Must be." Azul cut a small carrot into two equal pieces.

Tobias cast her an appreciative smile. "You are the only one who thinks that. Everyone else thinks that I'm a dreary, humorless block." He skewered a piece of meat on his fork and put it in his mouth.

"That can't be true."

"It is." He pinned her with his blue stare. "You bring out something in me that I didn't even know was there. I don't think that I've ever bantered and flirted as much with anyone, and I'm having so much fun that I never want it to end."

Was he feeding her lines to seduce her?

If he was, it was working.

"I'm glad." She shifted her eyes away from his intense gaze and lifted a piece of carrot to her mouth.

For the next several minutes, they ate in silence, enjoying her mother's vegetables and her father's smoked meat and washing it down with homemade mead.

When they were done, Azul cleaned their plates and utensils with a cloth napkin before putting them back in the basket.

She was a little buzzed from the mead, not tipsy, but loosened enough to overcome her inhibitions.

Stretched on the blanket on his side, Tobias braced his upper body on his forearm. His black wings were tucked against his back and sprawled behind him like a wet leather cloak.

Azul wanted to touch them, to run her hands over the

smooth, leathery ridges. Were they sensitive? Would she elicit a shiver out of him?

Rising to her knees, she closed the distance between them and cupped his cheeks. "I think it's time for your kiss, my knight with shining wings."

"Our kiss." He didn't move a muscle as he waited for her to bring their mouths together.

Slowly, she lowered her head until their lips touched, gently pressing them against his. When she flicked her tongue out and licked at the seam, he groaned, and the next moment she was on her back, with him poised above her.

"Don't be scared," he murmured against her lips and kissed her like she'd never been kissed before.

Scared? She wasn't scared of him, but the inferno of desire rioting through her body terrified her.

Threading her fingers through his hair, she moaned into his mouth and got lost in the kiss.

In those moments, nothing outside the two of them existed. With his wings wrapped around them, they were in their own bubble of lust that Azul was in no hurry to leave anytime soon.

42

TOVEN/TOBIAS

As Azul writhed under him, Tobias fought the urge to tear both of their clothes off and have her right there in the open amphitheater.

Wasn't that what he'd had in mind when he'd brought the blanket?

Yeah, that was precisely what he had planned, but now it seemed wrong. Azul wasn't just a romp in the hay to him, and she wasn't the type of girl who was okay with someone walking in on them making love. The village was small, and it wouldn't take long before everyone knew that she'd been caught in a compromising position. It would embarrass not only her but also her parents.

He couldn't do that to her.

Azul deserved better than to be taken on a wooden stage in the center of her village. When he made love to her, it would be in a bed fit for a queen.

Rolling to his side, he took her with him and turned her around so her back was pressed to his chest.

"Why did you stop?" she protested.

Struggling to compose his breathing, he kissed her

neck. "I didn't. I'm going to take care of you, my precious Azul."

As he brought his wing around them, cocooning her in its protective shield, she lifted her hand and traced a finger along one of the ridges, eliciting a shudder from him.

"I wondered whether they were sensitive," she murmured.

"Very." He tightened his arms around her, his hand reaching under her shirt to splay over the softness of her belly.

When she dragged a finger along another ridge, he pressed into her, grinding his hard shaft against her bottom.

This time, she didn't lurch forward as she'd done on the saddle. Instead, she pushed back.

His hand inched upward on her stomach, but her vest was too tight to allow him access, and when he did quick work of releasing the clasps holding it together, Azul didn't object.

Her breaths becoming soft pants, she trembled in his arms as he slid his hand right under the swell of her breast.

He kissed her neck. "Do you want me to touch you?"

"Please," she gasped.

Slipping his other hand under her shirt, he cupped both breasts, and as her peaked nipples scraped against his palms, he kissed her ear. "Perfect."

She arched, pressing her bottom to his shaft even harder. "More."

He smiled against her neck. "Your breasts are just the right size to fill my hands." He rubbed his palms over her nipples and then pinched them lightly between his thumbs and forefingers.

As she began twisting toward him, he held her in place. "Tonight is all about you."

"I want to touch you too."

He nipped her neck. "Then you'll have to see me again because it's not happening tonight."

"You're so bad."

"I'm so good." He let go of one taut nipple to slide his hand down her belly and under the band of her pants. "Will you let me touch you there?"

Even though he was sure that she would say yes, he inched lower slowly to give her a chance to say no.

"Please."

"Thank you." He kissed her neck as he reached lower and cupped her under her pants.

She was soaking wet, and as his thumb circled that sensitive spot at the apex of her thighs, she gasped, "Oh."

Gently teasing her nipple with the fingers of one hand while brushing his thumb against the sweet spot down below, he murmured endearments against her neck.

Azul murmured something incoherent back, but even though he couldn't understand the words, Tobias was pretty sure that it was either a complaint about not getting enough of what she needed or a demand to give it to her right now.

Tobias couldn't deny her. Not tonight when she was so sweetly surrendering to his ministrations. Maybe next time, he would keep her poised over the precipice longer, when they were in a proper bed, had proper privacy, and no one was waiting for her to return home.

"I've got you," he whispered in her ear as he rubbed his thumb in tighter and tighter circles around the center of her pleasure while teasing her nipples with the fingers of his other hand.

Bucking against his aching shaft, she mewled but hadn't climaxed, not yet. He could easily bring her to a screaming orgasm with his bite, but that would be like cheating in a race. He was skilled enough of a lover not to rely on the gods-given crutch his parents had sold thirty years of his life for.

Sliding a finger inside Azul's wet heat, he pumped it in and out a couple of times before adding another. She was so tight that he wondered whether the idiot boyfriend who'd left her had ever gotten a chance to deflower her.

Tobias didn't know whether to hope yes or no. On the one hand, he loved the idea of being Azul's first lover, but on the other hand, he didn't. A woman's first and even second time was never as pleasurable as the third, and he wanted her to know only pleasure with him.

Though given the sounds she was making and the way she was moving on his hand, Azul was experiencing no discomfort, and as he hooked his fingers inside her and pressed his thumb to that most sensitive bundle of nerves, she threw her head back and cried out softly.

Satisfaction washing over him, he helped her ride out her orgasm until she went limp in his arms.

Withdrawing his fingers, he brought them to his mouth and licked every last drop off of them.

43

MIA/AZUL

*A*s Azul's body stopped trembling and the haze of lust lifted, the reality of what she'd just done, or rather had allowed to be done, slammed into her.

She tried to summon shame for her loose behavior, or regret for allowing things to go much further than she'd planned, but all she felt was gratitude, which was the least expected feeling of all.

She was grateful for the incredible pleasure, but most of all for proof that she could climax with the right man. She wasn't defective as Nathan had implied without actually saying it.

There was nothing wrong with her.

Behind her, Tobias's hard body was like a shield of warmth, his erection a reminder that he hadn't had his release. Pressing soft kisses to her neck, her shoulder, her ear, he caressed the swell of her hip over her pants, her bare stomach under her shirt, and then her waist and down her hip again. The lazy strokes weren't meant to keep her arousal from waning but did so nonetheless.

She wanted her hands all over him, starting with his

muscular chest and trailing down to that hard length that she was about to worship.

He didn't try to stop her when she turned in his arms, but as she pressed on his chest and tried to push him on his back, he caught her hand and brought it to his lips. "Not tonight, precious." He kissed her fingers before taking her mouth in a soul-bending kiss.

That was the second time he'd called her precious. Had he really meant it? Was she precious to him?

When he finally let her come up for air, she put her hand on his chest again. "I want to touch you, Tobias. It's not fair that you got to touch me, but you don't allow me to do the same to you."

He dipped his head and kissed the top of her nose. "I'm a great believer in building up anticipation. Besides, when I take you fully, I want it to be in a proper bed, not on a stage." He grinned like a fiend. "Unless the stage comes with a bed and you are into live performances."

She slapped his chest. "All I offered was to return a favor. I didn't offer myself to you on a silver platter."

Liar.

"How about silver-colored silk bedding and down-filled pillows and blankets? One of the perks of being in Had-dar's personal guard is having a room to myself with a luxurious bed. Will you come to the temple tomorrow?"

Azul wanted to, oh boy, how she wanted to be with him in that bed. But she couldn't, and not just because everyone would know why she was there and with whom. She needed to end this thing between them before it got more serious.

Tobias was conscripted into service for the next twenty-five years, and as long as he held that position, he had to not only enforce the law but also uphold it as well. If they got fully intimate, and she admitted her use of contraceptives, he would have to report her.

Even if he were willing to lie for her, the god could pluck that information straight out of his head. She didn't know it for a fact, but it made sense that the gods would delve into their guards' minds from time to time to make sure they weren't plotting against them.

"I can't," she whispered. "I can't take another day off." It was the truth, just not the whole truth.

"Then I will. I'll return tomorrow evening and spend the night with you."

She smiled. "That doesn't solve the problem of us having no bed."

The calculating gleam in his eyes told her that she might have made a mistake. He had a solution in mind, one she might not be able to poke holes in. She would hate to tell him flat out that she never wanted to see him again.

It would be such a big fat lie that even a mere human would know it for what it was.

"I'll figure out something. What time should I get here? And where do you want to meet me?"

"Aren't you supposed to be guarding the god?"

"We take turns at night. I'm supposed to be on night duty tomorrow, but I'm owed enough favors from the other guards to free up the rest of the week." His arms tightened around her. "We can be together every night."

Despite all the self-talk, and despite it being a really bad idea, Azul nodded. "I would like that."

44

TOVEN/TOBIAS

*I*t was past midnight when Tobias got back to the temple and handed Thunder to the stable hand. "Take good care of him. He's had a long day."

"I will. Good night, sir." The guy walked Thunder to his designated stall.

The rain had stopped by the time Tobias had headed back, and he could have flown the distance between the village and the temple in twenty minutes instead of the three hours it had taken on horseback, but leaving Thunder in the village overnight was not an option. He might need him today to perform his duties, and he also didn't want to explain why his horse was missing.

He'd had a lot of time to think during those hours, and the only thing on his mind and in his heart was Azul.

How had she done that?

Tobias couldn't remember ever feeling so buoyant, even joyful. His former contract owner had complained about him being like a dark cloud, always brooding, never smiling, and silent. At the start of his service, Eshkada had found his brooding sexy, but she'd soon gotten bored with his indifference toward her and his unpleasant company and had shipped him off along with her son to one of the poorest and most mismanaged municipalities.

He couldn't even blame the lustful goddess or his enforced servitude for his cloudy disposition because he hadn't been any different as a child.

Growing up as the only boy with wings in his town had made him the target of envy and bullying, and the fact that he was smarter than all of those kids combined hadn't aided his popularity either.

Tobias had been a loner his entire life.

Things had gotten a little better when he'd been assigned to Had-dar, but nothing and no one had ever made him feel as alive as he felt with Azul.

Perhaps it was just the right time.

He'd turned twenty-five in April, the age when most men started looking for a bride. He'd thought it was a cultural construct, but maybe it was a biological need—nature's way of ensuring that people formed long-lasting unions in preparation for having offspring.

Before today, the idea of having a child of his own had never appealed to Tobias. He had twenty-five more years of service in front of him, and marriage or fatherhood were not part of the deal. He would have to wait until his contract expired. That part of his servitude had never bothered him before, but it did now.

Azul was still very young, but she would not wait twenty-five years to marry and build a home of her own.

He was going to lose her, and the prospect sent a bolt of pain through his chest, eradicating the happy feelings he'd carried with him from Patagonia all the way back to his bed. To disperse the dark cloud, he reminded himself that he was seeing Azul tomorrow, and he needed to somehow get his hands on a good-quality travel wagon.

Had-dar's hovercraft would have been best, but he doubted the god would allow him to borrow it.

The crafts were irreplaceable.

A wagon or a coach would have a hard time over the uneven terrain, but he could make it with one if he went slowly.

The other option was to pitch a tent and make a nice bed out of furs. It wasn't how he wanted his first time with Azul to be, but if he didn't secure a wagon, it might have to do.

A rented room over the tavern would most likely appeal to her even less than spending the night in his bedroom in the temple. That was where the other guards took their women.

When he finally got in bed at one in the morning, Tobias stroked himself to memories of Azul—the feel of her soft skin and the taut muscles underneath, the sounds she'd made as he pleasured her, the way she'd orgasmed around his fingers...

The climax tore out of him with a muffled shout, and even while he kept spending, he still needed more.

After orgasming two more times, he was finally exhausted enough to fall asleep.

But he didn't get to rest long.

A hand shook his shoulder. "Tobias, wake up."

"What is it?" he asked without opening his eyes. "Unless we are under attack, I'm not getting up."

"Mr. Navón, your virtual adventure is over, and you need to open your eyes and remember who you really are. You told me to use your son's name as a reminder. His name is Orlando."

Toven groaned. "It was supposed to last weeks or at least days. It's only been half a day."

"I'm sorry," the tech said. "It's different for every person. Some experience weeks in the span of the slotted three hours, usually when not much is happening. You must have packed a lot into the time you had."

"That might be true, but I have unfinished business with the lady. I need to schedule another session with her."

"Let me check if she marked it as an option." The tech looked at a screen that was out of Toven's line of sight. "I'm sorry. The lady checked off the box that said 'do not contact under any circumstances.' That doesn't leave room for misinterpretation."

Toven remembered that clause. He hadn't checked it.

"She might have changed her mind after our joint adventure. I'm not asking to meet her in real life. I just want to meet her again in the fantasy we've started."

The tech smiled. "If she does, she will let her technician know, but I'll inform our central office that you are interested in another session with the lady, and they will forward the message to her studio. Did you know that if you book the next session right after you finish your first one you get a twenty-five percent discount?"

By the time Ruben contacted headquarters, and someone over there contacted Azul's technician, she would be long gone. And even if they sent her an email later, she might refuse because the adventure would no longer be fresh in her mind.

"I couldn't care less about the discount." Toven started removing the sticky pads from his chest. "Can you check if she asked for another session?"

"I can't. I don't have access." The tech took over the pads' removal.

"You saw her answers, so you must have access."

"I don't. The only thing the other side is privy to is whether the person is open to meeting up again in real life or in the virtual world. I don't even know which studio she's in. But I'll forward your request to our central office." He grinned. "I suggest that you book your next adventure right away. That will give them an incentive to make an effort on your behalf."

"I will. Thanks for the advice."

Toven hadn't scented a lie on the tech, and since Ruben didn't have access to Azul's file or even know which studio she was in, there was no point in compelling him. All the tech could do was forward Toven's message to the central office.

Whatever the answer was, though, there was no way Toven was giving up on meeting Azul again. If he couldn't get her to join him on another virtual adventure, he would find out who she was in real life and take her out on a real date.

MIA

"*W*ake up, Mia," a gentle female voice said.

Azul's eyes popped open. This wasn't her bed in Patagonia, she wasn't five hundred years in the future, and Tobias was gone.

She was Mia Berkovich, age twenty-seven, and she lived with her grandparents in Arcadia, not Patagonia.

A sense of loss washed over her. She should have kept him with her, should have insisted on making love to him on that stage. Now she would never know how it could have been between them.

Fighting tears, she whispered, "It was too short."

"It's different for every person," Doctor Brenna said. "You must have done a lot in a short period of time." She unbuckled the left wrist restraint. "And since you've done very well, you can go back provided that your partner is interested in another round." She unbuckled the one on her right wrist.

"I can't." Mia closed her eyes and tried to remember Tobias's handsome face. "This was a birthday gift from my friends, and I can't afford another round."

Could she sell something? Mia didn't have anything

valuable, and she could never ask her grandparents to loan her the money for something as frivolous as a virtual hookup. They'd already sacrificed enough for her.

Brenna smiled. "I'm sure we can work something out. Everyone who books another session the day they complete their first one gets a twenty-five percent discount, and I can probably get you another twenty-five from our special needs fund."

Mia gritted her teeth so as not to snap at the doctor. She hated it when people treated her differently just because of her disability. She didn't have a lot of money because she was young and at the start of her career, not because she was limited in some ways. She had a talent most perfectly healthy people didn't.

Why were only physical challenges considered limiting?

Naturally, she said none of that to the nice doctor who was just trying to help.

"That's very kind of you to offer, but even with a fifty percent discount, I can't justify the expense." She gave her a tight smile. "I'll cherish the memories of one perfect day, with one perfect guy."

Brenna gently parted Mia's shirt lapels and started removing the sticky pads. "You can ask to meet with your partner in real life. That doesn't cost anything."

Right. As if that was an option.

What she wanted was to go back to the fantasy world, where her body functioned better than it ever had, where she had a mother and a father who doted on her, and a guy who could make her climax harder than she'd ever climaxed before just with his fingers.

"I don't want to spoil the fantasy." She rubbed the glue off her chest. "My perfect guy is probably an old man." She chuckled. "In fact, I'm sure of that. He was way too mature for his age."

"You never know. Worst case scenario, you'll have a nice chat with an older gentleman who rocked your world in dreamland."

The doctor pushed to her feet. "I'll tell your friend that she can come in, and in the meantime, I'll check whether your partner put in a request to meet you."

If he thought that she was as lovely in real life as she'd been in the virtual world, he would be greatly disappointed, and he would be even more disappointed if he imagined that she would make good on her promise in fantasy-land when they met in real life.

"I don't want to meet him," Mia called after the doctor. "I marked the box in the questionnaire that I don't want to be contacted under any circumstances."

Brenna looked at her over her shoulder. "I'll check anyway. Don't you want to know if he requested a meeting with you?"

Mia nodded. "I do, but not because I want to meet him. I just want to know if he enjoyed our virtual adventure as much as I did."

"Of course." Brenna smiled before opening the door.

"Mia!" Margo rushed in. "Are you okay? You have to tell me everything. Was it exciting?"

Mia chuckled. "I'm fine. And I'll tell you everything on the way home. There is so much to tell that it will take hours. The fantasy was very different from what I requested. I don't know if that was because Tobias wanted it that way or because the computer took all of the information from my questionnaire and decided to give me things I didn't even think to ask for." She swallowed the lump in her throat. "My mother was alive in the fantasy, or rather her avatar was, and I had a father who cared about me. They were both great. I would go back just to be with them one more day."

"Oh, Mia." Margo leaned over and wrapped her arms

around her. "It must have been so damn hard for you to wake up and realize that it wasn't real."

In the safety of her friend's arms, Mia let the tears loose. "I want to go back so badly, but that's stupid. Even if it wasn't so expensive, I can't live in a fantasy world while my body is strapped to a chair in a studio. This is supposed to be a once-in-a-lifetime adventure, not something people do every day. Can you imagine what would happen to the world if everyone lived inside a fantasy whenever they wanted to? It would fall apart."

Margo let go of her as the door opened, and Doctor Brenna walked in. "The good news is that your partner requested another adventure with you, which means that he enjoyed it at least as much as you did."

"I can't. But if that's the good news, what's the bad?"

"There is none." Brenna shrugged. "Except for your refusal. Would it help if I arranged a seventy-five percent discount for your next session?" She smirked. "I have the founder's ear."

"Yes," Margo answered for her. "She'll take it." She squeezed Mia's hand to stop her from protesting.

"Wonderful." The doctor smiled. "All I need is your credit card information, but don't worry, you won't be charged until the session is scheduled."

Mia groaned. "I guess I won't be upgrading my tablet this month. I'll have to wait for the next check from my publisher."

"It's worth it." Margo patted her shoulder.

Mia agreed. Her tablet was a little sluggish, but it still worked fine. It could wait. Tobias, on the other hand, could not. She had to have another adventure with him, one that would hopefully last weeks and not end after just half a day.

TOVEN

During the ten-minute drive from the Perfect Match studio to Toven's building, the taxi driver had tried to engage him in conversation, but he'd been too preoccupied to even pretend that he was listening.

The storyline that Brian, or perhaps the artificial intelligence, had come up with had been very different from what Toven had in mind, and it wasn't a case of misinterpretation because he'd been very clear and very descriptive.

It was also unlikely that Azul had requested the dystopian scenario. He doubted that she had come up with the story of humanity shrinking to a mere fifty million people in only five hundred years.

Was that even a thing?

What seemed to preoccupy human end-of-the-world prophets nowadays was climate change making Earth uninhabitable or artificial intelligence taking over the world. Before, it had been a nuclear war and a new Ice Age, and before that, it had been something else. There was always some horrible disaster looming on the horizon to make humans fearful, but it usually never came to pass.

The worst disasters in human history had not been anticipated or predicted, at least not decades in advance.

Toven might not be an optimist, but he wasn't a prophet of doom either. Humanity somehow always managed to overcome the challenges facing it, and he didn't foresee that changing in the future unless Earth was hit by a giant meteor or the sun went supernova.

Tobias's story was supposed to take place in the distant future that had borrowed heavily from science fiction books Toven had read, as well as some of his own musings about possible futures.

His adventure should have unfolded in a futuristic city with advanced technology that included space travel. The gods' return was not supposed to be about saving humanity or ruling over it, but about establishing diplomatic relationships and tourism.

The things that the program had gotten right were the genetic enhancements that made human bodies self-healing and prolonged their life span, as well as vanity enhancements like wings and pointy ears and many others. It had also gotten his avatar right—an enhanced human, a winged warrior.

He'd chosen to be a modified human in his adventure, and that had proven to be an excellent choice. It was more exciting to woo a female without the ability to sniff her emotions or her arousal. The guesswork made the chase much more interesting.

Being human had been incredibly liberating. Although, it could be that the lightness of heart he'd experienced in the virtual world had more to do with not being an ancient god, who carried around too many failures and regrets, than being a young human male, who wished to find love and settle down with a wife. Simple needs and simple desires that were easily attainable.

As the last god remaining, Toven had felt that it had

been his duty and his obligation to continue his people's mission of helping humanity become an advanced and civilized society. He had doggedly shouldered that burden for many centuries before finally giving up, then he'd spent many more centuries feeling guilty about abandoning his people's mission, and eventually, he'd reached the numb state of not giving a hoot about anything.

Humanity had survived just fine without him.

Except the guilt had not dissipated, living instead in his subconscious, and it seemed that he could get rid of it in its entirety only when playing a human inside a virtual reality adventure.

Still, the dystopian future bothered him. The computer wouldn't have created the scenario out of thin air. If neither he nor Azul had included it in their fantasy, then the artificial intelligence must have collected it from movies or books or news articles.

Was it even true that birth rates had been declining in recent years?

The only place that had actively reduced its population's birth rate had been China, but the unforeseen consequences of that policy had been devastating, and it had been amended, but not fully revoked.

Back at his apartment, Toven walked over to his desk, flipped open his laptop, and initiated a search. The internet would have the answer.

"I'll be damned," he murmured as the search results confirmed the virtual fantasy's grim prediction.

If that was a possible future, could he continue with his selfish and meaningless existence and do nothing to stop the decline? If nothing was done, that insidious threat, which hardly anyone was bothered by, would eventually wipe humanity out of existence.

Who would have thought that humanity would perish

not in a nuclear war or a massive solar flare but in a quiet, gradual atrophy?

If Toven did nothing, his father would be so disappointed in him. Ekin was humanity's champion, and he would have expected his son to prevent it from winking out.

Toven closed his laptop, grabbed the burner phone with Brian's number programmed into it, and swiveled his chair toward the view of the city below.

Perhaps the declining birth rate was just one more doomsday prediction that would never come to pass. After all, there had been so many before it. Only a decade ago, scientists had been worried about overpopulation and lack of resources to feed everyone. Then there was the Ice Age scare, predicting that everything north and south of the equator would become uninhabitable. The Year 2000 panic, predicting that the end of the world was coming.

It was just another alarmist speculation. Today's birth rates might be declining, but the trend might reverse in the next decade or the one after that. Things hardly ever moved in a linear way—they oscillated between extremes only to settle in a comfortable median.

Blowing out a relieved breath, Toven propped his feet on the window ledge and closed his eyes. A short nap would do him good, and when he was rested, and his mind was calmer, he would call Brian about another session with Azul.

DARLENE

*G*eraldine walked into the living room looking like a fresh daisy in her white shirt and yellow capris.

"Darlene, sweetie, why aren't you dressed yet?"

"Do I have to go? I'm exhausted. Kri worked Ronja and me until we were about to puke."

It was true, but that wasn't the reason Darlene was still wearing her exercise clothes, slouching on the couch in her mother's house, and watching a soap opera she was only marginally interested in.

Cassandra had probably invited yet another Guardian to dinner, and Darlene was tired of her sister's and Geraldine's matchmaking efforts.

Once her family had realized that she and William were just friends, they'd started a campaign of introducing her to a new guy nearly every day.

"You know that you can't just not show up. Cassandra cooked dinner."

"She brought takeout on her way back from work." Darlene let out a breath. "But you're right. Give me five minutes to get ready."

Geraldine grimaced. "It takes me longer to choose what

I want to wear. I don't know how you can be ready so quickly."

Translation—please make an effort to look nice for a change.

"It's the Brazilian blowout. I don't need to do my hair." She gave Geraldine a smile before walking to her room.

Humoring Geraldine, Darlene took a little longer in the shower, and after she threw on one of Geraldine's borrowed dresses, she brushed black mascara on her eyelashes and put pink-tinted gloss on her lips.

Her hair didn't need more than a quick comb through to look great.

As she looked in the mirror, she had to admit that even with that minimal effort, she looked better than she had in years. She'd lost a little weight, gained a little tone in her muscles, and her skin looked good even though she hadn't used foundation or concealer to hide its imperfections.

Drinking two liters of water every day had proven the best skincare routine, and she had Merlin to thank for it.

The doctor had made it his mission to get Ronja into the best physical shape of her life, so when her transition started, she would have a better chance of surviving it. Darlene was lucky that Ronja had come before her, and that Merlin had already researched the topic extensively and formulated an action plan. Then she'd roped William into joining as well, and their little group supported each other's efforts.

When she emerged from her room in the red borrowed dress, a dress she couldn't fit into only a week ago, Geraldine smiled brightly.

"You look beautiful, and it only took you an additional five minutes. Wasn't it worth it?"

"I guess. So who's the unlucky guy this time? Another one of Onegus's men?"

Geraldine threaded her arm through Darlene's. "I don't know him. Cassandra said that Ragnar runs one of the clan's hotels in New York." She opened the door and walked out of the house. "He's in the village for a short vacation."

They were really getting desperate if they were bringing out-of-towners to meet her.

"I thought that only the chef and one of the councilmen lived outside of the village." They took the steps down to the walkway.

"I thought so too, but apparently, the members who manage the clan hotels have homes in the village but spend a lot of time in those hotels. The clan has one in Hawaii that I'm dying to visit. Shai said that he would take me there as soon as he could get a few days off."

Darlene snorted. "Good luck with that. Kian works him to the bone."

"About that." Geraldine slowed down. "Shai has been looking for an assistant for a while now. Is that something you might be interested in?"

"Maybe. I have an administrative background, and I'm good at organizing things, but I don't want to rush into anything. I want to take my time and figure out what I want to do with the rest of my life."

Geraldine stopped and turned toward her. "It doesn't have to be a forever job. It could be something to do for now. Shai needs the help, and if he has a capable assistant, he might be able to take a vacation sooner than later."

She wasn't sure if working with her stepdad was a good idea. Shai was a nice guy, but working for family was complicated. Then again, most everyone in the village was related to everyone else, and they seemed to be fine working together.

Then there was Kian. The guy was intimidating even when he was trying to be nice, and if she worked for his assistant, it would be like working for him.

Thankfully, she didn't have to decide anything yet.

"Don't I have to transition before I take on a job? Because if I don't, I'll have to leave the village."

"Not true. No one expected Ronja to attempt transition, and yet Kian allowed her to stay in the village because she's David's mother. The same goes for you."

That was a relief.

"If that's so, why are you and Cassandra working so hard on finding me a match?"

Geraldine's eyes misted with tears. "Because we love you, and we want you to be with us forever, and because we want you to be happy."

"I can be happy without a mate."

Darlene had been married for a long time, and she hadn't been happy most of it, but at the same time, she didn't know how to be alone.

Geraldine smiled. "Of course. But you can be even happier with a good man by your side. Cassandra and I were doing perfectly fine before she met Onegus, and I met Shai. But we are both much happier now."

MIA

"Check your email," Margo said for the fifth time since they'd gotten in her car.

"I checked a minute ago."

Doctor Brenna had promised that someone from head-quarters would notify her whether Tobias wanted another session with her, but they were taking their sweet time.

Mia was pretty sure that he would want her to make good on her promise, but what if he couldn't afford another token?

Had they offered him the same big discount they'd offered her?

Probably not.

She'd gotten the discount because of her disability, and as much as she hated accepting it for that reason, she had no choice. As it was, the remaining twenty-five percent meant eight hundred dollars, which would put a serious dent in her budget, and that was when she was living with her grandparents and not having to pay rent or utilities.

She'd offered, but they'd refused to hear of it.

Her grandparents were the best, and she felt so damn guilty for ruining their retirement plans. The money they'd saved for the cruise around the world they'd dreamt about had been spent on her rehabilitation, and in the beginning, she'd needed so much help that they couldn't even think of going anywhere.

There had been no one else to take care of her.

Her mother had been an only child, so there were no aunts and uncles, and her father had disappeared shortly after contributing his sperm to her conception. She knew who he was, but she didn't know what had become of him, and she didn't care. He'd never shown any interest in the daughter he'd fathered.

Margo cast her a sidelong glance. "I know that you promised Frankie to wait until the three of us were all together, but you have to throw me a bone, or I'll die of curiosity, and that's a problem because I'm driving."

Mia was just as eager to share her adventure with her besties as they were to hear it.

"Frankie will chew my head off, but since you were with me the entire time, you deserve a bone." She smiled. "Tobias was even more handsome than the drawing I made, but he didn't look anything like Thor, and he had wings. The wings were probably his wish because I didn't put down anything about that." She waved a hand. "You know what I wanted. I wanted to be a fairy and to meet a fairy prince who looked like Thor but with dark hair, but neither of us was fae in the adventure. The software created a whole new storyline that was absolutely fascinating, with gods who genetically manipulated humans and gave some of them wings and others pointy ears or some other modifications. I wonder how much of it was influenced by Tobias's input." Winded from her monologue, Mia sucked in a breath.

Her expression serious, Margo reached over the center console and put her hand on Mia's arm. "Slow down, Mia. You are not supposed to get overexcited."

"I know." Mia took several calming breaths. "They did a great job keeping the level of excitement moderate throughout most of it and without it becoming boring even for a moment, but at the end, some excitement was unavoidable." She winked.

"Ooh!" Margo squealed. "I can't wait to hear all the naughty details, but Frankie will kill us if she finds out that you told me first."

Mia had no intention of giving either of them a blow-by-blow description of how Tobias gave her an orgasm, the first one she'd ever experienced with another person, but she would have to give them the highlights, or she would never hear the end of it.

"All I can say for now is that Tobias was gorgeous and that wings can be very sexy. He wrapped them around me to keep me warm."

"That's so romantic." Margo glanced at the phone clutched in Mia's hand. "Check again. It has been five minutes, and we are almost at your grandparents' house."

Letting out a breath, Mia lifted the phone and opened the email application.

Her heart skipped a beat when she saw the Perfect Match Virtual Fantasy Studios' name in her inbox.

Dreading rejection, she opened it and sighed in relief that the first sentence wasn't—'we are sorry to inform you'...

As she kept reading, a smile spread over her face. "Tobias requested another session with me right as he woke up from our adventure."

"Did you doubt that he would?"

Mia cast Margo a smile. "He might have faced the same problem I did. Lack of funds. For all I know, he also got a token as a birthday present from his friends."

"Nah." Margo pulled into Mia's grandparents' driveway. "No one has friends as fabulous as we are."

Frankie's car was parked on the street, and as Margo turned the engine off, the front door opened, and her other best friend waved both hands in the air in a victory dance.

"That's absolutely true." Mia grinned.

Frankie rushed over and opened her door. "I was biting my nails to the bone, holding off until you got home. I want to hear everything, and I mean every little thing."

"Are my grandparents home?"

"Yes, but you can give them the PG-13 version first and then tell us the rest later."

ALIYA

"Good afternoon, Aliya." Phinas sauntered over to the counter. "How have you been?"

"Great. And you?"

"Just another boring day at the office."

He stopped by every day after work, usually ordering a cappuccino and drinking it sitting at the counter so he could flirt with her.

Vrog spent his days working on his laptop in a shaded corner of the café and keeping an eye on her but rarely engaging her in conversation.

He was honoring her wishes and giving her space, and in his own way so was Phinas, with his daily half an hour at the counter and light banter. But even though she liked and was attracted to both, Aliya wasn't ready to commit to either one, or even the two together.

Not that they would ever agree to share. Perhaps Vrog would, but not Phinas.

Besides, she was still a virgin, and pretty clueless about how this whole thing of establishing a male harem worked. Some advice from a Kra-ell female would have been great, but since there were none, she was on her own.

Maybe when Emmett returned to the village, she would talk with him. He was already mated, so he wouldn't be a potential contender for a position in her harem, and he might give her some unbiased advice.

"Hey, pretty lady." A clan male walked up to the counter and leaned against it. "Can you hook me up with a latte and a Danish?"

She tried to remember his name. Was it Mathew or Mateo?

"Coming right up." She gave him a smile and turned to the La Marzocco cappuccino machine.

By now, she knew how to make all the different coffee drinks, but she still couldn't make fancy designs like Wonder could, which was why she hadn't earned the barista title yet.

Wonder leaned over and whispered in her ear. "Jackson should double your pay. Since you started working here, there's been an explosion of male coffee aficionados in the village."

Aliya stifled a smile. "I should bring it up the next time I see him."

Jackson was an awesome boss. Her interview had lasted one minute, with him welcoming her aboard and telling her what her hourly pay would be. It was more than generous.

"You do that." Wonder clapped her on the back.

"Here's your latte." She put the cup in front of Mathew or Mateo. "Enjoy."

"Thank you." He looked as if he wanted to say more, but a glare from Phinas caused him to reconsider.

She shook her head at Phinas.

He waited for the clan male to take his coffee to one of the tables before leaning forward. "Don't shake your head at me. He's not good for you."

"That's for me to decide, not you, but I'm curious to hear what makes you think that."

Leaning back, Phinas cast her a seductive smile. "Mateo is a programmer. Should I say more?"

"What's wrong with that? It means that he's smart."

"He's not a fighter. If you get even a little aggressive with him, he'll run away screaming."

The image he'd planted in her head made her laugh. "Maybe you'll run away screaming as well." She leaned closer. "As we both know, I can kick your butt."

"Indeed." His brown eyes flared with inner light, turning them a beautiful shade of amber.

He was such an attractive male, but the truth was that his physical weakness took away from his appeal.

Aliya craved a male who was stronger than her, who could pin her down and pleasure her into oblivion, but the only one who could do that never would.

For some reason, Vrog didn't possess the innate maleness that Phinas did.

They were both handsome, both smart, but they were very different people, and for some reason, she felt more at ease with Phinas.

"When is Emmett coming back, do you know?" she asked him.

"Not anytime soon. He and Eleanor are on a mission, and when they achieve their objectives, they will probably go straight to Safe Haven. Why?"

"He's older than Vrog and me, and he might know more about the tribe and the Kra-ell traditions than both of us. I would like to talk to him."

"I can get you his phone number." Phinas pulled his phone out of his pocket.

The kind of questions she wanted to ask Emmett needed to be asked face to face and without his mate within earshot. Eleanor might think that Aliya was after her male and challenge her to a fight. Aliya would win of course, but it might get her kicked out of the village.

"Never mind. I wouldn't want to upset Eleanor. She might have an issue with another female calling her male, especially a hybrid Kra-ell like him, and I don't want to make enemies."

Phinas cast her a calculating look. "Was that common in your tribe? Did the females fight over the males?"

"No, they shared them all. But if a female from another tribe made a move on one of theirs, that would have been considered a great offense and resulted in a challenge. Or at least that was what Jade told the younger females about how it used to be a long time ago. Females were never allowed to fight to the death, though. They were too scarce and precious."

"Did males fight to the death?"

"They used to, but it was outlawed at some point."

"You seem to know a lot more about the Kra-ell than Emmett and Vrog. Is that all from listening to the pure-blooded females talk?"

She nodded. "I was the bee on the wall. Is that the right expression?"

"I think it's the fly on the wall. What else did you learn about the old ways?"

Aliya thought back to the many conversations she'd overheard. Most of them had been about the tribe's finances and its various businesses, but on rare occasions, Jade had gotten nostalgic, and the conversation drifted to the Kra-ell history.

Aliya had found those the most interesting.

"Jade said that the disparity between males and females was the result of the queen's ban on tribal wars and challenges to the death between the males. Before that, so many males died in those wars and challenges that the numbers of males and females of child-bearing age had been about equal. It's chilling to think that out of every five males, only one survived to become a father. Maybe that's why their society didn't encourage love. Imagine having five sons and knowing that only one would survive." She shivered. "I'm glad that their queen put an end to it."

"How long ago was that?"

"I have no idea, but it must have been a very long time ago for their entire society to adapt and develop the harem system."

VROG

*A*s Vrog watched Phinas flirt with Aliya, the urge to get up and challenge the male to a fight was overwhelming. But it wouldn't be a fair fight, and therefore not satisfying.

Phinas was more experienced, but he was weaker.

How did Aliya not realize that?

Her job as a Kra-ell female was to choose the best male to father strong children, and that was Vrog, not Phinas.

Maybe she needed proof?

Perhaps he should fight the male, only to show her how wrong she was by entertaining thoughts of mating with immortal males.

The reason Kra-ell females kept a harem was not just the excess of males who needed a chance to father children. By pitting them against each other and letting only the strongest into their beds, they ensured the best outcome.

"Vrog, my man." Yamanu clapped him on the back. "How are things going?" The Guardian pulled out a chair and sat down.

"They are going as well as can be expected." Vrog closed

his laptop. "I'm able to do most of the recruiting for the school online, and Wang is sending me daily reports. I also watch the surveillance feed to check that the grounds and common areas are clean and that the teachers are doing their job."

"I didn't mean your school." Yamanu leaned back in the chair, stretching his long legs in front of him. "I mean a certain young lady who you are pining for."

Vrog waved a hand in Phinas's direction. "See for yourself. She's getting a lot of attention, and she's enjoying every moment of it."

Yamanu sat up and braced his elbows on the table. "She needs time to adjust to her new life, and you're being smart about giving her space. I doubt that I could have tolerated other males circling my mate like that, but then I never claimed to be smart." The Guardian laughed at his self-deprecating remark.

"I'm respecting Aliya's wishes, but it's not easy," Vrog admitted. "Especially since I know I'm the best choice for her, and that's not bragging. That's the truth."

"Hmm." Yamanu rubbed his square, clean-shaven jaw. "You probably need a new strategy, but since she's half Kra-ell, I don't know what your next move should be. She's not like human or even immortal females." He narrowed his eyes. "Monogamy might not be her thing. Could you tolerate sharing?"

Vrog shook his head. "If the other contenders for her affections were also Kra-ell, I might have reasoned with myself that this is our way to ensure the best and strongest offspring. But that's not the case."

"Got you." Yamanu nodded sagely. "Perhaps someone who has her ear needs to clarify it for her. It can't be you, though. Maybe I can have a chat with Wonder."

Vrog groaned. "Please, don't. It's bad enough that the

entire village is watching us and wondering who Aliya will choose."

"Do you have a better idea?"

"Yeah. Give her time to reach the right conclusion. Aliya is a smart female. Sooner or later, she will realize that I'm her only choice."

Yamanu made a hissing sound. "That's never a good thing to say to a female, or a male. No one wants to have just one option. Besides, you want to be chosen because she believes that you are the best for her, not because she has no choice. And that's true for anyone, male or female, human, immortal, or Kra-ell."

"True." Vrog let out a breath. "I'm better educated than Phinas, more refined, and I'm also much stronger. But he's charming, and he knows how to flirt. I'm too reserved and serious." He cast another glance at the counter and saw Aliya smiling at yet another male. "Maybe I should just go back to my school and lay low for a while. I don't think I can sit here and watch her flirt with males for much longer without losing my mind."

Yamanu shook his head. "Then you'll abdicate the fight and lose by default. Stay and fight for her."

"I don't know how."

"Let me think." Yamanu rubbed his jaw again. "You had a virtual adventure scheduled, right?"

He shouldn't be surprised that Yamanu knew about that. Keeping secrets in the village was impossible.

"I asked to postpone it indefinitely, and the female who matched with me graciously agreed."

"Perhaps you shouldn't wait. You should make Aliya think that she might lose you to another. Kra-ell females are competitive, right? She wouldn't like that one bit."

Yamanu was onto something.

Instead of spending his days in the café and letting her

see him pining for her, Vrog should start acting unin-terested.

"You are much smarter than you give yourself credit for." Vrog pushed to his feet and tucked his laptop under his arm. "Thank you for the advice."

"I have my moments." Following him up, Yamanu grinned and clapped him on the back. "Good luck, my friend."

TOVEN

When Toven opened his eyes, the sky outside his window had darkened. How long had he been asleep?

Lifting his hand, he glanced at his watch. It had been only a little over an hour, but it had felt like much longer.

He'd dreamt about the virtual world he'd left behind only a couple of hours ago. He'd lived in it, but not with Azul. Absurd obstacles had kept preventing him from seeing her night after night, and the frustration he'd felt in the dream lingered.

Rising to his feet, he put the phone that was still clutched in his hand on the desk and walked over to the kitchen to make himself an espresso. His pod machine brewed a perfect cup in under a minute, filling his kitchen with a wonderful aroma, and as he sipped it, he kept thinking about the dream. Was it a premonition of how things were about to unfold between him and Azul, or was it a reflection of his frustration over the difficulty of communicating with her?

When his cup was empty, he made himself another espresso and headed back to his study.

He put the cup on the desk, picked up the phone, and dialed Brian.

"Good afternoon, Tobias. How did you enjoy your adventure?"

Toven was no longer surprised that the guy always answered and was always ready to help.

"It wasn't what I'd envisioned, but I have to admit that I enjoyed it much more than I expected."

He'd felt alive for the first time in nearly a millennium.

"I'm glad you had fun, but I'm surprised that the adventure was so different from what you'd imagined. I programmed it to closely match your storyline."

"Some of the elements were there, but I didn't ask for a dystopian future where the world's population had shrunk back to what it was five thousand years ago."

Perhaps that was why the artificial intelligence decided on that number? That was the size of humanity during the gods' previous era, and because in Toven's story, the gods had returned, the computer recreated similar conditions.

That was very interesting. Perhaps the software had run simulations, and those conditions were the only ones that could support the gods' dominion over humans? Then again, his fantasy hadn't been about the gods ruling over humans. It was about coexistence and cooperation.

"Perhaps it was something your partner requested?"

"Don't you know whether she did or not?"

"I only added your gods to several existing environments and created avatars for them. The rest, including genetic modifications that gave humans wings, was already there. I didn't look over Azul's questionnaire, and even if I did, I wouldn't tell you what was in it, but just so you know, many people dream of a simpler world and a return to the basics. It might have been part of Azul's list of requests."

Toven doubted that Brian didn't know what was on her

wish list, but he also doubted she'd requested it. During their adventure, she'd petitioned the gods to revive manufacturing because she craved a world with all the comforts humans had gotten used to before everything had fallen apart.

Nevertheless, he wasn't going to press Brian for answers. He would rather find out what Azul's heart's desires were during their next joint adventure.

"I want another session with her."

"So I've been told. The doctor who attended to Azul during her session convinced her to go for another one with you by offering her a seventy-five percent discount."

That was great news. If Azul also wanted to continue their story, she must have enjoyed their time together.

But there were a couple of clues in Brian's statement that had given Toven pause.

"Why did she need a doctor to attend her session? I only had a technician attend mine."

"I'm not at liberty to disclose this information. Doctor Brenna is the wife of one of our two founders, and she often attends sessions for research purposes."

"Did she attend this one in that capacity?"

Brian chuckled. "As I said, I'm not allowed to disclose that information."

Toven considered using compulsion to get Brian to tell him the truth, but he decided against it. Compulsion was a last resort weapon, and he used it sparingly.

The guy's comment about the discount was the other clue Toven needed to clarify. "The discount that the founder's wife offered Azul implies that she couldn't afford more sessions."

"I can't comment on that either, but I can talk in generalities. Most people can't afford more than one session, but since Azul asked not to be offered a face-to-face meeting with her partner, the only way you could continue seeing her was to find a solution to the affordability issue. We know that you can pay for yourself, so it made perfect business sense to offer her the discount."

Toven was still stuck on Azul's refusal to meet face to face with her virtual adventure partner. It hadn't occurred to him before, but perhaps she hadn't wanted to be contacted because she was married?

It hadn't bothered him going in, but it did now. He wanted her to be his exclusively for as long as they had a relationship, first in the virtual world, and later in the real one.

No, that wasn't a good idea.

He was still under the influence of the virtual story, and in his mind, he and Azul were both genetically enhanced humans with the same lifespan. In reality, he could never have a long-lasting relationship with a human.

The virtual world was the only place they could be with each other as equals. Still, it would detract from his enjoyment if he knew that she was in a committed relationship with another male.

"Do you know why she checked off that box? I hope she's not married."

"Dear Tobias. You know that I can't answer that. But you might have a chance of convincing her to change her mind during your next adventure."

Toven was a skilled lover, but Azul was stubborn, and he doubted he could do that in just one more session with her.

"I'll pay for her tokens, including what remains of the current one after the discount, but I don't want her to know that." She was way too proud to accept that. "Can you tell her that she won twenty sessions for being the one-thousandth customer or something along those lines?"

"I don't know much about your lady, but given your interest in her, she must be intelligent, which means that she will see right through it and will want nothing to do with you because you tried to trick her."

Toven let out an exasperated breath. "This whole thing is one big trickery. We are using avatars to play fake versions of ourselves in a virtual fantasy."

"True, but lying to her about winning free sessions will happen in the real world, not the fantasy."

"Then what do you suggest I do?"

"I suggest that you talk to her and come up with a compelling reason for her to agree to let you pay for her sessions. I can check with her whether she would be willing to chat with you on the private chat portal on our website. Your identities will be fully protected."

"You mean a chat as in exchanging messages, not actually talking?"

"Correct."

He hadn't known that Perfect Match offered that option. Toven had been under the impression that communication between adventure partners had to go through an intermediary in the company unless both agreed to disclose their real identities to each other.

"Where can I find the chat portal on your website? I didn't see it when I browsed it before."

"I'll send you the login instructions tomorrow."

"Why tomorrow?" Toven switched the phone to his other ear. "I want to chat with her today."

Brian loosed a breath. "Azul is most likely exhausted after the adventure and needs sleep to regenerate and reorganize her mind. Besides, both of you should cool down before you communicate with each other."

Toven felt ashamed that Brian had to remind him that Azul was just a fragile human in this reality, with no enhancement and no three-hundred-year life span.

She needed the rest, and he needed to come up with a

very convincing argument for why she should let him pay for her virtual adventure.

Her avatar's personality was a reflection of her real-life one, and Azul was a proud woman who wouldn't like the idea of some rich guy paying for her tokens.

"Very well. Tomorrow morning, though, I hope to see an email from you with the instructions."

"If the lady agrees, you will."

"Thank you for your continued assistance, Brian."

"It's my pleasure. Good night, Tobias."

"Good night, Brian."

After ending the call, Toven pulled out a fresh sketchbook from his desk drawer and started working on his first portrait of Azul.

He sketched for hours, completing one portrait and continuing to the next, until the entire sketchbook was filled with Azul in different poses and with different expressions on her lovely face.

It was after three in the morning when he fell asleep with the sketchbook on his chest, hoping it would help transport him into the dream world where he and Azul were together.

52

MIA

"*M*ia, breakfast is ready," her grandmother called.

"I'll be there in a minute."

Frustrated, Mia tore out the page she'd been working on, crumpled it, and threw it into her nearly full basket of discards.

She'd spent most of the morning sketching Tobias, her virtual parents, the virtual landscape, the ziggurat temple, the massive doors that led to its main hall, the perfect face of the god in charge of it, and the god on his throne with Tobias and the other winged warrior standing like guardian angels behind him. And while committing every detail she could remember to paper, she'd also checked her inbox every few minutes.

Yesterday's email had promised that today she would get a schedule for their next session, but so far nothing had come in, and she feared that Tobias had changed his mind.

But she had work to do, and after filling up an entire sketchbook worth of memories, she tried to switch gears and to do that. She needed to come up with at least one of the lineup of fuzzy creatures that her publisher wanted her to create for her next children's book.

Perhaps she was reluctant to start because she didn't want to make the story about cute imaginary characters. Mia had wanted to make it about a group of children, but her publisher had other ideas, and he was the god in her little universe.

What her publisher wanted, her publisher got. It wasn't as if she had other options and could play the diva.

Glancing once more at her computer screen, she almost missed the email from someone named Brian from the Perfect Match Studios.

That was odd. Usually, their emails had their company name as the sender.

Clicking it open, she read through the short email twice to make sure that she understood it correctly.

"Mia!" Her grandmother stood in the doorway with her hands on her hips. "Your omelet is getting cold!"

"I need to answer an email, Grandma. I'll be there as soon as I'm done. It's from Perfect Match."

Her grandmother smiled. "Take your time. I'll give your omelet to your grandfather and make you a new one when you're ready."

Mia shook her head. "He's supposed to watch his cholesterol."

Her grandmother waved a dismissive hand. "I won't give him any eggs tomorrow."

Mia shifted her eyes back to her computer screen and read the email for the third time.

Tobias had requested a chat with her, and Brian was asking whether she would be willing to do so through their company's secure chat interface. He promised that it was completely anonymous, with no sound or video, just typed messages exchanged between her and Tobias that were inaccessible to anyone other than them, not even the people working for Perfect Match.

Wow.

She leaned back in her chair. It was an opportunity to learn more about the man behind the avatar without having to actually meet him.

Of course, she was willing.

Clicking on the link Brian had provided, she entered the code that was included in the email and registered a chat box under her avatar's name. Once the registration was completed, she was instructed to add the chat-box to the notifications function on her computer so she would get a ping when Tobias was ready to chat.

Since there was no way she could concentrate on creating a new furry creature now, she decided to flip through the files she kept for inspiration.

Whenever she saw something she liked, be it a certain facial expression or an interesting color combination, or a quote that spoke to her, Mia saved it to one of her inspiration files.

She remembered saving the pictures of a bunch of cuddly toys a few months ago. Maybe they could inspire a creature or two.

They should be under the visuals folder. Or maybe it was the future story ideas folder?

As she opened the first one, pictures of Margo and Frankie and her grandparents came up first, reminding her that she wanted to create story characters based on the most important people in her life.

Mia smiled at an old picture of her with her grandparents in Disneyland. That had been fun, but nothing could compare to experiencing a virtual adventure.

Her grandparents had been so relieved to hear that her adventure had been mild and that nothing overly stressful or exciting had happened. When they asked for more details, she told them that she'd had a wonderful time and promised to show them her sketches of the virtual world and the handsome winged warrior she'd met as soon as she had them ready.

Naturally, she hadn't told them about the last part of her evening with Tobias, and they had been tactful enough not to ask.

Frankie and Margo hadn't been.

They'd grilled Mia for details until she'd told them more than she'd planned to, blushing so hard that they had finally relented because it was getting dangerous for her to be so flustered.

53

TOVEN

*W*hen Toven's laptop pinged with an incoming email, he put his book down, pushed to his feet, and walked over to his desk.

The email he'd been expecting from Brian had finally dropped into his inbox, and as he opened it, he was relieved to find a link to the company's secret chat interface.

He'd spent the night thinking about convincing arguments for Azul, and he believed that he'd come up with a good one. It was a total fabrication, which he didn't like, but then there would be a lot more of that coming up during their chat.

She would probably ask him what he did for a living, where he was from, where was his family, and a thousand other personal questions he couldn't answer truthfully.

If he did, she would think that he was nuts and hang up on him.

Once the chat-box was set up, Toven got up, made himself an espresso, and then sat back down and wrote his first message to Azul.

Hello, this is Tobias. Are you free to chat?

Her answer came a moment later. *Hi, Tobias. It's nice to hear from you in the real world. How have you been?*

He smiled. *I didn't sleep much. I was thinking about our adventure, replaying every moment of it in my mind and craving more.* At least that part of their conversation was true. Soon, he would have to start making up lies.

Same here, she admitted. *I filled an entire sketchbook with sketches of you, Had-dar, the village, my parents. It was such an incredible experience, and I didn't want to forget any of it.*

Azul was an artist.

He should have realized that from the sketch she'd provided of her avatar. The artificial intelligence had changed it significantly, which was why he'd forgotten about it. But she'd also sketched his avatar inside the virtual adventure.

I did the same. I fell asleep with my sketchbook on my chest, and I drew only you. I have about thirty portraits of you.

Perhaps he shouldn't have said that. She would think that he was obsessed with her, and she wouldn't be wrong.

Wow. I'm flattered. Are you an artist?

He'd never thought of himself as one. He used to be an explorer, a researcher, a philosopher. Now he was a bored god who filled his time writing love stories.

I am a storyteller who sketches. I'm not a visual artist. Are you?

He much preferred talking about her than about himself.

That's incredible. I'm sort of a writer myself, but I tell stories through illustrations because my audience is small children.

Adorable.

Tell me about your books.

It took several long moments for her to answer.

I don't want to reveal too much about myself. I would like this to remain anonymous. What kind of books do you write?

Toven wanted to ask why she wanted to hide behind

her avatar, but since he preferred it that way as well, he didn't.

I write love stories, which brings me to the reason for this chat. The storyline the software created for us is very different from what I had in mind. Did you ask for a dystopian world?

He hoped his question wouldn't spook her.

Not at all. I asked for a fairytale with a handsome fae prince.

Toven chuckled. *You must be disappointed. Instead of a prince you got a winged warrior who's more or less an indentured slave. And before you ask, that wasn't what I asked for. I wanted to have wings as a genetic modification in a futuristic world.*

The three dots blinked for a while, but she must have written and erased her question because when it appeared, it was only one line.

What about the gods? Was that your idea?

He could have said no, but he wanted to minimize the lies to only what was necessary.

It was. I thought it would be cool to include mythology in our fantasy. And to hide any potential thoughts he might have had about being a god.

I thought that it had to do with your god complex.

Toven laughed. *In real life, I don't have one. But back to the reason for this chat. I love the storyline the computer created, and I want to use it in a future book, but I will need many more sessions to really learn this world and to collect enough anecdotes to write about. To me, this is a veritable goldmine. Now, I know the service is costly, and I can't expect you to keep purchasing tokens. From now on, I will cover all the costs, even transportation to and from the studios. I can deduct everything on my tax returns as a research expense, so in reality, I would be paying just my share anyway.*

He hoped she understood enough about taxes to realize that what he was telling her made sense.

Aren't you worried that I'll figure out who you are? Once you publish your book, that will no longer be a secret.

Toven let out a relieved breath. If that was her only concern, he'd already won the argument.

I write under several pen names, and none of my readers know who I am.

He waited for her response with bated breath.

You must be doing very well if you are in the top tax bracket.

Was he a lucky god or what?

She'd understood perfectly what he'd been trying to communicate.

I'm a prolific writer. I don't produce any literary master-pieces, but people like my stories, and I'm doing very well. So, do I get a yes?

He held his breath.

I would love to assist you in your research while spending a wonderful time in our own virtual world. But I have a life, and I have work that needs to be done. I can't move into the studios. How many sessions do you think you'll need for your book?

Many years of them.

He'd enjoyed very much being a human with wings, carefree and in love.

Was he in love with Azul?

That was impossible. He had lost the ability to feel love a long time ago. Tobias, the human winged warrior, might fall in love with Azul, but Toven the god could not fall in love with the girl behind the beautiful avatar.

Two to three a week until we call it quits. I would gladly pay you for your time. That would qualify as a research expense as well.

Hopefully, he hadn't gone too far with that offer.

That's a hard no. I'll accept the tokens and nothing more.

He'd had a feeling that she would say that. His Azul was a proud lady.

Can I at least pay for transportation expenses to and from the studios?

I have a car, and I can drive myself. I had a friend drive me yesterday because I was a little scared, and I didn't know if I would be okay to drive after the adventure was over, but since I felt perfectly fine, I see no reason to bother my friend again.

He hoped that it had nothing to do with the reason her session had been supervised by a doctor.

If you change your mind, my offer stands. It was a pleasure chatting with you, Azul, and I can't wait until our next shared adventure.

He stared at the three blinking dots as she typed up her answer.

Do you know whether our adventure will continue from where we left off?

He hoped so. They had unfinished business that he was eager for.

I believe so, but I expect more surprises. The neural network of that artificial intelligence is very creative.

Her answer came faster this time.

If everything was predictable, it wouldn't be exciting. I bid you farewell until we meet again in the virtual world, Tobias.

He smiled and leaned back in his chair. *Until tomorrow, farewell, my lady Azul.*

54

RONJA

*E*arbuds blasting music in her ears, Ronja swayed to the rhythm as she peeled potatoes. Her arms hurt from lifting weights earlier, but it was a good kind of pain, indicating that her workouts were effective, and she was building muscle.

Whether all that effort helped with her transition remained to be seen, but at least it made her feel like she was proactively doing something to improve her chances of success and wasn't totally at the mercy of fate. It might be an illusion, and nothing she did would mitigate the risk, but it helped alleviate her anxiety to some extent, if not entirely, and that was better than nothing.

Lisa walked into the kitchen and mouthed, "I love you, Mom." She kissed Ronja's cheek.

Ronja removed her earbuds and put them in her apron pocket. "I love you too, sweetie. Dinner will be ready in forty-five minutes."

Lisa nodded. "Do you want me to peel the potatoes?"

Her daughter never volunteered to help in the kitchen. Her chores were to vacuum the floors, set the table, and wash the dishes after meals, which she considered to be more than her fair share of household duties.

When she was all sweet kisses and smiles and offered to help with cooking, she usually wanted something.

Ronja handed her the peeler. "You can peel while you make your pitch. What is it this time? A new pair of sneakers?"

The downside of having her daughter enrolled in an expensive private school was the rich kids that attended it. Collecting sneakers was a new craze that had swept over the entire school, including Lisa and Parker. The two were following auctions on new limited releases, placing bids, and offering their cleaning services to pay for their newfound expensive hobby.

"It's not sneakers this time." Smiling slyly, Lisa took the peeler and started on the next potato. "Parker and I are meeting some friends from school at the Santa Monica pier this Saturday, and someone suggested that we all go parasailing."

"That's a hard no. It's too dangerous."

"Sheesh, let me finish. I'm not done yet."

"Go ahead, but I'm not going to give you a different answer."

Lisa rolled her eyes. "First of all, it can't be dangerous if they let six-year-old kids do it, and secondly, Parker and I are going to do it together. If anything happens, which it won't, Parker is going to save me. And thirdly, you can look at the company's track record and see that they have a perfect safety record. No one has died on them. Parasailing is the safest, easiest, and most exciting water-sport activity. I checked the forecast, and the weather on Saturday is going to be perfect for parasailing—not too cold and not too hot, and no wind is forecasted either." Lisa had delivered the entire speech without stopping to take a breath, and there was almost nothing left of the potato she'd been peeling.

Ronja took the peeler out of her daughter's hand and waited for her to catch her breath. "How high above the water will you be flying?"

"I think it's about three hundred feet."

"A fall from that height is like hitting concrete, and that's certain death. Any malfunction and you plummet to your death, God forbid."

"Why would there be a malfunction? They test their equipment to make sure it's in perfect working order."

"It's a no, Lisa, and I don't want to hear any more about it. Parker shouldn't do it either, even though he's immortal. I doubt even his immortal body could recover from such massive injuries. Let me reiterate. Falling into the water from three hundred feet is like hitting concrete. It's not like in the movies where you see someone jump out of an airplane, fall into the ocean, surface, and swim away. I know that you don't like to hear the gory details, but maybe you should go online and find out what happens to a person's body when it hits the water from even a lesser height."

Lisa's pale cheeks reddened with anger. "Everything can be potentially deadly. Even going to school can be dangerous, and we could both be killed in a car accident. Does that mean that we shouldn't go anywhere? I'm sure that if I check the statistics, I have more chance of dying in a car crash than from a parasailing accident."

"The difference is that driving places is necessary, and avoiding it would impair the quality of our lives. Parasailing is an unnecessary risk that I don't want you to take. I'm not forbidding it to be mean. I just don't want to lose you."

Lisa huffed. "Why are you allowed to take risks with your life, and I'm not?"

"That's not a fair comparison, and you know it. I'm taking a risk, but the upside is immortality. What's your upside? Twenty minutes of fun? Impressing your friends?"

"Ugh." Lisa threw her hands in the air and stormed out. "I can't wait to be an adult." She walked out the door and slammed it shut behind her.

Wiping the sweat off her brow, Ronja let out a long-suffering breath. She hated fighting with her children and tried to avoid it by reasoning with them instead. Usually, nothing more was needed because her kids were smart people. Well, that was true for David and Lisa, but Jonah had been a handful.

God, she missed him. Not a day had gone by that she hadn't thought of him, of Michael, of Frank, her parents—all the people she had loved and lost.

As her eyes misted with tears, Ronja wiped them away with a corner of her apron.

The build-up of stress over Ronja's impending transition was getting to Lisa. She was only fifteen, and she'd already lost a brother and a father. The fear of also losing her mother must be overwhelming, and the longer it took for the transition to start, the more stressed and fearful Lisa had become.

It had been three weeks since she and Merlin had started working on it, and nothing was happening. Perhaps her body was too old to transition, and all the work she'd put into making it healthier was not enough.

Still rattled over the confrontation with Lisa, Ronja felt a stress headache coming on. If she didn't relax, it would turn into a migraine, making her miserable for the rest of the day or longer.

With a sigh, she pulled out a bottle of wine from the fridge and poured herself a glass. A few moments sitting in the backyard with a book and a little wine would do her good.

55

MERLIN

.

*M*erlin glanced at the clock hanging on his kitchen wall.

Since the kitchen had been fully converted into a laboratory and no longer served its original purpose, it was time to replace the old relic with a more accurate time-keeping device that he could rely on for his experiments.

As he took his eyes away from it, a rumble from his stomach reminded him why he'd glanced at the clock to begin with.

It was dinner time, but neither Ronja nor Lisa had called to remind him like they usually did.

Patting his coat pockets, he was relieved to find the phone and pulled it out. Perhaps Ronja had had a mishap preparing dinner and was running late. If that was indeed the case, he could finish his reading before heading home for the day.

Merlin smiled.

At some point, Ronja and Lisa's place had become home. Apparently, the human saying was right, and home was where the heart was.

When Ronja didn't answer, he called Lisa.

"Hi, Merlin. I'm having dinner at Parker's house."

"Why? Did Ronja burn the roast again?"

"I don't know. I'm not home. You should call her."

He hadn't missed the sour note in Lisa's tone and wondered whether mother and daughter had had a fight. It was on the tip of his tongue to ask, but he stopped himself.

It wasn't his place. He wasn't Lisa's father, and he should count his blessings that she hadn't objected to him moving in. Butting into her and Ronja's relationship would be a mistake.

"I called. She's not answering."

"Call her again. She might have been in the bathroom and didn't take the phone with her, or she might be blasting music on her earphones and didn't hear the ringing."

"Will do. Say hi to Parker and his parents for me."

"They say hi back."

They all lived on the same street, or rather walkway since there were no streets in the village, and the houses didn't have numbers. Parker was a frequent guest in Merlin's lab as well as in Ronja's home, and occasionally so were his parents.

Merlin called Ronja's phone again, and this time let it ring until it went to voicemail.

Unease creeping up his spine, he rushed out the door and jogged over to her place. She was still human, and there were a thousand ways for her to get hurt. Poisoning from a gas leak, a fall from a ladder, or electrocution from a defective electric kettle or hairdryer.

Bursting through the door, the first thing Merlin noticed was the smell of burning meat coming out of the oven.

Ignoring it, he ran through the house, searching for Ronja. Her phone was nowhere to be seen, so maybe she'd gone somewhere and had forgotten to turn off the oven?

But if the phone was on her, she should have answered. Pulling his own phone out of his pocket, he dialed her number again, and a moment later, he heard it ringing outside in the backyard.

Ronja must have fallen asleep on the lounger.

Huffing out a relieved breath, he slid the patio doors open and walked out.

As he'd suspected, Ronja was asleep on the lounger, an open book resting on her chest, and an empty wine glass perched on the edge of the side table.

"Good evening, my sleeping beauty." He crouched next to her and planted a soft kiss on her lips.

When she didn't wake up, he kissed her again and then shook her shoulder. "Ronja, darling, it's time to wake up."

Her eyelids rose with obvious effort. "I don't feel well," she murmured.

Her lips had felt a little warm, but he'd thought nothing of it. Pressing his lips to her forehead, he confirmed that it was warm as well.

"Your temperature is slightly elevated. You might have caught a cold or flu. When did you start feeling unwell?"

When she didn't answer, and her eyelids slid shut again, his heart lurched with fear.

Was she transitioning?

The mild fever might be the first sign, and she might start burning up in minutes. He had to get her to the clinic.

Scooping Ronja in his arms, Merlin straightened up and started jogging. He should have called ahead and had Bridget meet him at the clinic.

Except, he'd left the phone on the kitchen counter, which reminded him that there was something burning in the oven, and he should tell someone to turn the thing off before the house caught on fire.

As he jogged past Magnus and Vivian's place, he came up with the solution. Turning around, he ran up to their front door and banged on it with his foot. "Open up. It's an emergency."

A split second later, Magnus threw the door open, took one look at Ronja, and knew right away what was going on. "Is she transitioning?"

"Oh, my God." Lisa rushed out. "Is she unconscious?"

"She's just sleeping very deeply," Merlin said to calm the girl down, and turned to Magnus. "Call Bridget and tell her to meet me at the clinic, and I need someone to turn off the oven in Ronja's house before it catches fire and to bring me my phone. I left it on the kitchen counter."

"I'm on it." Magnus pulled out his phone while running toward Ronja's place.

"I'm coming with you," Lisa said.

"And so am I." Parker put his hand on Lisa's shoulder.

Merlin nodded. "Try to keep up." He broke into a fast jog again.

"I'll pack a bag for Ronja!" Vivian called out from behind them. "I'll bring it to the clinic."

"Thank you!" Lisa shouted back, her voice breaking up.

His heart went out to the girl, but he had no time to comfort her. Parker was with her, though, and he could count on the kid to provide her with support.

LISA

*P*anic, hot and acrid, filled Lisa's veins.

She'd lost her father only a few months ago. She couldn't lose her mother.

Fate couldn't be so cruel, right?

Except, fate had no mercy, and shit happened to good people all the time.

Was she good people, though? She'd left the house in a huff, slammed the door, and stayed at Parker's house without even calling her mom to tell her that she wasn't having dinner with her and Merlin.

Oh, hell, what if those angry words were the last she'd ever speak to her mother?

Parker squeezed her hand. "It's going to be alright. Your mom has two doctors at her side. Bridget hasn't lost a Dormant yet, and she's not going to lose your mother, and Merlin is not going to let her slip away."

Lisa blew out a breath. "I pray that you are right, but I'm scared. I can't imagine losing her. I just can't. My heart won't survive it." She rubbed a hand over her chest. "It can't take any more sorrow."

As Parker wrapped an arm around her, she leaned her

head on his shoulder. He was just a boy, but he was all she had, and she was grateful for his presence and support. He might be younger than her, but he was rock solid.

Parker's dad was there as well. Magnus had brought Merlin's phone and stayed, probably to provide moral support.

She also had Merlin, but he needed to take care of her mother, and she had David and Sari, but they were in Scotland.

"Oh, damn." Lisa lifted her head off Parker's shoulder. "I need to call David."

"Right, you do." Parker shifted to the side so she could pull her phone out of her pocket. "David should get here as soon as he can. For you and for your mother."

"And also for himself." Lisa's hands shook as she pulled up her list of favorite contacts and touched David's picture. "He wanted to fly over as soon as I told him that our mother and Merlin were attempting her transition, but she told him to wait until it actually started. Now I wish that he hadn't listened to her."

As the phone kept ringing, Lisa calculated the time difference in her head. Seven in the evening in Los Angeles was three in the morning in Scotland.

Her brother was asleep.

"Come on, David. Wake up." She clutched the phone to her ear.

After another four rings, he finally answered. "What happened?" His words were slurred from sleep.

"Mom is transitioning. You should get here as soon as you can."

"What's her condition?" His sleepiness was gone in an instant, and he sounded all business.

"I don't know. Doctor Bridget is with her, and so is Merlin."

"Tell me what happened," David commanded.

In the background, Lisa heard Sari talking with someone about arranging a flight for her and David.

"Merlin found Mom half passed out on the lounger outside. She must have felt tired and went to lie down."

"What do you mean half passed out? Was she responsive or not?"

In her panic, Lisa had forgotten that her brother was not only a psychologist but also a psychiatrist—a trained medical doctor.

"I heard Merlin tell Bridget that he found Mom asleep. When he woke her up, she told him that she wasn't feeling well. Then he asked her another question, but she didn't respond. He carried her to Parker's house and told us to call Doctor Bridget and to turn off the stove. When I asked him if she was unconscious, he told me that she was in a deep sleep, but I think he lied to me because he ran all the way to the clinic carrying her, and I don't think he would have been in such a hurry if she was just sleeping."

"He was probably worried that she would slip into unconsciousness. Do you have someone with you?"

"Parker and his dad are here."

"Good. I don't want you to be alone. Sari is calling Kian and Syssi, and one of them will come over to keep you company until Sari and I arrive."

Lisa cast a sidelong glance at Parker. "Tell Sari not to bother them. It's not like they can do anything to help. Parker and Magnus will keep me company, and Vivian is on her way with an overnight bag for Mom. If I need anything, I can ask them."

"I'm glad that you are not alone, and I'm grateful to Parker and his family for taking care of you, but I also want Kian to stop by. Sari asks if you called Annani."

"I don't even have her number, but maybe Merlin called her? Can Sari check?"

"She's calling Annani right now."

ANNANI

"They are adorable," Annani whispered as she and Alena passed by the two teenagers sleeping in the clinic's waiting room.

Lisa and Parker had fallen asleep with their heads leaning on one another.

Alena smiled. "They look good together. One day they will make a nice couple."

Annani leaned closer to her eldest daughter and whispered in her ear. "I think they already are."

Alena had verified with Merlin that Magnus and Vivian had gone home before they headed out to the clinic.

Under the guise of visiting her dear friend, Annani was going to help Ronja, or rather see if she needed her help right away. According to Merlin, her vitals were good, and she was not in a critical condition.

Bridget had also left, leaving Ronja in Merlin's capable hands, so unless the teenagers woke up, he was the only obstacle to overcome to having privacy with Ronja.

Merlin opened the door and beckoned them inside. "Thank you so much for coming. I thought that perhaps a preemptive blessing might be a good idea."

Annani and Alena exchanged glances, both thinking the same thing. They suspected that Merlin had guessed the truth about her *blessing*, but the three of them pretended as if he had not.

But that was neither here nor there. Merlin was right. Why wait until Ronja was in trouble when a little transfusion could shore her up and ease her transition?

The problem was getting rid of Merlin, but that could be easily solved. Annani could play her diva card and demand to be alone with her friend, while Alena kept Merlin outside and made sure that she was not interrupted while providing Ronja with a little boost.

"How is she doing?" Annani asked.

"She's in a coma." Merlin did not sound alarmed.

Alena must have gotten the same impression. "You say that as if it's a good thing."

"It's a necessary thing." Merlin smoothed a hand over his much shorter beard. "Bridget and I agree that the transition induces coma to help the body change. It's a common medical practice to induce coma with drugs in order to help a patient heal from severe trauma, but that doesn't mean it is without risks. A medically induced coma is administered with drugs, and doctors have control over it. That's not the case when the coma is natural. We cannot wake Ronja up when we want to."

"And that is why you want me to give her a blessing even though she is stable?"

"Correct." He inclined his head. "You said to let you know right away when Ronja started her transition. I assumed that was why."

"I am concerned for her." Annani walked over to Ronja's bed and took the hand that had no tube attached to it. "I shall give her my blessing, but as you know, I require complete privacy for the ritual."

He nodded. "So I heard. I will wait outside until you tell me that it is okay to come in. How long does it take?"

Annani shrugged. "It depends on the Dormant. Some need more infusion of my energy than others." She glanced at the camera mounted near the ceiling. "I need you to turn this off."

"No problem. What about the rest of the monitoring equipment? Is it okay to leave it on?"

"Of course." She gave him a smile. "The privacy is for me, not for Ronja."

Alena opened the door. "I'll help Merlin turn the camera off."

As the two left the room, Annani locked the door and then walked back to Ronja's bed and hopped up on it. One more perk of having privacy was that she did not need to act regal.

"My darling Ronja." She leaned to kiss her friend's pale cheek. "If you can hear me, I want you to know that you are in good hands, and we are all working together to help you pull through."

Annani started singing an old song in an even older language. If Ronja was aware, as some people in a coma were, she would remember Annani singing what sounded like a prayer.

She would not feel the small pinprick of the needle or the tiny infusion of Annani's blood entering her system.

Pulling the syringe from a hidden pocket in her gown, Annani removed the wrapping, inserted the needle into the plunger, and pricked her own arm. Only a tiny amount was needed, and once the container was one-quarter full, she pulled it out and pricked Ronja's arm.

The entire procedure took less than thirty seconds, during which Annani continued singing softly. When it was done, she returned the syringe to the hidden pocket and took her friend's hand.

"All will be well, my dear Ronja. You and Merlin are going to have eternity together, and Fates willing, you will give Lisa a little brother or sister."

MIA

*A*t precisely two o'clock in the afternoon, Mia was back in the Perfect Match Studios, back in the same small room with all the beeping and blinking monitors, and back in the same chair that looked like a torture device from a science fiction movie.

She'd better get used to the setup and make herself comfortable. Thanks to Tobias's generosity and clever tax planning, she was going to spend many pleasurable hours in that chair.

As he'd promised, Tobias had covered the cost of their second session the same way he was going to cover all the others.

It was a dream come true. She would get to spend time with a wonderful man in the virtual world, chat with him in the real one about their adventure, and maybe even pick his brains about authorship.

He was a successful author, and he could probably give her advice that would help propel her career.

For an unlucky girl, that was an unbelievably good stroke of luck. Heck, it was a windfall.

Mia smiled. She would never have dared to call herself unlucky within her grandmother's earshot. Her grandma always reminded Mia that she needed to count her blessings. She was alive, she had loving grandparents, great friends, and a talent that would hopefully support her one day.

It could have been worse.

Mia glanced at the door to the small room. The technician had left a while ago, promising to be back in a moment, and Mia wondered what was keeping her. These machines probably cost a fortune, and every moment they were not in use was a waste.

As the door opened and Doctor Brenna walked in, Mia got her answer. "Hello, doc. I didn't know that you were coming to supervise this session as well."

"I'm going to supervise all of your sessions." Brenna pulled out the rolling stool and sat down. "You're an important test subject. When I collect enough clinical data from your sessions, I will be able to sell the therapeutic benefits of this device to hospitals and nursing homes. Besides, I'm not taking any risks with you."

Mia shifted her gaze away from the doctor to hide her disappointment. Since Tobias was funding her sessions, Perfect Match was not doing her any favors, and she should be treated like every other paying customer and not a case study.

But if the goal was to collect data that would enable Perfect Match to provide relief to others who were in even more serious situations than hers, how could she refuse?

"Do you know if my adventure will continue from where Tobias and I left off two days ago?"

"More or less." The doctor started to attach wires with sticky pads to Mia's chest. "It might start a few hours later, or a few days. It depends on the content of your adventure, and what was going on when the previous one ended."

"The previous one ended with me going to sleep. When I woke up, I thought that I was at my parents' house in Patagonia."

Brenna arched a brow. "Your adventure was located in South America?"

Mia chuckled. "A small village called Patagonia in the municipality governed by the god Had-dar."

"I see." The doctor attached another wire. "So it's a fantasy land."

"More like a dystopian future. Neither Tobias nor I requested it, but for some reason, the computer decided to put us five hundred years in the future, in a world with a population that had shrunk to less than fifty million people worldwide."

"Ha." Brenna paused with her next sticky pad. "I should tell Gabriel about your adventure. He and Hunter should take a look and figure out what went wrong."

"I didn't say that it was wrong. Tobias and I enjoyed our adventure very much. It's just that neither of us expected it to be in a dystopian future."

Brenna frowned. "How do you know that Tobias didn't request it?"

"I chatted with him on your secure chat application. Didn't you know that?"

"I didn't." Brenna parted Mia's shirt further to attach more pads. "I got a message from headquarters that both of you wanted more sessions and that Tobias purchased a bunch of tokens for you both. We do our best to provide our clients with maximum anonymity, which means that people in our different departments don't discuss clients among themselves. The information is fed into the servers, and the computer does the rest."

"Smart computer." Mia put her arms on the armrest for the doctor to fasten the restraints over.

"That's artificial intelligence for you." Brenna fastened

the left one. "It has its limitations, but even so, I'm awed at what it can do."

59

TOVEN/TOBIAS

*A*s the wagon's wheels got stuck in the mud once again, Tobias released a string of curses that would have made a sailor blush and dismounted for the umpteenth time.

It had seemed like such a fantastic idea to secure a plush wagon for his and Azul's first night together as lovers, a night that would set the tone for the rest of their relationship, a night both of them would cherish for years to come, but at the rate he was going, he would arrive covered in mud like a vagabond, and Azul's parents would never allow her to spend the night with him by the lake.

Well, that was a bit melodramatic. Being a winged warrior might work in his favor and compensate for his less than pristine appearance.

Everyone respected the winged guard. As the law enforcers and protectors of the municipality, they were known to uphold the law to the letter, and Azul's parents would know that no harm could come to their daughter while she was with him.

No one would dare to lay a finger on her, and as for him, nothing would happen without her explicit consent.

Bracing against the slippery ground as best he could, Tobias pushed the wagon from behind.

"Pull!" he commanded Thunder.

Finally, when horse and man managed to release the wheel, the accursed wagon surged forward with a splatter of mud that covered Tobias from head to toe.

Wiping his face with his sleeve, he thanked his foresight to bring a change of clothes. It looked like he would have to dunk himself in the freezing lake and change before arriving on Azul's doorstep.

He should have asked Had-dar for the hovercraft, and the young god would have probably allowed him to borrow it for one night.

After reading Azul's well-thought-out appeal to the gods, Had-dar had been impressed not only with her ideas but also with the clarity of her writing, and he had been very sympathetic to Tobias's request for a day off to pursue the lovely young lady.

The god even joked that if Tobias ever lost interest in the girl, he might offer her a place in the temple as one of his courtesans.

Perhaps that was the reason Tobias hadn't asked for the hovercraft.

After that comment, he could hardly think past the haze of anger, and it had taken all of his formidable self-control not to punch the god in his handsome face.

Had-dar had laughed, wished him best of luck, and offered him the use of his own plush wagon that was equipped with all the comforts a lady might require—all except the ability to hover above the ground and smoothly traverse uneven terrain. But at that point, Tobias had been in no position to negotiate. He was lucky to have a good-natured god like Had-dar as his boss. Eshkada would have reached into his mind and subjected him to unimaginable torment for daring to get angry at her.

After making a detour to the lake and washing the mud off, Tobias donned the civilian clothes that he'd packed for the next day and headed to Azul's village.

Half an hour or so later, Tobias stood in front of Azul's front door, holding gifts for her and her parents.

Hopefully, she wouldn't be too upset about him coming to her home instead of meeting her at the amphitheater. She hadn't wanted him to meet her parents yet, but since he wanted to take her out for the entire night and most of the next day, he needed to introduce himself and make a good impression first.

The door opened before he had a chance to knock, and Azul stepped out, but instead of inviting him in, she closed the door behind her.

She looked just as beautiful as he remembered, and he was pleased to see that she'd dressed up for him. Her short black hair was shiny, her large green eyes were outlined with some kohl, and an earring dangled from her pointy fae ear. She wore tight riding pants, a cream-colored blouse, and an embroidered vest that was a little more festive than the one she'd worn the day before.

"What are you doing here?" she hissed.

He'd expected her to be surprised, and maybe just a little upset, but he hadn't expected such hostility. "We had a date, remember?"

She glared at him. "I didn't forget. But we were supposed to meet in the amphitheater, not here." She put her hand on the small of his back. "Let's go."

He stood his ground. "I want to introduce myself to your parents and ask their permission to take you out to the lake tonight." He smiled. "I secured Had-dar's personal wagon for us."

"That's lovely, but I'm an adult, and I don't need my parents' permission. I just need to let them know that I'll be spending the night with you."

She sounded nervous and not at all eager for the night of passion he'd planned for them.

Perhaps he'd read her all wrong? "Are you having second thoughts about us?"

Azul looked up at him and loosed a breath. "I was looking forward to our second date, or first as it may be, but frankly, I didn't plan on being gone all night and certainly not on introducing you to my parents."

He cupped her cheek. "I want our first time together to be special. I want us to fall asleep together and wake up together to watch the sunrise over the lake. Is that such a bad thing? I thought that you would love my plan."

"I do." She didn't sound convinced. "It's a lovely idea. Just give me a moment to tell my parents, and we can be on our way."

He narrowed his eyes at her. "Are you embarrassed to be with me? Is that why you don't want me to meet your parents?" He lifted the gifts he'd brought for them. "I don't understand your reluctance to let me come inside. I brought presents for you and your parents."

She rolled her eyes. "I'm not embarrassed to be with you. I'm embarrassed about my parents' house. It's a mess, and I don't want you to see it like that. If you'd given me an hour or two warning, I would have cleaned it up."

She was lying.

Tobias might not have a god's sense of smell, but he was a trained law enforcer, and he knew how to read people.

"What are you hiding in there, Azul? Do you have another guy in the house?"

"No, of course not. I told you. It's a mess."

What a pretty little liar.

Maybe everything she'd told him had been a lie?

What if she was living with a man? What if she was married and she'd just been amusing herself with him at the amphitheater?

Playing around wasn't a crime, but she shouldn't mislead him. That was just manipulative and cruel. Had she sought to gain favor with a god's guard?

She wouldn't be the first female to come up with the idea of seducing a guard to get favors from the god or goddess they worked for.

Fury clouding his vision, Tobias forced a smile. "Messes don't scare me." He took a step back, turned around, and depressed the handle. "Are you coming in? Or do you want to stay out here while I introduce myself to your parents?"

60

MIA/AZUL

*A*zul's heart hammered against her chest.

She'd just brought ruin to her family. The mess hadn't been a lie. Brewing equipment on the dining table, bunches of herbs drying on the hearth, small bottles of tonic filling the bookshelves—there was no mistaking the illegal trade that was going on in their home.

She'd expected her parents to panic when Tobias stormed in, but since he was in civilian clothes and his wings were tucked against his back, they didn't realize right away what he was.

She hadn't told them that the man who'd escorted her home was a winged warrior. She'd told them that he was a temple guard, which wasn't the same. The regular guards weren't in charge of upholding the law.

Her mother smiled. "Hello. You must be Tobias. I'm Helena, Azul's mother." She walked up to him and offered him her hand.

Standing with his back to the open door, Tobias didn't move a muscle, but his eyes darted around, taking everything in before shifting to her mother. "Hello, Helena." He took her hand. "Now I see who Azul got her beauty from."

"You must be talking about me." Her father rose to his feet and walked over to Tobias. "Just joking." He offered his hand as well. "Azul is fortunate to have taken after Helena, not me. I'm Javier."

Tobias forced a smile as he shook her father's hand.

"Please, come in." Her father said. "Can I offer you a drink?"

Her heart beating frantically in her chest, Azul took Tobias's hand. "We need to go." She tugged on it. "Tobias is taking me to the lake, and we are going to spend the night there."

Maybe she could convince him not to report what he was seeing. If he cared for her, he might be persuaded to turn a blind eye to the illegal substance trade.

"Not yet." He pulled his hand out of hers. "What's in the vials, Azul?" As he pointed at the bookshelf, he turned just enough for his wings to show.

Her mother gasped, and her father took a step back.

"Perfumes," Azul said quickly. "We make perfumes from herbs and flowers we collect near the lake."

"How ingenious." He handed her the gifts he'd brought and walked over to the bookshelf. "Are they for men or women?" He reached for one of the vials, uncorked it, and sniffed. "That doesn't smell too good." He cast Azul an accusing glance. "Should I try another?"

"They are not ready yet," her mother said. "The process takes several rounds of brewing and combining until we get the right combination."

It was a good lie, and if Tobias cared about her, he would leave it at that. Plausible deniability was all he needed to cover his own ass in case they were ever caught.

"I see." He replaced the cork and put the vial back on the shelf. "Let me know when you have a batch that's ready to sell. I will buy some for my mother."

Was he playing along, or had he bought the lie?

"Of course," her mother said in a surprisingly steady voice. "But since you're dating our daughter, it'll be on the house."

What game was her mother playing? Was there an implied message in what she'd told him?

He cast Helena a smile that looked more like a threat. "That's very generous of you." He dipped his head. "Thank you." He took Azul's hand. "We'd better be going. I hope it's okay with you if I return your daughter to you tomorrow morning."

"Azul's a big girl," her father said. "If that's her wish, she's free to do as she pleases."

Right now, Azul didn't feel like a big girl, and what she wished for was to erase the last two days from existence, so she would never have met Tobias.

Given the cold look he was giving her, he hadn't bought the lies. But since he hadn't confronted her parents about it, he must have something else in mind.

Perhaps he realized the truth but was going to pretend that he believed them?

Or was he giving himself time to decide what to do?

She needed to get out of there and get some fresh air. Tobias had sucked all the air out of the room, and she felt that she was suffocating.

"Let's go." She tugged on his hand.

He didn't budge. "Don't you want to pack a bag?"

"I don't feel so good." She let go of his hand and stepped outside.

Leaning against the railing, she opened her mouth to gulp more air, but her lungs refused to expand, and the suffocating sensation got worse.

When black dots started swimming in front of her eyes, she heard Tobias's worried voice as if through a tunnel. "What's wrong, Azul? Talk to me."

She felt his hands on her shoulders but lacked the strength to turn around, and then her knees gave out, and she was falling, but she never got to hit the ground.

61

TOVEN/TOBIAS

*O*ne moment Tobias's hands were on Azul's shoulders, and the next, she was gone, winked out of existence. Reaching the only conclusion his mind could fathom, he turned around, expecting to see Had-dar.

Only a god could plant in his mind such a realistic illusion of Azul disappearing right before his eyes, right from under his hands.

But all he saw through the open door were Azul's parents, frozen in place inside their house. What was happening? Were they in shock just as he was?

As he opened his mouth to ask, everything around him winked out of existence, and in the next instance, he felt someone shaking his shoulder.

"Wake up, Tobias!" A frantic male voice. "Come on, man. Don't do this to me. Open your eyes. Orlando, that's your son's name, remember Orlando?"

Toven opened his eyes. "What happened?"

The tech let out a relieved breath. "Thank God. You gave me one hell of a scare. I've been trying to get you to wake up for over twenty minutes. I've never had anyone remain in the virtual world for so long after the program was terminated. How did you do that?"

"I have no idea."

Was it that long? Only seconds had passed between Azul's disappearance and him waking up.

"What happened?"

"They ended the session on the other side."

"Why?"

The tech looked worried. "The only time a session is terminated with no prior warning is when there is a medical emergency. But don't worry. You'll get a full refund."

As if he gave a fuck about the money.

Azul had felt faint. She'd clutched at her chest before walking out to get fresh air. That hadn't been part of the fantasy. That was her body in the real world getting distressed.

Pulling his hands out of the restraints, Toven started tearing the sticky pads off. "Find out what happened," he imbued his voice with compulsion.

His eyes glazing over, the tech reached for the phone and dialed a number. "This is Ruben from the Manhattan branch. We had a session suddenly terminated. Can you find out what happened?"

"Give me a moment," a female voice said on the other side. "I'll check with the other branch."

So that was how it worked. He should have thought of it the first time Ruben said that everything had to go through headquarters. All he needed to do was to have the tech contact someone in the main office, and in turn, they could contact the branch Azul was in.

"Medical emergency," the woman said. "She was taken to a hospital."

"Ask her what happened to her," Toven commanded. "Is she alive?" He frantically removed the rest of the pads.

Ruben repeated the questions, and the woman on the other side repeated them to someone else.

"The session was supervised by Doctor Brenna because the client had a heart condition. The doc called an ambulance and went with the client to the hospital, so she must be alive."

"Ask her which hospital and where."

"I don't know," the woman's voice said after Reuben repeated the question. "But I can find out."

"Give me the phone," Toven commanded.

When Reuben handed it over, Toven dialed up the level of compulsion in his voice. "Put me on the line with the other branch."

When she did as he commanded, another female voice sounded. "Who is this?"

"This is Tobias Navón. Tell me Azul's real first and last name and the name of the hospital she was taken to."

"Her name is Mia Berkovich," the woman said. "Give me a moment, and I'll find out where she was taken."

"Don't disconnect." He needed to keep the compulsion going. "Keep me on the line while you call from another phone. If they ask why you need to know, tell them that you need to put it in the client's file."

"Yes, sir.

He waited impatiently as the woman made the call.

"Hi, Doctor Brenna. This is Stacy. Which hospital is Mia going to? I need to put it in her file and notify her emergency contact."

"Cedars-Sinai Medical Center. I've already called her family and they are on their way. You don't need to call anyone."

Mia was in Los Angeles. As far as Toven knew, Cedars-Sinai had no hospitals outside of the Los Angeles metropolitan area.

"How is she doing?" Stacy asked.

"She's stable. It must have been too much excitement for her." The doctor continued to say something quietly that sounded like reassuring words.

Was she talking to Mia?

"I don't know what happened," the doctor said a little louder. "Something in the adventure must have stressed you more than your heart could handle."

She was talking to Mia, which meant that she was awake and responding.

A weight rolled off Toven's chest.

"I know," the doctor said. "It was supposed to be only moderately exciting. But maybe the adventure had nothing to do with it? You might have forgotten to take your medication."

Mia must have answered something too quietly for him to hear or just shook her head.

He was listening to a conversation through the line Stacy had left open and the other one she dialed. Even his godly hearing had difficulty with that.

"I'm just glad that I was there to terminate the session in time."

It was his fault, or rather Tobias's.

He'd known right away what had been going on in Azul's parents' home. They'd been making illegal drugs in there.

Toven had to remind himself that other than his and Mia's thoughts and feelings, nothing in that virtual reality had been real.

But if Mia wasn't allowed to experience stress, why the hell had Brian included the production of illegal drugs in their fantasy?

The guy should have known better. What he had done qualified as reckless endangerment.

He was going to call the guy and give him a piece of his mind.

Then again, Brian had told him that he hadn't known what was in Mia's questionnaire, so it was the artificial intelligence's fault.

Wasn't someone supposed to check, though?

No wonder the Perfect Match people had their clients sign page after page of disclaimers. They made sure that no one could hold them responsible for any health consequences of participating in a virtual adventure, including death.

62

MIA

"Your phone is making noises, Mia." Her grandmother handed her the phone.

Tobias had been trying to reach her through the private chat-box on the Perfect Match chat application, but Mia had ignored him.

Had he been told what had happened?

Doctor Brenna had said that he wouldn't be, that it was against their company policy to reveal any information about their clients without their permission, but he'd probably been told that the session had been terminated because of a medical emergency.

What else were they going to tell him?

That there had been a malfunction? They wouldn't lie to cover for her. They'd either told him the truth without going into details or avoided even that and told him that they couldn't release the information. But given his frantic attempts to communicate with her, he was worried.

If the roles were reversed, she would have been going out of her mind with worry. She hoped that he had at least been told that she was alive, and that they were keeping her in the hospital for observation but were going to release her in a few hours.

Mia's regular doctor had arrived to replace Brenna, and after checking all of her vitals and making a slight adjustment to her medication, she'd admonished Mia for doing a reckless thing like going on a virtual adventure and had gotten her to promise that she would never do that again.

That was why Mia wasn't answering Tobias. What was she going to tell him? That they were never going to meet again?

It was too difficult to do even through a chat-box, and she wasn't supposed to get upset.

Eventually, he would figure it out on his own and find a different partner to continue the adventure with.

Was that even possible?

"Don't look so sad," her grandmother said. "You got a scare, but you are all right. Doctor Sheila said that you can go home tonight and resume all of your normal activities."

Mia nodded. "I know. I'm sad because I'll never get to be with Tobias again."

"That's not true." Frankie moved the curtain aside and walked over to her bed. "You can still chat with him." She gave Mia a gentle hug. "How are you feeling?"

"I've been better. You shouldn't have left work to be with me."

"As if." Frankie sat on the bed. "Margo is on her way too."

Her grandmother pushed to her feet. "Since you're here, I'll join Grandpa in the hospital cafeteria. Call me if you need to leave. I don't want Mia to be alone."

"No problem, but I'm not going anywhere. I took the rest of the day off."

"You're the best." Mia waited until her grandmother was out of earshot. "They don't allow more than two visitors at a time in the emergency room. That's why she left. She made room for Margo."

"I love your grandmother. She's awesome."

"I know." As a tear slid down Mia's cheek, she wiped it away angrily.

"Oh, Mia." Frankie took her hand. "These tears are not about you getting emotional, right? You are already grieving your relationship with Tobias."

Frankie had a way of distilling things to their bare essence, making the bitter pill that much harder to swallow.

"Yeah." Mia wiped away another tear. "It's over. Even if my doctor approved, they are not going to allow me in the Perfect Match Studios ever again."

"I figured as much. But you can still chat with him. I'm sure that they wouldn't be so mean as to revoke your login credentials into their chat interface. And even if they do, you can chat with him over the phone."

"What for? It will just drag the misery out more. The only place I could be with him was in the virtual world. Besides, that's how it was supposed to be from the start. I had fun, but I didn't plan to return. I got roped into it by the discount they offered me, by Margo, who bullied me into accepting it, and later by Tobias, who offered to finance all of our future sessions. I should have known that Mia Berkovich wasn't that lucky."

Thankfully, her grandmother wasn't there to hear her say that.

Frankie let out a sigh. "You could meet him in real life."

"I can't."

"It's not that you can't, it's that you won't. You don't have the guts to put yourself out there because you assume that no one would want you, but that's not true. People in your situation fall in love, get married, and have babies. You need to give yourself a chance to meet someone."

Mia grimaced. "It's not like I've been hiding in my grandparents' house for the past four years. I go out with you and Margo, and I go shopping and to the bank. What else am I supposed to do? Sit in coffee shops and bat my eyelashes at guys?"

"Dating apps." Frankie threw her hands in the air. "That's the only way to meet people. I told you that a hundred times, but you refuse to listen."

"You also told me that I need to put my condition in the 'about me' section, so guys would know what to expect. Do you really think anyone would want to go on a date with me after reading that?"

"You are beautiful, Mia. Inside and out. I'm positive that there are guys out there who face difficulties of their own and would love to connect with a pretty, smart, talented woman who understands them."

And pigs might fly, but Mia didn't say that out loud because she didn't have the energy to argue with Frankie.

"Maybe. But right now, I don't want to talk about dating apps, or being brave, or overcoming difficulties." She closed her eyes. "Can I just be sad and tired for a little bit?"

"You can be sad today. But tomorrow, I'm signing you up for all the dating apps that I use, and if you don't want me to compile your profile, you'd better start thinking about what you want to put on there."

63

TOVEN

*A*s the taxi inched along the congested street, Toven pulled out a couple of twenties, handed them to the driver, and got out.

He could get back to his Manhattan apartment faster on foot, and much faster if he ran. Breaking into a jog that was much slower than what he was capable of, he was at the building's front door less than ten minutes later.

"Good afternoon, sir." The doorman held the door open for him.

"Good afternoon." Toven rushed by him into the elevator.

He'd left the burner phone with Brian's number on his desk, and since he hadn't bothered to memorize it, he had to get back to the apartment to call the guy.

Curiously, no one at the Manhattan branch had known who Brian was. The answer Toven had gotten was that the company headquarters employed hundreds of people, and that if he wanted to speak with someone from there, he had to call the front desk and have them locate the person he was looking for.

When he'd done that, the receptionist asked for Brian's

last name, and when he'd told her that he didn't have it, she'd told him that she couldn't help him. Their directory went by last names and first initials. There was no way she could find one guy named Brian without knowing his last name.

Frustration couldn't begin to describe how Toven felt.

He was a powerful god with compulsion at his disposal, and even he couldn't get through to one annoying guy.

Back in his apartment, he snatched the phone from his desk and dialed Brian's number.

"My favorite client," the guy chirped. "How was today's adventure?"

"You don't know?"

"Know what?"

"The session was terminated because of a medical emergency. Did you know that Mia had a heart condition and wasn't supposed to get overly stressed or excited?"

"I didn't. People mark the level of excitement they desire in the questionnaire, and the algorithm adjusts the adventure accordingly. Is she okay?"

"She's alive. That's all I know, but I'm sure that you know more than you are willing to admit. I want you to tell me her phone number and her address," Toven imbued his voice with compulsion.

"I'm sorry, but I don't have it. You can contact her via the chat application. I will make sure that both of you have continued access to it."

The guy either really didn't have the information, or he was immune to compulsion.

"I tried that many times. She's not responding, and I don't know whether it's because she's in a coma or just doesn't have her phone on her, and I'm going out of my mind with worry."

"Did you try to find her on the internet?"

Toven frowned. "What do you mean?"

"You seem to have gotten her real name somehow. You might be able to find her profile on social media."

Toven had no social life, and therefore he had no use for social media. He had no idea how to even start looking for someone's profile. "Can you do that for me? I'm too frantic to think."

"I'm sorry, Tobias. That's as much as I dare to hint at. You'll have to figure out the rest on your own. Good luck." Brian ended the call.

Toven gaped at the device at his hand. Had the guy just hung up on him?

What was he supposed to do now?

He could search the internet and find instructions on how to search for Mia on the damn social media sites, but that would take too long. He needed to find someone to do it for him.

Everyone under the age of seventy would most likely know how to navigate social media, including the doorman downstairs.

Grabbing another phone, he headed out the door and took the elevator down.

As soon as the elevator door opened, the doorman asked, "Can I call a taxi for you, Mr. Neisman?"

Toven plastered a smile on his face. "I have a favor to ask. Do you know your way around social media?"

Looking confused, the guy nodded. "How can I help you?"

"I'm looking for a lady named Mia Berkovich. I was told that I might be able to find where she lives using social media."

"Only if she wasn't careful. Smart people don't put their addresses on their profiles. But if she posted a picture of her home, and her geolocation wasn't turned off, you might be able to find where that home is."

Toven affected an embarrassed smile. "I'm ashamed to

admit that, but I'm a total ignoramus when it comes to social media. Can you check for me?" He pulled out a hundred-dollar bill and handed it to the guy. "I would really appreciate it."

"I'll do what I can." The doorman took the bill and tucked it in his pocket. "But if I'm unsuccessful, I know a guy who can find anything you want for a couple of Benjamins."

64

LISA

"David!" Lisa burst into tears as she ran to hug her brother. "I'm so glad that you are here."

He embraced her tightly. "Did you spend all night in the clinic?"

She nodded. "Parker brought me a change of clothes, and I showered in the other patient room. Mom is unconscious but stable, and Doctor Bridget says that her vitals are good."

"Fantastic news." David gave her a gentle push and dislodged himself from her arms. "Is Doctor Bridget around?"

"I am." The doctor walked out of her office.

As the two exchanged medical jargon, Sari pulled Lisa into a soft hug.

"How are you holding up, kiddo?" she asked.

"I'm better now that you are here. How was your flight?"

The Scottish arm of the clan didn't own a jet, which meant that Sari and David had flown on a commercial airline.

"It was very comfortable, but neither David nor I

managed to get any sleep. We were too worried. This must be so difficult for you."

Lisa wanted to say that she was fine, but that would be a lie. "It's even worse than when my mom and dad went missing," she admitted. "I didn't know that it would end badly, and I hoped that we would find them and they would be alright and that we would all have a laugh because it was some silly misunderstanding. But then they were found, and my father died, and my mother barely made it, and I was never the same again." The tears were flowing even worse than when David hugged her.

"Oh, sweetie." Sari stroked her hair. "You've been through so much."

"I hate being here," she whispered in Sari's ear. "It's like the hospital where my father died. All the medical equipment and the noises it makes, and even the waiting room, it all brings it back."

"Then let's get out of here." Sari looped an arm around her waist and looked over her shoulder at Parker. "You too, young man. I'm taking you both out for lunch in the café."

"We already had lunch. Parker's mom brought us food to the waiting room. We both missed school today, and we are not going tomorrow either." She looked at Parker. "You are staying with me, right?"

"I'm not going anywhere."

"Except to the café." Sari pulled the door open.

Parker followed them out. "Can I ask you a question?"

"Sure." Sari smiled encouragingly.

"How come you and David don't have bodyguards?"

Lisa stifled an eye roll. Guys were so weird. That was what Parker had been thinking about?

"I like to travel light," Sari said. "Just don't mention this in front of my mother. She might get inspired to shackle me with bodyguards like she did to Kian. If it was up to him, he wouldn't have any either."

As Sari and Parker discussed the pros and cons of having bodyguards, Lisa discreetly wiped her eyes. It was one thing to have a crying fit in the clinic, and another thing to have puffy red eyes in public.

Sari led them to a table and motioned for them to sit down. "What would you like?"

Parker shook his head. "I'll order for us. You've just come off a long flight."

Leaning closer to him, Sari whispered. "I have an ulterior motive. I heard that Aliya is working in the café, and I want to meet her."

Parker's face brightened. "She's really cool. People say that she looks strange, but I think that she's hot."

Lisa didn't like that comment one bit.

"She's thirty, Parker. Way too old for you and way too tall. Besides, I heard that she's as strong as two Guardians."

"So? I think that's hot."

"You think that a stick with boobs is hot," she murmured under her breath.

Sari laughed. "I'll leave you two to bicker while I get us some pastries. Do you kids drink coffee?"

"We do," Lisa said. "Thank you."

When Sari walked away, Parker regarded her with a sly smile on his face. "Are you jealous that I think Aliya is sexy?"

Lisa shrugged. "Why would I be jealous? I just don't think she's attractive. She's pretty, but in a strange way. Her eyes are too big, her waist is too narrow, and she has no breasts to speak of. She looks like a stretched-out porcelain doll."

He leaned closer. "You are much prettier, and your eyes are just the right size. You have no reason to be jealous."

"I'm not."

"Yes, you are. Admit it."

She rolled her eyes. "You are so full of yourself, Parker.

We are just friends, and you can lust after whoever you want."

He was still smiling like a Cheshire Cat. "We are much more than friends, but you just don't want to admit that you really like me because I'm a year younger than you. But that's okay. One day, you'll realize what an awesome guy I am."

"You are awesome, Parker. But our friendship is too important to me to risk on some stupid romantic stuff. Let's wait until we are both off to college."

65

KIAN

*I*t was a rare occasion that Kian had all his three sisters and his mother at his dining table, and it felt damn good. He even liked that Kalugal and Jacki had become such an integral part of the family that it was the most natural thing to include them in every family gathering.

"Where are Andrew and Nathalie?" Sari asked. "I hoped to see them tonight."

"They are trying to keep Phoenix on a normal sleeping schedule, at least during the week," Syssi said. "Nathalie enrolled her in a preschool that's an hour drive away from the village, which means that they have to leave their house at seven in the morning. A cranky little girl is no fun to deal with, so late-night dinners are out."

"Isn't it dangerous to enroll an immortal toddler in a human preschool?" Sari asked. "Phoenix can't be expected to keep secrets."

"Nathalie told the teacher that Phoenix has a wild imagination. They are not going to take anything she says seriously."

"What about her fast-healing ability?" David asked. "If she scrapes her knee, it will heal in moments."

Syssi sighed. "Then someone will have to go there and deal with the teacher's memories. Phoenix needs to be with other kids her age."

"That's true," Sari relented.

"I wish Lisa were here." Syssi handed David the bread-basket. "She doesn't need to stay with your mother twenty-four-seven. Ronja has Merlin with her, and I hear that she's doing very well, all things considered."

Kian had a good idea why Ronja was doing so well, and a quick glance at his mother confirmed his suspicion.

"Lisa is scared of losing her," David said. "I should have realized that she hasn't recovered from the unexpected death of her father yet. She's too good at faking that she's fine, but that's not an excuse. I'm not only her brother but also a trained professional."

"Did she show any signs of PTSD?" Amanda asked.

"None, but then I wasn't here. The only one who was with her is unconscious, and I can't ask her."

"You can ask Parker," Sari suggested. "And Merlin. Lisa spends a lot of time with both of them."

David nodded. "I'm so grateful that she has them in her life. When we are done, I'll go back to the clinic and talk with Merlin. Although with how absentminded he is, he might have not noticed that Lisa was exhibiting any of the symptoms."

"Merlin would have noticed," Annani said. "He might be disorganized and forgetful, but he is a keen observer. Not only that, but he would also have called you to let you know."

David blew out a relieved breath. "Thank you for telling me that. I have been riddled with guilt."

"That is natural." Annani smiled sadly. "We think that we are in control of our destiny and that of our loved ones, and when something goes wrong, we assume that we have made a mistake, or that there was more we could have done. But I can tell you as a goddess and as someone who has lived for a very long time that you cannot foresee every difficulty or prevent every catastrophe."

"Way to spoil the mood." Amanda unfurled her napkin and placed it on top of her belly. "Can we eat?"

She had one week to go, and given the size of that belly, it might happen sooner. Both Amanda and Dalhu were tall, and their daughter would probably come out the size of a six-month-old baby.

"Of course." Syssi motioned to Okidu to bring out dinner.

"On a happier note," Kian said. "The new section of the village will be ready to move into by the time your baby comes. I saw Ingrid earlier today, and she said that you should stop by her design center to choose things for the nursery."

Amanda waved a dismissive hand. "Already done. I'm having everything delivered after Choocha is born."

Kian arched a brow. "Choocha?"

"It's a placeholder name. Dalhu and I decided not to name her until she arrives, so we can see what name fits her best."

"Where did you buy the things for the nursery?" Jacki asked.

"I can text you the store's website. You can order everything you want, and they will hold it for you until after your baby is born."

"Thanks. Except for the nursery and a few artwork pieces that Kalugal commissioned, our place is done." Jacki turned to Alena. "Did you and Orion choose one of the new houses? Or are you happy with the one you've got now?"

Alena cast a quick glance at their mother before

answering. "We haven't decided where we are going to live yet, so the loaner house will do for now."

"What are the options you are considering?" Jacki asked.

"It's either the village or the Sanctuary." Alena smiled at Orion. "I thought that we would tour the world before settling on a place, and we can still do that, just not for as long as I planned. Six months tops."

"And the wedding?" Syssi asked. "Did you decide on the when and where?"

Alena shook her head. "Do you remember Amanda's idea for Kian's birthday?"

Amanda dropped her fork. "You want to have your wedding on a cruise ship?"

"Why not? An Alaskan cruise. We can fit the entire clan in one of those huge ships with room to spare, and instead of celebrating for one day, we can celebrate for a week."

"I love it." Amanda cast a look at Kian. "What do you think?"

"I'm not dismissing it, but I want to run it by Turner and see what he thinks."

Amanda chuckled. "Are you thinking of having a submarine escort for the ship? Because I don't think even Turner can get that for you."

66

MIA

"*M*ia, sweetheart." Her grandmother walked into the room. "Grandpa and I need to go grocery shopping."

"Is it Friday already?"

Her grandmother smiled. "All day long."

On Fridays, her grandparents did their weekly grocery shopping at Costco, starting right as the store opened to beat the crowds. They usually spent a couple of hours leisurely strolling through the warehouse and tasting all the samples. After getting the supplies, they liked to stop for Costco's famous quarter-pound beef hot dogs and wash them down with Diet Pepsi.

"Have fun."

"Are you going to be okay here on your own?

"I'm fine, Grandma. Enjoy your shopping trip."

"If you need us for any reason, call. We can be back here in minutes."

"I know. Don't worry about me."

Her grandmother gave her a look that said it was her job to worry about her family, leaned down, and kissed her cheek. "Do you want us to bring you a hot dog?"

Mia laughed. "You ask me that every Friday, and my answer is always the same. I don't know how you can eat that stuff, but enjoy."

"Oh, we certainly will. It's your loss."

When her grandparents were gone and the house got too quiet, Mia un-muted her desktop and put on her favorite classical channel.

The reason she'd silenced her computer was Tobias's incessant messaging.

The pings had stopped coming after midnight last night, and she assumed that he'd gone to sleep, but when she'd woken up this morning, she'd found two new ones he'd sent at three and five in the morning.

She didn't read them, not because she didn't care, but because she was afraid that once she did, she would cave in and answer him, which would be like reopening the wound.

The smart thing to do was to let the wound scab over until it stopped hurting, burning, and itching.

With a sigh, she turned her tablet on and resumed drawing. Her first creature was coming along nicely. She'd finally gotten the concept down and was working on finalizing the shape. He was going to be a little blue alien with antennae sticking out of his head, a cat's tail, and purple puppy eyes.

With the music playing softly in the background, Mia immersed herself in the creative process, enjoying the calm bliss of drawing and sketching. She was in her element, and the outside world didn't exist when she was working.

Except, it did, and sometimes it got noisy and annoying.

A car stopped in front of her house with the engine idling, disturbing her bliss.

It couldn't be her grandparents already. It was too early for them to be back.

Swiveling her chair around, she looked out her bedroom window.

A taxi was idling next to the curb, and a moment later, the back passenger door opened, and a man got out. She didn't get a chance to see his face because he stood with his back to the window, waiting on the sidewalk as the taxi driver opened the trunk and took out a rolling carryon. She could appreciate his fine backside, though. He wore tailored slacks, so it wasn't as well defined as it would have been in a pair of jeans, but the view was still impressive.

He also wore a dress shirt, which meant that he was either a realtor or a businessman interested in her neighbors' house.

It was for sale, and it attracted a lot of out-of-towners. For some reason, Arcadia had become very popular with rich Asians, and they snatched up properties as soon as they hit the market, turning them into mini mansions. Her grandparents' house was one of the few on the block that was still the original structure from the early seventies.

Hopefully, the guy would realize that he was in front of the wrong house before ringing her front door. Mia was in no state to be seen by anyone, but she was curious to see the face that went with that body and waited for him to turn around.

When he did, her heart started a dangerously fast beat.

It was Tobias. She had no doubt about it. He didn't look exactly like his avatar, but close enough, and unbelievably, even better.

Who looked like that? The man was absolutely stunning.

Mia couldn't think of a movie star who could match that level of perfection. She must be hallucinating.

Should she pinch herself?

How had he even known where to find her? She'd been

assured that her information was a hundred percent confidential.

Except, deep down, she'd known that Tobias would find a way, that he wouldn't give up on Azul, but she hadn't expected him to be able to do it so quickly.

He must have flown in if he arrived by taxi and had luggage with him, which meant that he'd found out who she was and where she lived within hours of their disrupted adventure.

She shouldn't be surprised, though. He was a rich man, and money bought information.

The problem was that he had come looking for Azul, but he would find Mia instead, and his disappointment would devastate her.

When he had finished tipping the taxi driver and grabbed the handle of his carry-on, Mia ducked her head so he wouldn't see her, and she didn't dare lift it until she heard him rolling it toward her front door.

He rang the doorbell a moment later.

"Shit," she cursed under her breath.

What was she going to do now? There was no way she was letting him see her like this, and she didn't have time to do anything about it.

She could pretend that she wasn't home and not answer the door. Or maybe she could message him and tell him to come back in an hour?

That would give her enough time to get ready.

What for, though?

There was no hiding what was wrong with her, and he would leave no matter how she dressed up.

He wouldn't leave right away, though. He would stay for a little while, making small talk and pretending that it didn't bother him, and then he'd tell her that he would call, or come visit again, but he never would.

It was better to get it over with sooner rather than later.

Rip the Band-Aid off in one brutal tug instead of peeling it off a millimeter at a time.

She would let him in, show herself to him at her worst, and give him five minutes to squirm before coming up with an excuse for why he needed to leave.

TOVEN

*T*oven rang the bell again.

He knew that Mia was in there. He could sense her anxious energy and wondered whether he'd made a mistake by coming over uninvited, unexpected, and probably unwanted.

He'd told her he was coming via the Perfect Match chat application, but she hadn't opened any of the numerous messages he'd sent her.

Stress was dangerous to Mia, and he'd been the cause of her distress during their adventure, he didn't want to cause any more damage by coming to see her.

Except in this world, he was a god and he could help her, while in the virtual world, he'd been just a helpless human. One of the scariest moments in his long life had been watching her wink out of existence and not being able to do anything to stop it.

But that had been just an illusion. A virtual game.

He was, and always would be, a god. He'd just played at being human for a few hours and had enjoyed it very much. It had been such a relief not to carry the combined weight of his experiences, the guilt over his failures, and for all the things he could have done and hadn't.

It had also been wonderfully refreshing not to be able to scent anyone's emotions. He'd enjoyed using his mind and knowledge of human nature to figure out whether Azul liked him or not, what pleased her and what didn't.

Should he leave?

He hadn't thought it through when he'd booked the first direct flight from New York to Los Angeles. He could have slept on the lie-flat seat in first class, but he hadn't. Instead, he'd been consumed by thoughts of Mia and how he was going to convince her to give him a chance.

Except, he hadn't arrived at any breakthroughs during the six-hour flight or the two-hour taxi drive. The god of wisdom and knowledge had no answers because he didn't have enough data to analyze the situation.

Mia had refused to chat with him, so he didn't know why she was ignoring his communication attempts. The one good thing about that was that she hadn't told him to stay away.

It was quite obvious, though, that she didn't want to see him, but he needed to find out why.

Was it because of her heart condition?

Perhaps she couldn't get intimate without a doctor supervising her through it? Maybe the virtual world was the only place she could enjoy intimacy without fear?

He had to find the answers to his questions, and then convince her that no matter what her difficulties were, he could help her.

With his money, he could get her the best specialists in the world, and if that wasn't enough, he might even try giving her some of his blood and see if the rumors had been right.

No, that was too risky.

His blood might kill her instead of saving her. He didn't

know what it did or how it did it. The gods had been reluctant to use that method to save humans who they'd cared about for a reason. He had never tried it on anyone before, and he sure as hell wouldn't start with Mia.

Pulling out his phone, he was about to type up another message for her when he heard a rolling sound from the other side of the door, and a moment later, Mia's nervous energy hit him right in the chest.

As he waited for the door to open, he took a step back and held his breath.

Seconds turned to minutes in his mind as he heard the deadbolt release, the knob handle twist, and then finally the door inch open.

When he saw her, his heart nearly stopped, and then he was on his knees in front of her. "Did I do this?"

She frowned. "Do what?"

"Your heart. The wheelchair."

She had a blanket draped over her thighs, but unless she had her legs folded under her, she was missing most of both.

For a long moment, she gaped at him, bewildered by his response.

Toven gaped back.

She was beautiful, but right now, she looked sick. Her big green eyes, so much like Azul's, were puffy from lack of sleep or maybe from crying, and there were dark circles under them. Her short dark hair was identical to the picture she'd drawn of her avatar, but it was messy and dull, not shiny and healthy like Azul's.

His little sprite was not well, and he had a feeling that he'd made things ten times worse for her.

"Tobias," she whispered. "None of this is your fault. Why would you think that it was?"

Shaking his head, he realized that he was still kneeling

on her doorstep, making a spectacle of himself and probably embarrassing her in front of her neighbors.

"May I come in?"

"Yes, of course." She wheeled the chair back.

The first thing he was going to do was buy her a motorized chair. It would make moving around much easier.

As Mia turned the chair around and wheeled herself inside, Toven rose to his feet, walked in, and closed the door behind him. Leaving his carry-on by the door, he followed her into the living room.

MIA

When Tobias had dropped to his knees, Mia had thought that he was going to embrace her, and her stupid little heart got all excited—in a good way.

But he didn't wrap his arms around her, hadn't kissed her, and hadn't told her that she was perfect the way she was. His expression was full of sorrow and guilt, as if her condition was his fault.

What a strange and stunning man.

What reason could he have for seeking a lover in the virtual world?

Tobias didn't need to hide behind an avatar. He could have supermodels and actresses, but perhaps he was seeking something else, something that he couldn't find in the real world.

Beauty didn't guarantee love or happiness, but it sure as hell didn't stand in their way. Mia had been beautiful before, or so she'd been told. She'd been elected home-coming queen, and in college, her picture had been used in their advertising campaign. But that was all in the past, and she'd made her peace with it.

"May I sit down?" Tobias asked from behind her.

"Yes, of course." She turned her chair around. "Where are my manners." She waved toward the couch.

When he sat down, she asked, "How did you find me?"

He smiled slyly. "I can be very persuasive when I need to be."

She wondered about the persuasion methods he'd used. Was it money? A charming smile? Threats?

It didn't matter.

"Why are you here, Tobias?"

The smile slid off his gorgeous face. "I was worried. I knew that you were alive, but I didn't know whether you were well, and I can see that you're not, and I feel responsible. I need to make it up to you." He leaned forward, giving her a smile that was all about sex. "Once you feel better, of course."

Was he serious? Did he think that they would just continue where they'd left off in the virtual world?

Now she knew why a stunning guy like him was looking for love in a virtual fantasy. He wasn't right in the head.

"You should leave."

"You don't mean it." All levity was gone from Tobias's face. He was dead serious. "Talk to me, Mia. Tell me what's on your mind. After the initial shock of seeing you in a wheelchair, I realized that the loss of your legs couldn't possibly be my fault. You would still be in the hospital if it was."

"So now that you know it wasn't your fault, you should no longer feel guilty, and you don't need to make it up to me. I had a great time with you in the virtual world, and I wish I could continue our adventures, but after the scare I gave everyone, Perfect Match Studios are forever barred to me. I'm too much of a risk."

He tilted his head. "Forever is a very long time, and I

have the means and the motivation to fulfill nearly every wish you might dream of." He glanced down at her legs. "I can't give you back what you lost, but I can get you the best, custom-made prosthetics money can buy."

It was such a condescending thing to say, but she didn't have the energy to get angry. Besides, he meant well. He just didn't know any better.

Mia let out a sigh. "I have prosthetics, very good ones in fact, and I worked very hard to be able to walk again. It took many months of rehabilitation. But I was too tired today to bother with them." She smoothed a hand over her messy hair. "Also, I usually don't look this bad. I had a difficult day yesterday, and my mood is in the dumpster, but I'm not going to let myself wallow much longer, so you have nothing to worry about, and you can go back to wherever you came from. I'll be fine."

She needed him to go so she could be done with the torment of looking at him and knowing that he was an impossible dream, have a good cry, and then pull herself out of the dumpster and go back to her routine.

"Why are you so adamant about getting rid of me? I thought that we had something special. I don't want it to end. I want to be with you."

The guy was unbelievable.

"Seriously? Do you have a savior complex?" Mia whipped off the blanket she'd thrown over her lap. "Don't pretend like this doesn't bother you. I don't want your pity, and I don't want your charity. If you really want to help me, you can give me advice on becoming a successful author. That's the only help I'm willing to accept from you, and we can do that via emails and chats."

TOVEN

*T*hat was a start, and Toven could work with it. As long as Mia allowed him in her life in any capacity, he could convince her over time that there was so much more to her than what was missing.

Extending his hand, he smiled. "I can work with that. But we are going to do it in person, not via email or chat."

Mia didn't take his hand. Instead, she glanced at the carry-on he'd left by the door. "Don't you have a home you need to return to? A family?"

He had a son, but he'd driven him away and would probably never see him again.

"I don't. I'm a loner, a traveler, a nomad, and a collector of experiences. I don't own a home anywhere." He looked out the window. "That being said, I find Arcadia quite charming, and I'm of a mind to stay here for a while. I saw a for-sale sign on the neighboring house. I'm going to contact the realtor and make an offer."

She narrowed her eyes at him. "You just said that you're a nomad who doesn't own a home, and yet you are talking about buying the neighbors' house."

Smiling, he crossed his legs at the ankles. "That's the

beauty of my nomadic lifestyle. I can settle down anywhere I choose, anytime I want."

Mia shook her head. "You're crazy."

She wasn't wrong about that. It was illogical to pursue a human, and it would only lead to heartache for both of them, heartache that Mia couldn't afford to feel.

Was that why she was so adamant about driving him away?

He desperately needed a doctor's advice, and he was going to get the best whether she wanted it or not.

"I suspect that you don't like talking about it, but how did you lose your legs? Was it a car accident?"

She leveled her big green eyes on his. "Four years ago, my heart suddenly gave out. I collapsed and was brought to the hospital. I was revived, but my heart kept stopping, and the doctors fought to keep me alive. I was shocked, induced into a coma, and they hooked me to a machine to keep my heart beating. But it only pumped at a fraction of what it was supposed to, and not enough blood got to my legs. The doctors had to amputate both of them above the knee to prevent septic shock and keep me alive. Later, they figured out that I have a rare genetic condition that causes an abnormal heart rhythm. I was put on medication, and when that wasn't enough, I got a cardioverter defibrillator implanted."

His brave, brave sprite. What incredible odds she'd had to overcome. He was awed by her courage and so proud of her for not giving up.

"That's a remarkable story of survival and perseverance. I'm impressed, and I'm not a man easily impressed." Toven reached for her hand, but she cast him a look that said stay away. "That being said, I can't believe that the Perfect Match people allowed you to participate in the adventure. I don't know whether to applaud them for giving you a chance despite the risks, or to berate them for being greedy bastards. In either case, I'm thankful to them for pairing us, and I'm glad that I got to share an amazing adventure with you. I wish we could go back and have many more."

She tilted her head. "Are you doing all of this for research for your new book?" She gave him a haughty look. "Talk about immersing yourself in the creative process. I thought that I was obsessed, but you are taking it to a whole new level."

He could have lied and said that his motivation was collecting material for a future book, but it would be one more lie on top of many he would have to tell her. Besides, it wasn't what she wanted to hear, and he didn't even need to enter her mind to figure that out.

"I might write about you, Mia, and I might fill journal after journal with portraits of you, but I will never publish this story."

"Why? Because it's too sad?"

"No, because it's our story, and starting tomorrow, we are going to write it together. I don't want to share it with anyone but you."

If he were a mortal, he would have added that he might want to share it with their children one day, but that was a fantasy better left for the virtual world. In the real world, the chances of him fathering another child were nearly non-existent, and even if that wasn't a problem, Mia's fragile heart was.

"What happens tomorrow?" Mia whispered.

Toven smiled. "Tomorrow, my dear Mia, we will start our new adventure with a proper visit. I'll come in the evening, after you and your grandparents have had dinner, I will introduce myself as your new next-door neighbor, and we will take it from there."

COMING UP NEXT
The Children of the Gods Book 60
Dark God's Reviviscence

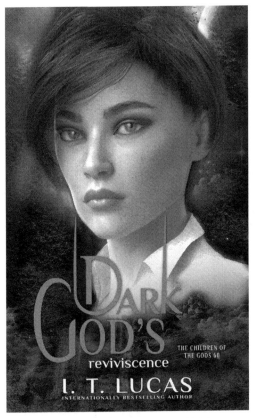

To read the first 3 chapters JOIN the VIP club at
ITLUCAS.COM

Dear reader,

Thank you for reading the ***Children of the Gods***.

As an independent author, I rely on your support to

spread the word. So if you enjoyed the story, please share your experience with others, and if it isn't too much trouble, I would greatly appreciate a brief review on Amazon.

Love & happy reading,
    Isabell

To find out what's included in your free membership, flip to the last page.

If you're already a subscriber, you'll receive a download link for my next book's preview chapters in the new release announcement email. If you are not getting my emails, your provider is sending them to your junk folder, and you are missing out on **important updates, side characters' portraits, additional content, and other goodies.** To fix that, add isabell@itlucas.com to your email contacts or your email VIP list.

THE CHILDREN OF THE GODS SERIES

THE CHILDREN OF THE GODS ORIGINS

1: GODDESS'S CHOICE

When gods and immortals still ruled the ancient world, one young goddess risked everything for love.

2: GODDESS'S HOPE

Hungry for power and infatuated with the beautiful Areana, Navuh plots his father's demise. After all, by getting rid of the insane god he would be doing the world a favor. Except, when gods and immortals conspire against each other, humanity pays the price.

But things are not what they seem, and prophecies should not to be trusted...

THE CHILDREN OF THE GODS

1: DARK STRANGER THE DREAM

Syssi's paranormal foresight lands her a job at Dr. Amanda Dokani's neuroscience lab, but it fails to predict the thrilling yet terrifying turn her life will take. Syssi has no clue that her boss is an immortal who'll drag her into a secret, millennia-old battle over humanity's future. Nor does she realize that the professor's imposing brother is the mysterious stranger who's been starring in her dreams.

Since the dawn of human civilization, two warring factions of immortals—the descendants of the gods of old—have been secretly shaping its destiny. Leading the clandestine battle from his luxurious Los Angeles high-rise, Kian is surrounded by his clan, yet alone. Descending from a single goddess, clan members are forbidden to each other. And as the only other immortals are their hated enemies, Kian and his kin have been long resigned to a lonely existence of fleeting trysts with human partners. That is, until his sister makes a game-changing discovery—a mortal seeress who she believes is a dormant carrier of their genes. Ever the realist, Kian is skeptical and refuses Amanda's plea to attempt Syssi's activation. But when his enemies learn of the Dormant's existence, he's forced to rush her to the safety of his keep. Inexorably drawn to Syssi, Kian wrestles with his conscience as he is tempted to explore her budding interest in the darker shades of sensuality.

2: DARK STRANGER REVEALED

While sheltered in the clan's stronghold, Syssi is unaware that Kian and Amanda are not human, and neither are the supposedly religious fanatics that are after her. She feels a powerful connection to Kian, and as he introduces her to a world of pleasure she never dared imagine, his dominant sexuality is a revelation. Considering that she's completely out of her element, Syssi feels comfortable and safe letting go with him. That is, until she begins to suspect that all is not as it seems. Piecing the puzzle together, she draws a scary, yet wrong conclusion...

3: DARK STRANGER IMMORTAL

When Kian confesses his true nature, Syssi is not as much shocked by the revelation as she is wounded by what she perceives as his callous plans for her.

If she doesn't turn, he'll be forced to erase her memories and let her go. His family's safety demands secrecy – no one in the mortal world is allowed to know that immortals exist.

Resigned to the cruel reality that even if she stays on to never again leave the keep, she'll get old while Kian won't, Syssi is determined to enjoy what little time she has with him, one day at a time.

Can Kian let go of the mortal woman he loves? Will Syssi turn? And if she does, will she survive the dangerous transition?

4: DARK ENEMY TAKEN

Dalhu can't believe his luck when he stumbles upon the beautiful immortal professor. Presented with a once in a lifetime opportunity to grab an immortal female for himself, he kidnaps her and runs. If he ever gets caught, either by her people or his, his life is forfeit. But for a chance of a loving mate and a family of his own, Dalhu is prepared to do everything in his power to win Amanda's heart, and that includes leaving the Doom brotherhood and his old life behind.

Amanda soon discovers that there is more to the handsome Doomer than his dark past and a hulking, sexy body. But succumbing to her enemy's seduction, or worse, developing feelings for a ruthless killer is out of the question. No man is worth life on the run, not even the one and only immortal male she could claim as her own...

Her clan and her research must come first...

5: Dark Enemy Captive

When the rescue team returns with Amanda and the chained Dalhu to the keep, Amanda is not as thrilled to be back as she thought she'd be. Between Kian's contempt for her and Dalhu's imprisonment, Amanda's budding relationship with Dalhu seems doomed. Things start to look up when Annani offers her help, and together with Syssi they resolve to find a way for Amanda to be with Dalhu. But will she still want him when she realizes that he is responsible for her nephew's murder? Could she? Will she take the easy way out and choose Andrew instead?

6: Dark Enemy Redeemed

Amanda suspects that something fishy is going on onboard the Anna. But when her investigation of the peculiar all-female Russian crew fails to uncover anything other than more speculation, she decides it's time to stop playing detective and face her real problem—a man she shouldn't want but can't live without.

6.5: My Dark Amazon

When Michael and Kri fight off a gang of humans, Michael gets stabbed. The injury to his immortal body recovers fast, but the one to his ego takes longer, putting a strain on his relationship with Kri.

7: Dark Warrior Mine

When Andrew is forced to retire from active duty, he believes that all he has to look forward to is a boring desk job. His glory days in special ops are over. But as it turns out, his thrill ride has just begun. Andrew discovers not only that immortals exist and have been manipulating global affairs since antiquity, but that he and his sister are rare possessors of the immortal genes.

Problem is, Andrew might be too old to attempt the activation process. His sister, who is fourteen years his junior, barely made it through the transition, so the odds of him coming out of it alive, let alone immortal, are slim.

But fate may force his hand.

Helping a friend find his long-lost daughter, Andrew finds a woman who's worth taking the risk for. Nathalie might be a Dormant, but the only way to find out for sure requires fangs and venom.

8: Dark Warrior's Promise

Andrew and Nathalie's love flourishes, but the secrets they keep from each other taint their relationship with doubts and suspicions. In the meantime, Sebastian and his men are getting bolder, and the storm that's brewing will shift the balance of power in the millennia-old conflict between Annani's clan and its enemies.

9: Dark Warrior's Destiny

The new ghost in Nathalie's head remembers who he was in life, providing Andrew and her with indisputable proof that he is real and not a figment of her imagination.

Convinced that she is a Dormant, Andrew decides to go forward with his transition immediately after the rescue mission at the Doomers' HQ.

Fearing for his life, Nathalie pleads with him to reconsider. She'd rather spend the rest of her mortal days with Andrew than risk what they have for the fickle promise of immortality.

While the clan gets ready for battle, Carol gets help from an unlikely ally. Sebastian's second-in-command can no longer ignore the torment she suffers at the hands of his commander and offers to help her, but only if she agrees to his terms.

10: Dark Warrior's Legacy

Andrew's acclimation to his post-transition body isn't easy. His senses are sharper, he's bigger, stronger, and hungrier. Nathalie fears that the changes in the man she loves are more than physical. Measuring up to this new version of him is going to be a challenge.

Carol and Robert are disillusioned with each other. They are not destined mates, and love is not on the horizon. When Robert's three months are up, he might be left with nothing to show for his sacrifice.

Lana contacts Anandur with disturbing news; the yacht and its human cargo are in Mexico. Kian must find a way to apprehend Alex and rescue the women on board without causing an international incident.

11: Dark Guardian Found

What would you do if you stopped aging?

Eva runs. The ex-DEA agent doesn't know what caused her strange mutation, only that if discovered, she'll be dissected like a lab rat. What Eva doesn't know, though, is that she's a descendant of the gods, and that she is not alone. The man who rocked her world in one life-changing encounter over thirty years ago is an immortal as well.

To keep his people's existence secret, Bhathian was forced to turn his back on the only woman who ever captured his heart, but he's never forgotten and never stopped looking for her.

12: Dark Guardian Craved

Cautious after a lifetime of disappointments, Eva is mistrustful of Bhathian's professed feelings of love. She accepts him as a lover and a confidant but not as a life partner.

Jackson suspects that Tessa is his true love mate, but unless she overcomes her fears, he might never find out.

Carol gets an offer she can't refuse—a chance to prove that there is more to her than meets the eye. Robert believes she's about to commit a deadly mistake, but when he tries to dissuade her, she tells him to leave.

13: Dark Guardian's Mate

Prepare for the heart-warming culmination of Eva and Bhathian's story!

14: Dark Angel's Obsession

The cold and stoic warrior is an enigma even to those closest to him. His secrets are about to unravel...

15: Dark Angel's Seduction

Brundar is fighting a losing battle. Calypso is slowly chipping away his icy armor from the outside, while his need for her is melting it from the inside.

He can't allow it to happen. Calypso is a human with none of the Dormant indicators. There is no way he can keep her for more than a few weeks.

16: Dark Angel's Surrender

Get ready for the heart pounding conclusion to Brundar and Calypso's story.

Callie still couldn't wrap her head around it, nor could she summon even a smidgen of sorrow or regret. After all, she had some memories with him that weren't horrible. She should've felt something. But there was nothing, not even shock. Not even horror at what had transpired over the last couple of hours.

Maybe it was a typical response for survivors--feeling euphoric for the simple reason that they were alive. Especially when that survival was nothing short of miraculous.

Brundar's cold hand closed around hers, reminding her that they weren't out of the woods yet. Her injuries were superficial, and the most she had to worry about was some scarring. But, despite his and Anandur's reassurances, Brundar might never walk again.

If he ended up crippled because of her, she would never forgive herself for getting him involved in her crap.

"Are you okay, sweetling? Are you in pain?" Brundar asked.

Her injuries were nothing compared to his, and yet he was concerned about her. God, she loved this man. The thing was, if she told him that, he would run off, or crawl away as was the case.

Hey, maybe this was the perfect opportunity to spring it on him.

17: Dark Operative: A Shadow of Death

As a brilliant strategist and the only human entrusted with the secret of immortals' existence, Turner is both an asset and a liability to the clan. His request to attempt transition into immortality as an alternative to cancer treatments cannot be denied without risking the clan's exposure. On the other hand, approving it means risking his premature death. In both scenarios, the clan will lose a valuable ally.

When the decision is left to the clan's physician, Turner makes plans to manipulate her by taking advantage of her interest in him.

Will Bridget fall for the cold, calculated operative? Or will Turner fall into his own trap?

18: Dark Operative: A Glimmer of Hope

As Turner and Bridget's relationship deepens, living together seems like the right move, but to make it work both need to make concessions.

Bridget is realistic and keeps her expectations low. Turner could never be the truelove mate she yearns for, but he is as good as she's going to get. Other than his emotional limitations, he's perfect in every way.

Turner's hard shell is starting to show cracks. He wants immortality, he wants to be part of the clan, and he wants Bridget, but he doesn't want to cause her pain.

His options are either abandon his quest for immortality and give Bridget his few remaining decades, or abandon Bridget by going for the transition and most likely dying. His rational mind dictates that he chooses the former, but his gut pulls him toward the latter. Which one is he going to trust?

19: Dark Operative: The Dawn of Love

Get ready for the exciting finale of Bridget and Turner's story!

20: Dark Survivor Awakened

This was a strange new world she had awakened to.

Her memory loss must have been catastrophic because almost nothing was familiar. The language was foreign to her, with only a few words bearing some similarity to the language she thought in. Still, a full moon cycle had passed since her awakening, and little by little she was gaining basic understanding of it--only a few words and phrases, but she was learning more each day.

A week or so ago, a little girl on the street had tugged on her mother's sleeve and pointed at her. "Look, Mama, Wonder Woman!"

The mother smiled apologetically, saying something in the language these people spoke, then scurried away with the child looking behind her shoulder and grinning.

When it happened again with another child on the same day, it was settled.

Wonder Woman must have been the name of someone important in this strange world she had awoken to, and since both times it had been said with a smile it must have been a good one.

Wonder had a nice ring to it.

She just wished she knew what it meant.

21: Dark Survivor Echoes of Love

Wonder's journey continues in *Dark Survivor Echoes of Love*.

22: Dark Survivor Reunited

The exciting finale of Wonder and Anandur's story.

23: Dark Widow's Secret

Vivian and her daughter share a powerful telepathic connection, so when Ella can't be reached by conventional or psychic means, her mother fears the worst.

Help arrives from an unexpected source when Vivian gets a call from the young doctor she met at a psychic convention. Turns out Julian belongs to a private organization specializing in retrieving missing girls.

As Julian's clan mobilizes its considerable resources to rescue the daughter, Magnus is charged with keeping the gorgeous young mother safe.

Worry for Ella and the secrets Vivian and Magnus keep from each other should be enough to prevent the sparks of attraction from kindling a blaze of desire. Except, these pesky sparks have a mind of their own.

24: Dark Widow's Curse

A simple rescue operation turns into mission impossible when the Russian mafia gets involved. Bad things are supposed to come in threes, but in Vivian's case, it seems like there is no limit to bad luck. Her family and everyone who gets close to her is affected by her curse.

Will Magnus and his people prove her wrong?

25: Dark Widow's Blessing

The thrilling finale of the Dark Widow trilogy!

26: Dark Dream's Temptation

Julian has known Ella is the one for him from the moment he saw her picture, but when he finally frees her from captivity, she seems indifferent to him. Could he have been mistaken?

Ella's rescue should've ended that chapter in her life, but it seems like the road back to normalcy has just begun and it's full of obstacles. Between the pitying looks she gets and her mother's attempts to get her into therapy, Ella feels like she's typecast as a victim, when nothing could be further from the truth. She's a tough survivor, and she's going to prove it.

Strangely, the only one who seems to understand is Logan, who keeps popping up in her dreams. But then, he's a figment of her imagination—or is he?

27: Dark Dream's Unraveling

While trying to figure out a way around Logan's silencing compulsion, Ella concocts an ambitious plan. What if instead of trying to keep him out of her dreams, she could pretend to like him and lure him into a trap?

Catching Navuh's son would be a major boon for the clan, as well as for Ella. She will have her revenge, turning the tables on another scumbag out to get her.

28: Dark Dream's Trap

The trap is set, but who is the hunter and who is the prey? Find out in this heart-pounding conclusion to the *Dark Dream* trilogy.

29: Dark Prince's Enigma

As the son of the most dangerous male on the planet, Lokan lives by three rules:

Don't trust a soul.

Don't show emotions.

And don't get attached.

Will one extraordinary woman make him break all three?

30: Dark Prince's Dilemma

Will Kian decide that the benefits of trusting Lokan outweigh the risks?

Will Lokan betray his father and brothers for the greater good of his people?

Are Carol and Lokan true-love mates, or is one of them playing the other?

So many questions, the path ahead is anything but clear.

31: Dark Prince's Agenda

While Turner and Kian work out the details of Areana's rescue plan, Carol and Lokan's tumultuous relationship hits another snag. Is it a sign of things to come?

32 : Dark Queen's Quest

A former beauty queen, a retired undercover agent, and a successful model, Mey is not the typical damsel in distress. But when her sister drops off the radar and then someone starts following her around, she panics.

Following a vague clue that Kalugal might be in New York, Kian sends a team headed by Yamanu to search for him.

As Mey and Yamanu's paths cross, he offers her his help and protection, but will that be all?

33: Dark Queen's Knight

As the only member of his clan with a godlike power over human minds, Yamanu has been shielding his people for centuries, but that power comes at a steep price. When Mey enters his life, he's faced with the most difficult choice.

The safety of his clan or a future with his fated mate.

34: Dark Queen's Army

As Mey anxiously waits for her transition to begin and for Yamanu to test whether his godlike powers are gone, the clan sets out to solve two mysteries:

Where is Jin, and is she there voluntarily?

Where is Kalugal, and what is he up to?

35: Dark Spy Conscripted

Jin possesses a unique paranormal ability. Just by touching someone, she can insert a mental hook into their psyche and tie a string of her consciousness to it, creating a tether. That doesn't make her a spy, though, not unless her talent is discovered by those seeking to exploit it.

36: Dark Spy's Mission

Jin's first spying mission is supposed to be easy. Walk into the club, touch Kalugal to tether her consciousness to him, and walk out.

Except, they should have known better.

37: Dark Spy's Resolution

The best-laid plans often go awry...

38: Dark Overlord New Horizon

Jacki has two talents that set her apart from the rest of the human race.

She has unpredictable glimpses of other people's futures, and she is immune to mind manipulation.

Unfortunately, both talents are pretty useless for finding a job other than the one she had in the government's paranormal division.

It seemed like a sweet deal, until she found out that the director planned on producing super babies by compelling the recruits into pairing up. When an opportunity to escape the program presented itself, she took it, only to find out that humans are not at the top of the food chain.

Immortals are real, and at the very top of the hierarchy is Kalugal, the most powerful, arrogant, and sexiest male she has ever met.

With one look, he sets her blood on fire, but Jacki is not a fool. A man like him will never think of her as anything more than a tasty snack, while she will never settle for anything less than his heart.

39: Dark Overlord's Wife

Jacki is still clinging to her all-or-nothing policy, but Kalugal is chipping away at her resistance. Perhaps it's time to ease up on her convictions. A little less than all is still much better than nothing, and a couple of decades with a demigod is probably worth more than a lifetime with a mere mortal.

40: Dark Overlord's Clan

As Jacki and Kalugal prepare to celebrate their union, Kian takes every precaution to safeguard his people. Except, Kalugal and his men are not his only potential adversaries, and compulsion is not the only power he should fear.

41: Dark Choices The Quandary

When Rufsur and Edna meet, the attraction is as unexpected as it is undeniable. Except, she's the clan's judge and councilwoman, and he's Kalugal's second-in-command. Will loyalty and duty to their people keep them apart?

42: Dark Choices Paradigm Shift

Edna and Rufsur are miserable without each other, and their two-week separation seems like an eternity. Long-distance relationships are difficult, but for immortal couples they are impossible. Unless one of them is willing to leave everything behind for the other, things are just going to get worse. Except, the cost of compromise is far greater than giving up their comfortable lives and hard-earned positions. The future of their people is on the line.

43: Dark Choices The Accord

The winds of change blowing over the village demand hard choices. For better or worse, Kian's decisions will alter the trajectory of the clan's future, and he is not ready to take the plunge. But as Edna and Rufsur's plight gains widespread support, his resistance slowly begins to erode.

44: Dark Secrets Resurgence

On a sabbatical from his Stanford teaching position, Professor David Levinson finally has time to write the sci-fi novel he's been thinking about for years.

The phenomena of past life memories and near-death experiences are too controversial to include in his formal psychiatric research, while fiction is the perfect outlet for his esoteric ideas.

Hoping that a change of pace will provide the inspiration he needs, David accepts a friend's invitation to an old Scottish castle.

45: Dark Secrets Unveiled

When Professor David Levinson accepts a friend's invitation to an old Scottish castle, what he finds there is more fantastical than his most outlandish theories. The castle is home to a clan of immortals, their leader is a stunning demigoddess, and even more shockingly, it might be precisely where he belongs.

Except, the clan founder is hiding a secret that might cast a dark shadow on David's relationship with her daughter.

Nevertheless, when offered a chance at immortality, he agrees to undergo the dangerous induction process.

Will David survive his transition into immortality? And if he does, will his relationship with Sari survive the unveiling of her mother's secret?

46: Dark Secrets Absolved

Absolution.

David had given and received it.

The few short hours since he'd emerged from the coma had felt incredible. He'd finally been free of the guilt and pain, and for the first time since Jonah's death, he had felt truly happy and optimistic about the future.

He'd survived the transition into immortality, had been accepted into the clan, and was about to marry the best woman on the face of the planet, his true love mate, his salvation, his everything.

What could have possibly gone wrong?

Just about everything.

47: Dark haven Illusion

Welcome to Safe Haven, where not everything is what it seems.

On a quest to process personal pain, Anastasia joins the Safe Haven Spiritual Retreat.

Through meditation, self-reflection, and hard work, she hopes to make peace with the voices in her head.

This is where she belongs.

Except, membership comes with a hefty price, doubts are sacrilege, and leaving is not as easy as walking out the front gate.

Is living in utopia worth the sacrifice?

Anastasia believes so until the arrival of a new acolyte changes everything.

Apparently, the gods of old were not a myth, their immortal descendants share the planet with humans, and she might be a carrier of their genes.

48: Dark Haven Unmasked

As Anastasia leaves Safe Haven for a week-long romantic vacation with Leon, she hopes to explore her newly discovered passionate side, their budding relationship, and perhaps also solve the mystery of the voices in her head. What she discovers exceeds her wildest expectations.

In the meantime, Eleanor and Peter hope to solve another mystery. Who is Emmett Haderech, and what is he up to?

49: Dark Haven Found

Anastasia is growing suspicious, and Leon is running out of excuses.

Risking death for a chance at immortality should've been her choice to make. Will she ever forgive him for taking it away from her?

50: Dark Power Untamed

Attending a charity gala as the clan's figurehead, Onegus is ready for the pesky socialites he'll have a hard time keeping away. Instead, he encounters an intriguing beauty who won't give him the time of day.

Bad things happen when Cassandra gets all worked up, and given her fiery temper, the destructive power is difficult to tame. When she meets a gorgeous, cocky billionaire at a charity event, things just might start blowing up again.

51: DARK POWER UNLEASHED

Cassandra's power is unpredictable, uncontrollable, and destructive. If she doesn't learn to harness it, people might get hurt.

Onegus's self-control is legendary. Even his fangs and venom glands obey his commands.

They say that opposites attract, and perhaps it's true, but are they any good for each other?

52: DARK POWER CONVERGENCE

The threads of fate converge, mysteries unfold, and the clan's future is forever altered in the least expected way.

53: DARK MEMORIES SUBMERGED

Geraldine's memories are spotty at best, and many of them are pure fiction. While her family attempts to solve the puzzle with far too many pieces missing, she's forced to confront a past life that she can't remember, a present that's more fantastic than her wildest made-up stories, and a future that might be better than her most heartfelt fantasies. But as more clues are uncovered, the picture starting to emerge is beyond anything she or her family could have ever imagined.

54: DARK MEMORIES EMERGE

The more clues emerge about Geraldine's past, the more questions arise.

Did she really have a twin sister who drowned?

Who is the mysterious benefactor in her hazy recollections?

Did he have anything to do with her becoming immortal?

Thankfully, she doesn't have to find the answers alone.

Cassandra and Onegus are there for her, and so is Shai, the immortal who sets her body on fire.

As they work together to solve the mystery, the four of them stumble upon a millennia-old secret that could tip the balance of power between the clan and its enemies.

55: Dark Memories Restored

As the past collides with the present, a new future emerges.

56: Dark Hunter's Query

For most of his five centuries of existence, Orion has walked the earth alone, searching for answers.

Why is he immortal?

Where did his powers come from?

Is he the only one of his kind?

When fate puts Orion face to face with the god who sired him, he learns the secret behind his immortality and that he might not be the only one.

As the goddess's eldest daughter and a mother of thirteen, Alena deserves the title of Clan Mother just as much as Annani, but she's not interested in honorifics. Being her mother's companion and keeping the mischievous goddess out of trouble is a rewarding, full-time job. Lately, though, Alena's love for her mother and the clan's gratitude is not enough.

She craves adventure, excitement, and perhaps a true-love mate of her own.

When Alena and Orion meet, sparks fly, but they both resist the pull. Alena could never bring herself to trust the powerful compeller, and Orion could never allow himself to fall in love again.

57: Dark Hunter's Prey

When Alena and Orion join Kalugal and Jacki on a romantic vacation to the enchanting Lake Lugo in China, they anticipate a couple of visits to Kalugal's archeological dig, some sightseeing, and a lot of lovemaking.

Their excursion takes an unexpected turn when Jacki's vision sends them on a perilous hunt for the elusive Kra-ell.

As things progress from bad to worse, Alena beseeches the Fates to keep everyone in their group alive. She can't fathom losing any of them, but most of all, Orion.

For over two thousand years, she walked the earth alone, but after mere days with him at her side, she can't imagine life without him.

58: Dark Hunter's Boon

As Orion and Alena's relationship blooms and solidifies, the two investigative teams combine their recent discoveries to piece together more of the Kra-ell mystery.

Attacking the puzzle from another angle, Eleanor works on gaining access to Echelon's powerful AI spy network.

Together, they are getting dangerously close to finding the elusive Kra-ell.

59: Dark God's Avatar

Unaware of the time bomb ticking inside her, Mia had lived the perfect life until it all came to a screeching halt, but despite the difficulties she faces, she doggedly pursues her dreams.

Once known as the god of knowledge and wisdom, Toven has grown cold and indifferent. Disillusioned with humanity, he travels the world and pens novels about the love he can no longer feel.

Seeking to escape his ever-present ennui, Toven gives a cutting-edge virtual experience a try. When his avatar meets Mia's, their sizzling virtual romance unexpectedly turns into something deeper and more meaningful.

Will it endure in the real world?

60: Dark God's Reviviscence

Toven might have failed in his attempts to improve humanity's condition, but he isn't going to fail to improve Mia's life, making it the best it can be despite her fragile health, and he can do that not as a god, but as a man who possesses the means, the smarts, and the determination to do it.

No effort is enough to repay Mia for reviving his deadened heart and making him excited for the next day, but the flip side of his reviviscence is the fear of losing its catalyst.

Given Mia's condition, Toven doesn't dare to over excite her. His venom is a powerful aphrodisiac, euphoric, and an all-around health booster, but it's also extremely potent. It might kill her instead of making her better.

———

FOR EXCLUSIVE PEEKS AT UPCOMING RELEASES & A FREE COMPANION BOOK

Join my *VIP Club* and gain access to the VIP portal at
ITLUCAS.COM
(http://eepurl.com/blMTpD)

Included in your free membership:

- **FREE** Children of the Gods companion book 1
- **FREE** narration of Goddess's Choice—Book 1 in The Children of the Gods Origins series.
- Preview chapters of upcoming releases.
- And other exclusive content offered only to my VIPs.

If you're already a subscriber, you'll receive a download link for my next book's preview chapters in the new release announcement email. If you are not getting my emails, your provider is sending them to your junk folder, and you are missing out on **important updates, side characters' portraits, additional content, and other goodies.** To fix that, add isabell@itlucas.com to your email contacts or your email VIP list.